Jamila

Peter Newton

Published by New Generation Publishing in 2024

Copyright © Peter Newton 2024

First Edition

The author asserts the moral right under the Copyright, Designs and Patents Act 1988 to be identified as the author of this work.

All Rights reserved. No part of this publication may be reproduced, stored in a retrieval system or transmitted, in any form or by any means without the prior consent of the author, nor be otherwise circulated in any form of binding or cover other than that which it is published and without a similar condition being imposed on the subsequent purchaser.

Paperback ISBN: 978-1-83563-303-8
Hardback ISBN: 978-1-83563-304-5
eBook ISBN: 978-1-83563-305-2

www.newgeneration-publishing.com

New Generation Publishing

Sidi Sayfa

Morocco 1948

The stony floor of the cave above the Yellow Rock is streaked with blood, made visible by the slivers and shafts of daylight penetrating from secret corners of rock and debris, catching the outline of a figure, squatting on the stones, scarf dishevelled, hair falling knotted, black cloak rolled and drawn up above her knees. She groans and draws in deep breaths. Around her mouth, mucus has accumulated and despite the cool air, sweat is running from her face, soaking into her scarf. Fears assault her. She feels deeply tired, afraid for her body, running on instinct, trapped by tightness, assailed by her loneliness, crouching balanced on her heels, her hands beneath her clothes, where she grasps at the emerging head of her baby. She clutches, pushes, deep down onto the child, actions repeated, penetrating pain echoing, resonating in the granite dome. She sways on her haunches as she draws wet breaths, gasps, presses her feet onto the unwelcome and bloody floor of the cave, easing the child from the safety of her womb.

With a supreme effort, her baby, a girl, slips free as in the same movement the new mother lifts her child, rocks, guides her onto her lap, ties a piece of ragged string close and tight around the birth cord. She takes the sharp flint she has kept beside her and cuts the cord, wraps her child in her scarf and shawl and brings her to her mouth where she draws the mucus from the baby's nostrils and spits it to the cave floor as the baby whimpers a little and struggles to a breath, a new life in a dark place.

When the mother watched her own sister give birth more than a year ago, she would never have believed that so soon she would give thanks for that generous lesson. Preparing to give birth safe in the sanctuary of her cave, in her chosen place, she had planned her actions, rehearsed her memories, stored them in her heart and placed them in her mind so these actions had become an instinct undeclared.

As she embraces her baby, tears of relief stream from the mother's eyes, wash across the child's bloodied and smudged cheeks and forehead and mingle with the fluids that she has carried on her flesh from within her mother. The mother feels herself wanting to press down again, to pant and heave and so, still a servant to her sister's lesson, she pushes what remains of the birth, warm debris sliding, slipping onto the floor of the cave. That done she presses herself backwards along the cave floor, a little away from the discarded fragments of birth, to rest her back against a rock. 'Jamila,' she whispers onto her child, 'my Jamila.' She pulls her wet and stained cloak around herself, presses Jamila against her heaving breast, kisses her warm cheeks, wipes more mucus from her face, touches her lips against the child's slight breath and clears her still bloodied mouth once more, spitting the waste to the floor of the cave.

So intent has the mother been, absorbed in the inevitability of her birthing, that all else seems not to matter, her circumstances so much less important than the advent of her child. But now that Jamila breathes free the mother turns, furtive, towards the shafts of sun that flash on her clear eyes. She peers into the space where the light gains entry and her fear surges for the intolerable pain she has yet to face. Her courage has never deserted her, her faith in the integrity of her new-born child sustains her but despite her resolution the loss she faces now feels unendurable. She opens her shawl slightly so she can brush her lips against the soft flesh she has mothered, touches the breath she has created, gathers up the sweet scent of the child she has made but far too soon, she hears voices.

Latifa stumbles as she rises, clutches Jamila tighter, glances around, her instincts sharp as she takes her first steps towards the daylight filtering through to her darkened space from the brightness beyond and uncomfortably edges her aching body forwards as she lifts her child on a murmured prayer of mercy.

1

1966

Jamila travelled the breadth of Morocco but only when she found the boat in Algiers was she shaken by her emerging fears. As she climbed on board she glimpsed the sea beneath the gangplank detaching her from the land, severing her from the familiar. She never felt resentful during her self-imposed journey, using her movement and the purpose it pretended, to chase away the bitterness; but now she stepped away from the land she was alone, her back to her people, her village and now her country and she was assailed by self-doubt, by questions, by the certainty that turning back was no longer an option but going forward more of a challenge than she so far acknowledged. Jamila had never travelled on the sea, never left the mountains, never been so isolated and never felt so agitated as questions started to course through her mind whilst the boat turned itself around to face towards France. She leant on the sticky railings, scanning the unfamiliar horizon and others around her chattered and joked whilst she was grasping the enormity of what she'd done. Finding her way across country Jamila had been alone for several days and all that time as her resentment grew, she absorbed her disbelief at how she'd been treated and the inevitable choice she made. Now she felt she could contain no more. Simultaneous anger and fear fed her misgiving as it seethed within her.

As the ship turned away from her homeland and set course for France she started to doubt. Maybe it was my fault, she thought. Did I somehow make it all happen, ask for it to happen to prove I was right all along? Was I wrong and was Ismail simply being a good father to me and to Nadeem? He cared about us all; he loved me. I know that. My mother loved me; she was a good woman and I have let her down terribly. I have stolen from her and from Ismail and why should I be forgiven? The more she thought the worse she felt; deep inside her heart was guilt, self-questioning. She stood on the sunny deck of the ferry, and soon convinced herself that she had made the most dreadful mistake and asked for trouble, trouble she now deserved. She drummed on the rusty railings, pressing the tension into the ends of her fingers. Jamila started to feel that her own moral values were violated and yet until now she saw that they were values she didn't recognise in herself and so to feel responsible for that violation affirmed her morality, but she was alarmed to see at that moment that what had become violated was her sense of herself, her confidence in her character and her ability to sustain her own honour. She felt worthless and devalued even though she knew she'd done nothing wrong. She now questioned the justification for her self-belief. She was astonished to discover that she even questioned in herself her own adequacy and felt herself inferior to all those around, travelling on this boat, even though they were strangers. 'Does it show?' she asked herself. 'Can these people see my shame?' Why should she feel ashamed as if she had brought events upon herself? She knew she hadn't but that made no difference. She wondered how her remorse could be justified when nothing was her fault.

Deep in thought she flinched when the ship's horn roared as they set out across the water. The noise wrenched her out of her anguish. She'd seen photographs of boats like this and never considered she would be a passenger. The smoking chimney towered above her, steam streaming out behind and the whole vessel shuddered and rattled as it started to race through the water. She drew in the salt scent, tasting the sea air. She'd certainly not imagined so much water, never understood the sea until today, curved, reaching from horizon to horizon. The river below her village in the mountains burst its banks in the winter and before today she thought that was a lot of water; memories invaded her and fed her fears; that river was where she learnt to swim, although it was as if she never learnt; all the children could swim. Zohra, little Hammed, Adel; all swam and played together except Nadeem. 'Your brown skin washed off, didn't it?' He always whispered that in her ear and Ismail always told Jamila to take no notice, but he did not discern her pain and how she was made to feel disconnected, floundering before Nadeem's sarcasm. Comment about her skin was the least of her worries made so much harder to bear when set against the unconditional love she was given by the rest of her family.

'Hello. You look as if you might be on your own.' Jamila heard the voice but not the words. 'Sorry. Did I disturb you.' The same voice and then Jamila realised that someone was speaking to her. She turned to a young woman like her, holding the same railing, looking out across the sea. 'Are you on your own?' she asked.

'Oh. Sorry,' said Jamila. 'I was thinking. I'm on my own, yes. I've never been on a boat like this before.'

'I'm on my own as well.' They both smiled. 'I'm Marie.'

'I'm Jamila. Are you living in Morocco?'

Jamila soon knew that Marie did not live in Morocco. She was from Marseille, on her way back home from visiting her brother in Algiers. 'He is working as an engineer,' Marie chattered on, cheerful and beguiling. 'He's still repairing war damage to the old railways to the east of the city. I've had a wonderful time meeting his friends, talking and exploring.' Marie's chattering and the cheerful flow of her conversation calmed Jamila, brushed away some of the discomfort she was feeling and diverted her self-criticism. Jamila soon learnt that Marie loved North Africa and as most Algerians spoke French, she could find her way around with no trouble. Then it was Jamila's turn. She explained how she learnt French from her sister who enjoyed classes with a real French lady for a teacher. She told Marie she was lucky and that there were still plenty of girls who didn't get even that chance and it wasn't long before Jamila began to put the pain of her earlier reflections to one side and began to enjoy Marie's commentary, their conversation, her stories of Marseille and her own family. By now they were sitting on benches at the bow of the boat, wrapped in ship's blankets, both happy in each other's company. They'd each carried a little food onto the boat, which they shared, bought a hot tea from the ship's cafe and then curled up to get some sleep. As they settled down Jamila reflected that Marie was just what she needed, a companion to share the next piece of her journey, able now to admit to herself that she had been lonely when she boarded the boat and that someone to talk to was an unexpected bonus.

*

Darkness came and they both slept but a few hours later Jamila awoke again feeling troubled. She looked at her new friend, asleep beside her and felt relief that she was still there as the comfort of friendship acted as a foil for her thoughts and she wondered what she would tell Marie about herself today. Jamila knew she wanted to tell Marie something but did not want her new friend to think badly of her even though she believed she had done nothing wrong. But where would she start? Rolling out of her chair, she left her worn, leather bag and her blanket next to Marie and walked around the decks reflecting that there was still another day and night on the ferry and so plenty of time to go over her own story.

Marie was awake when Jamila returned and she straightaway suggested a hot drink and a baguette from the ship's café and went off to find them, leaving Jamila to take her turn looking after the bags. As Marie found the café, she admitted to herself that she was curious to know more of her new friend. Soon back and sipping coffee she asked, 'When are you returning home, Jamila?'

'I've a one-way ticket. I'm not going back.'

Marie stayed quiet, surprised, straight away unsure how far to probe. She was thinking that Jamila remained quiet yesterday leaving her to ponder if all was well and this morning, both girls were thoughtful as they wrapped themselves up, hugging the warmth of the tea mugs. They didn't want to move elsewhere on the boat for fear of losing the bench space they'd slept on and thankfully the clear sky offered the prospect of a warmer day ahead than the chilly night just gone by.

Jamila scoured the horizon but at the moment there was no land in sight. 'There's so much water,' she said.

Marie smiled. 'Where did you live, Jamila?'

'In a village in the Moroccan mountains. Our house is on the valley side looking down to where the river flows and the sheep and goats graze.' She was leaving it behind, but she found herself saying 'our house'.

'That sounds beautiful,' said Marie, 'and yet you have left it all. How did that happen?'

'It is beautiful, Marie, you're right. When I was a child, I loved to play in the river with my brothers, precious Adel, Hammed and Zohra my sister. I have another brother Nadeem, but he never played with us. He is the oldest you see, Marie. He and I were not the same age, and he was the oldest boy, so he was always a little spoiled, especially by Ismail. Ismail was everyone's father except mine, but he was good to me.' Jamila paused. Her life had so far been so much in the present that self-questioning was unusual. It was a new experience for her to tell her own story, so she was comforted when Marie was attentive but sensing pain in her new friend Marie put her hand onto Jamila's arm. Jamila liked this. It helped her feel safe. 'Ismail was gruff and serious, but gentle.' Jamila continued: 'He worked hard to support us, growing food on the land near to the river and making leather goods to sell on the family leather stall outside our home in the village. I was nursed by Habiba, and I called her my mother and she always felt like I believed a mother should. Habiba died when I was a young girl and I missed her terribly. I still do.' Jamila paused and looked at Marie, calmed by her kindness and warmed by her attentiveness. 'It's good to talk to you, Marie. Tell me if I need to stop.'

Talking about herself, Jamila felt a surge of pride about her life that she never felt before. She was pleased to talk of herself, and Marie wanted to know and that gave Jamila courage, and she recognised that Marie knew nothing, with no preconceptions and that gave Jamila fresh confidence to be honest with herself as well as with Marie. So, sitting warmly wrapped, on the deck of a ferry and after so many days travelling alone, Jamila understood with relief that she'd stopped running. With that self-realisation she shed silent tears, overwhelmed by a sense of feeling safe. Seeing her emotions, Marie offered Jamila her arm, wrapped it around her shoulders and held her for several minutes. Her quietness encouraged Jamila who found herself snuggling into the comfort of her newfound friend.

'You were quite a large family. I have just one brother,' Marie said softly, already sensing hidden truths.

'We were a large family. Zohra and I were always friends. It's her I miss the most. She was like Habiba, never asking for herself but always giving to others. She was sent to school although she didn't work hard. The school was run by the French and so I learnt to speak French and English by talking with Zohra. I borrowed her schoolbooks as well. Nadeem didn't like it that I could speak other languages. I think he was jealous of me, only a girl, and he didn't want me to learn. It was even worse that the languages made me useful to Ismail with travellers on the leather stall and Nadeem didn't like that.'

'There's so many North Africans who speak French,' said Marie. 'That's why my brother likes working in Algeria so much.'

'Yes,' said Jamila, 'but many of the men in my village don't like the French. They call them the white colonialists.'

'My uncle was killed fighting in Morocco,' said Marie. 'My mother said it was the German soldiers who blew-up his tank.'

'I'm so sorry. That's hard for you. The French helped us in Morocco, didn't they? Zohra always said that we must thank them, but not everyone agrees. Anyway, Zohra and I became good companions as we grew older, and she began to think about who in the village would marry her and she always said she didn't want to marry a Frenchman. That made her laugh. I never thought like that. I planned to talk about marriage with Habiba someday but she died before I could.'

'What is your home like, Jamila? I'd love to know.'

Even as she'd travelled from the mountains to Algiers, Jamila never spoke of herself to anyone and so to speak with Marie like this was liberating. She found herself talking about Habiba, her pride in her children and her pride in her home. 'It's mudbrick, kind of hard and soft at the same time. We look out on the mountains across the valley and like all the villages the walls are burnt brown in the sun and worn by the mountain winds.'

Jamila was thinking how proud Habiba was of the hardwood door painted the colours of sunshine and the one window space that faced the hills and was decorated by a curled and twisted iron grating. Ornaments like that are expensive to find in the mountains. 'At the front of our house a rush mat roof covers a workbench and a stall set out with leather goods. We sell them to travellers who wander through the village from time-to-time, in search of peace, they always say. When travellers say that it makes Zohra and me laugh.' Jamila paused in thought. 'How strange that I would have to leave that village to try to find my own peace.' Marie could see that Jamila was wondering where her heart was taking her. 'We sell fresh leaved sweet tea at a small table and chairs, next to the leather goods. Prayer mats fill the open spaces, there for the buying.'

As they talked Jamila began to like herself more, to question herself and seek for her own motives as she spoke, and Marie listened closely to her new friend, quite sure now that there was more to this story and that she would need to be patient, to wait until Jamila was ready to tell her. She was wondering why Jamila was leaving such a good place to live. Marie just saw herself as a tourist, but she now recognised that Jamila was almost a refugee. The romance of that notion appealed to Marie although she thought that maybe Jamila simply ran away, but that was still interesting. It wasn't everyday she met someone with Jamila's courage and determination to leave their own country so Marie figured Jamila must have a good reason.

*

The following morning at the crack of dawn Jamila and Marie joined a small throng of passengers watching the French coast emerge from the sea mist and the screaming seagulls diving and dipping into the turbulent wake. It wasn't long before Marie was pointing across the horizon. 'There's Marseille,' she declared. 'Look. There's the Cathedral. Can you see, Jamila. On the hill. The Notre-Dame de la Garde.'

Jamila looked in wonder where Marie pointed and indeed, she could see. 'It's beautiful and so high up. Will you take me there, Marie? I would love to see it. I have never been to a cathedral.'

'Of course, I will. I've been thinking in the night Jamila, would you like to come and stay with me for a few days while you decide what to do next?' Jamila was pleased and so it was decided, and the two girls were firm friends.

As their ferry came alongside the harbour wall, they eased themselves onto the gangplank and dropped down to the quay delighted to be back on firm ground. Jamila was nervous to show her travel papers. She hadn't told Marie that she had no papers of her own. It was her secret that she'd taken her dead mother's papers from their box at home and wrapped herself in her mother's old scarf, so her face was covered but no one looked at the papers whilst she travelled across Morocco. At the French border she gave her papers to the uniformed official as he sat importantly at his greasy desk. 'How long are you staying?' he asked, picking his teeth.

'A few weeks I think,' she replied. He glanced at Jamila as he stamped the document. 'Well, that was easy,' she said to herself as she scurried away before he changed his mind.

A few minutes later they were on a tram, heading for Marie's apartment in Saint Lazare. Jamila was fascinated to look out from their bus and see the city passing. Walking the streets were men in berets and others in trilbies, women with heads wrapped in bright scarves shopping from stalls laden variously with clothes, books, fish and fruits; children laughing and chattering, running here and there, old men bent double and girls and boys, hand-in-hand and ignored by all. She had never seen that before. She noticed a stall selling baskets and oils and cooking pots and pans and more old men sitting slightly apart on a wall, legs crossed, engulfed by cigarette smoke, resting their hands on sticks, all facing the same way and seeming to ignore each other, an apparent indifference that made her smile. Why was it that old men easily looked so grumpy, she wondered. They look just like that in my village.

Marie looked at Jamila as the bus made headway and couldn't help grinning at her, as she turned this way and that, always distracted. Her childlike enthusiasm was contagious. They left the tram, walked a few steps across the busy road, entered a tall building by a small side entrance and then climbed several flights of stairs, finding the door to Marie's apartment. Jamila had never climbed so many steps in a house. After a good wash they were ready to go out again. Marie lost no time taking Jamila to her favourite café where they talked for a long time as Jamila absorbed the change in her life and Marie enjoyed her new friendship. Jamila felt liberated with Marie. Both knew that they would soon turn back to Jamila's reasons for leaving her village and abandoning her family; both felt the time wasn't right.

*

As they climbed the hill to the Cathedral, Jamila remembered her visit to the Kutubiyya minaret in Marrakech with her mother and with Zohra. It was the event of her life back then. Standing under this Cathedral, scanning the city of Marseille before her she felt she jumped from child to adult as she crossed the sea, left behind her dependence, her reliance and the familiar and discovered a new world where she was on an unequal footing to the rest and so free to choose. Today everything of her old life felt like years ago as if a chasm opened between Jamila and her past. As a child she could not have imagined anything as grand, as tall, as impressive as the Kutubiyya minaret in Marrakech and yet before her now was the Notre Dame de la Garde, towers and spires, topped with a huge statue of Mary and Jesus, ornate, perched on a hill from where Jamila felt she could see the whole world. But she felt so small, so overwhelmed by its beauty and she gasped as she discovered ornate decoration, statues, tombs, pictures of Jesus and his disciples, the waxy scent from votive candles glowing in every nook and cranny. 'Why am I here?' she was asking herself as she stretched up to see the golden domes above her. 'What am I running away from?' Pulling herself back together she joined Marie who knelt and was praying.

'It's beautiful,' said Jamila, as Marie sat back on the bench. 'Our mosques are beautiful but plain and empty where here everything is decorated, ornate, alive with painted figures and statues and yet I can't help but feel it's the same God in both places.'

'I'm not really a Christian,' said Marie. 'But I was brought up a Catholic and so it's a habit for me to pray. When I do, I often wonder how I would know it was God or just good luck if a prayer was answered? I suppose the only difference between Allah and God is the difference between Arabic and English.'

'The trouble is I haven't read the Bible or the Koran,' said Jamila. 'If I had read them, I'd know which of these books meant the most to me, which of them was closest to what I expect to hear from a God? But I have no idea what to expect. There's so much for me to understand.'

'Let's leave it until tomorrow then, shall we?' Marie smiled and they both laughed.

*

Marie had given up her job so she could go and visit her brother in Algeria and Jamila had almost none of the money left that she'd 'borrowed' from Ismail, so they both needed work. Marie knew several cafés where they might find a job and so they left the cathedral behind them and set out to search. They were jostled and bumped by the crowds at corners and road crossings and every so often a bus would pass by, horn blaring, constant intrusions into their limitless chattering. Before long they stopped for a rest and a couple of men eyed them both and smiled, cheeky grins on their shaven faces. No sooner did the girls notice than the men scurried away, laughing together, so they set off again walking along the street, arm-in-arm, carefully picking their way, lost in their thoughts. It wasn't long before they turned a corner and found themselves in a street where almost every shop was a café and every café spilled out onto the pavement. This was where Marie was sure they'd find work and indeed, within ten minutes they both found a job at the same café starting that night.

'Did you pray for that job?' asked Jamila, laughing.

'Well, as a matter of fact, I did,' said Marie. 'But was it God that found it for us or good luck?' They skipped away, arm-in-arm, giggling. 'I better tell you,' said Marie as they crossed a road. 'It wasn't God or good luck. I know Pierre, the owner of that café. That might have something to do with it.' Marie winked. Jamila laughed again. She had hardly thought of home all day.

*

Jamila and Marie worked at the café for a week or so; they were enjoying it, the customers liked them, and they didn't have to work as hard they thought they might have to, and a few customers returned, which pleased Pierre. They were busy. The street led down to the harbour and in the evening teemed with animated parties and cheerful families. Most were French of course but one evening a group of English students were in and had taken a shine to Marie, who'd told them as plainly as she dared, that she had a boyfriend and to keep their eyes on their food. Even so, they turned up again, a couple of nights later. Out the back Marie persuaded Jamila to take their table so she could keep herself clear of them and they'd soon made sure that Jamila had reason to remember them. They laughed and joked all evening. Jamila liked them. She spoke English quite well, thanks to Zohra and found herself enjoying their relaxed comments and jokes. It was good to hear people laughing.

A couple of days later they came again and Jamila took their table. There were four of them this time and one was a little older, a man with smiley eyes and a chirpy laugh. 'He's charming,' said Marie, out the back in the kitchen. Jamila blushed slightly, although she didn't know why and Marie laughed. She'd noticed. Jamila heard the men talking about buying brushes and pegs from the market and how many they'd need and she thought it an odd thing for them to be talking about.

'Where do you come from?' the older man asked Jamila as she cleared away some plates. Jamila told him and he seemed interested. 'Why are you in Marseille?' he asked and this time Jamila didn't know what to say so mumbled a few words in Arabic as she walked away from their table and on the way, she heard one of the younger men laugh as he said, 'She's a bit young for you isn't she, Donald?' Despite her unease Jamila found herself remembering the name. Such free and easy relationships surprised her more than she realised. After all, at home in Morocco, convention would hold them all apart and an easy association between a man and woman would attract criticism. This was a freedom she had not pondered or been prepared for.

The following day Jamila and Marie were walking to work when they noticed the same man sitting at a café table. As they walked past, they saw that in front of him was a worn, leather notebook with its pages open and printed on them were what looked like plans of a building. He was alone, scribbling and as they both approached the waiter brought him a fresh glass of wine. He looked up from his work and spotted them and Jamila smiled, so he waved a little and watched as they passed by. Despite herself Jamila was drawn to his smile, and she turned as they walked away and was surprised to see him looking at them. Donald smiled to himself as he noticed Jamila look back and he watched them walk into the distance, called for his bill and strolled away, thoughtfully.

'You seem to like him,' Marie commented as they walked to her apartment.

'Maybe,' said Jamila. 'I think he's English. I've always wanted to go to England.'

'Whatever for? What's wrong with France? I need you here with me.' So, saying she grasped Jamila by the hand and twisted her in a mock dance move on the pavement. Both girls were giggling.

'I've had a lovely day again,' said Jamila.

'Good. So have I. How about we walk down to the harbour, watch the moon on the sea and then get the tram back to the apartment?' said Marie. And they did.

2

Something in his eyes when they'd been talking had left Marie expecting to see the English gentleman again, so she wasn't surprised when it happened a couple of days later. He was sitting at the same café with his notebook and this time he stood up when he saw them both and asked them if they'd like to share a drink or a coffee with him. 'Why not?' they said to each other and before long the three of them were chatting in the sunshine. Jamila was used to the travellers passing through her village and stopping at their stall but even so was surprised at how this intimate conversation absorbed her interest. It was as if a new taste had crossed her palate and provoked her curiosity.

He introduced himself as Donald and told them about Scotland and his family home in the hills. Jamila was charmed and she didn't find it hard to tell him that her home was in the hills above a fierce river and Marie did the French thing and was very engaging, so he learnt a little about them both and they about him. Jamila was struck by his quiet voice. He seemed polite and gentle. 'Do you work at the café up the road all the time?' he asked.

So, they told him. Marie talked about her friend Pierre and her trip to Morocco to see her brother. Donald was interested and started to tell them about the trains in Scotland but quickly realised that they were bored so he changed the subject to his own work. 'Why are you in Marseille?' Marie asked.

'I'm an archaeologist,' he said. 'I work with things we find buried in fields and caves and under buildings. I'm working near Marseille now with some students looking for human teeth and other remains to work out what food they may have eaten in an old village thousands of years ago.'

'Teeth,' said Jamila. 'Just teeth. Why would you do that?' Jamila was taken by the notion that a grown man could spend his time searching for old teeth as it seemed to her a strange thing to do and so naturally assumed that it had some greater purpose. 'What will you do when you find the teeth?' she asked.

'Take them back to Scotland,' he replied. 'Take them to my laboratory for us to analyse.'

What Donald said impressed Jamila although she had little idea what it all meant but she was pleased he had not had the chance to ask her why she was in Marseille and why she had left home. 'How do you find teeth?' Jamila asked and Donald explained, whilst Marie was keeping her counsel but felt a little excluded and was thinking to herself that Donald was perhaps putting on a bit of a show to impress.

Marie was pleased when Donald said he was sorry but needed to finish his work and so couldn't talk anymore. She anticipated they would soon be free of him until as they were about to say goodbye, and seemingly as an afterthought, he asked, 'Would you like to come and see us working?'

Marie and Jamila exchanged smiles and as Marie raised her eyebrows.

'I'd like to,' said Jamila.

'We have a day off work on Friday, perhaps we could come then?' Marie, despite her discomfort, arranged the visit, there seemed no obstacles and at the end of the week they found themselves walking onto an archaeological dig a bus ride away from Marseille.

*

Jamila might say that from the outset she was fascinated and that by the end she wasn't sure why and Marie might say she only went along with it for the sake of her friend. Whatever their reasons they were both pleased to see Donald again as they dismounted from the bus and he sauntered over to greet them, clean shaven with dusty smudges on his cheeks and a knitted tartan hat pulled over his ears leaving his hair spilling out above his forehead and bobbing about as he pulled a mock bow and welcomed them like long-lost friends. They both liked this. Jamila was charmed by such ease and warmth and seeing him again she was pleased to think he looked younger than she remembered. Marie was pleased because they had to make the effort to get there, and she thought he might have forgotten them.

Donald hadn't forgotten, far from it. Without hesitation he appointed himself their guide. They straightway found themselves in an expansive field, with a few tents and a small marquee on one side and several broad areas of bare earth and stones on the other. Trestle tables and canvas seats were scattered untidily around and in the open spaces shallow trenches and piles of soil defined the landscape. Jamila had never seen anything like this at home. Here and there the men she'd served in the cafe were kneeling on the ground scraping, dusting, brushing, gathering dirt in small heaps with little spades and pans. That's what they were talking about she realised, buying brushes. Brushes to do this with. They were students she concluded, and they were busy studying each other's work.

It was meticulous labour. Donald was talking, describing what they were doing but Jamila wasn't listening, so fascinated was she by the activity in front of her. If she had been listening, she would have heard him explaining the process they were all going through and she would have heard his excitement, but she wasn't, she was absorbed by the scraping and brushing, the measuring and marking whilst Marie was listening and would later recount to Jamila the key bits of Donald's guided tour. Marie preferred his voice to the busyness of digging. She was surprised to find his Gaelic lilt appealing to her Frenchness. She thought of it as posh English with a twang. She learnt that the team of students came from his university, in Edinburgh, 'Capital of Scotland', they were here for a few more weeks and due to return to Edinburgh when they'd finished. He sounded important.

For Jamila it was the first time she had felt drawn to a man, attracted by what she saw as thoughtfulness, his ability to concentrate and the warm feeling she was left with. This surprised her. Only much later did she realise that he was good looking as well. What she hardly realised was that the troubles that preoccupied her on the boat had been sidelined for the time being by Donald's enthusiasm as he stopped them outside the largest marquee where one of the students left his work and came over to speak. Jamila immediately noticed that the student was not much older than they were, he wore tortoiseshell glasses and seemed different from Donald, his voice less musical and more serious.

'Excuse me, girls,' said Donald, 'I need to speak with David for just a moment,' and he turned on his heels to talk.

Marie caught Jamila's eye and made a mock bow and Jamila sniggered. 'We're "the girls" now,' she whispered, mocking his accent. 'Excuse me, girls.'

David was talking. 'When shall we open that new stretch, Donald? We're nearly there now. It's coming on jolly well.' Jamila noticed he was business-like, keen to get on with the job.

'Next week maybe. Let's not be in too much of a hurry. We need to be sure we're finished here before we move on.'

'We'll need a couple extra pairs of hands when we do move, though, to do the hard work, to shift the topsoil. Any chance you could find us a couple of good workers, Donald?' To their surprise David winked at Jamila and Marie and made sure they saw him.

'I'll see what I can do,' said Donald as David went back to his work, using a brush and dustpan to gather grains of soil from what looked like a bone buried in the ground.

Jamila was fascinated. 'Is that a human bone?' she asked Donald.

'We won't know for sure until we dig it out and test it in the laboratory, but I think it is,' he said. 'I think it might be a leg bone.' Marie observed her new friend absorbed and keen to know more. She also saw Donald's tendency to charm, to turn Jamila's interest with charisma. Donald showed them some pieces of pottery and several carefully cleaned segments of timber and stone that he said might have been used for building and he introduced them to a couple more students. Jamila was as attracted by the way everyone seemed to work together as she was impressed by the care everyone showed for the apparently random bits and pieces that they were collecting.

Then, with a theatrical swagger, Donald showed them what he described as 'his prize possession'. It was a small, wooden carton containing several brown and damaged teeth and he treated them like treasure. Watching him cautiously open the box Jamila thought of Habiba and the care she took of a few precious pieces of jewellery she kept in a small leather pouch in a cupboard, taking them down sometimes to check they were all there. 'These will be yours when I die,' she said, 'and there is another collection for Zohra.' Ismail gave Zohra her pouch when Habiba died but Jamila never received hers. She never mentioned it in case it made Ismail angry. Donald held his box closer to Jamila who bent to peer at the pieces.

'Where did you find them?' she asked Donald.

He touched her arm and whispered, as if in confidence. 'Out there in the field. They are the reason we are here.'

'But what is it you're doing?' asked Jamila, conscious of his hand now resting on her arm. 'Why are you doing it? What is an archaeologist? You're not collecting them for fun, are you?' Donald looked with kindness at Jamila, lifted his hand and rubbed his eyes and as he did so she felt he gathered himself up and thought about his answer. She was not conscious of the hook he dangled before her.

'We're doing many different things,' he said. He stretched and pointed out across the field. 'This field is our laboratory. Thousands of years ago people lived here in a village of stone, wood and straw houses and we are searching in the ground for traces of their lives, the animals they kept, the food they grew, their homes, their bodies and their treasures. We might find bones, pieces of timber, tools, fragments of ornaments, pieces of cloth.'

Jamila was drawn in. Donald's words seemed to her to be almost mystical and what he described was as unexpected as it was absorbing for her. So much of her own past was shrouded in mystery, seemingly inaccessible to her and yet here the ancient past of ancient people was being revealed with the help of a dustpan and brush. This group of men and women were working together to uncover history. 'We want to understand the diet of these people so we can work out what they grew and ate. We are searching what we believe is an ancient burial ground for fragments of bone and skulls.'

'How can that tell you what they ate?' Jamila thought how gentle a man must be who could care so much for something so fragile. Marie had hung back a little and for the first time since they met on the boat, she felt that Jamila was in a different place from her. Marie was in no doubt that Jamila was fascinated but she also was sceptical, cautious of Donald's allure. Mainly the ever practical Marie had her eye on the time.

'I'm sorry to interrupt you both but we must go,' said Marie. 'Our bus is coming soon and it's the last one back to the city.'

As he walked them back to the bus, playing the gentleman, Donald asked, 'Would you like to come and work here until we go back to Scotland? We can pay you a little.'

Marie's first thought was practical. 'Where would we stay?' she asked. 'It's too far to travel both ways every day.' Jamila hadn't thought about that but of course Marie was right.

'No problem,' said Donald. 'We can let you use a tent with a couple of camp beds, and you can eat with us. It's a bit basic but there are other girls here who manage quite well. You haven't met her yet, but Constance will look after you if you decide to say yes. She'll help you with everything you'll need. You must talk about it. If you come Monday morning with a few things in a bag you can have a job for a few weeks. You decide. Bye for now.'

Donald waved and bobbed down in a cheeky bow as he turned back into the field. 'They'll be back,' he said to himself with a wry smile.

*

The girls woke up just as their bus was driving into the city terminal. They'd missed the Saint Lazare stop so they walked the few steps down to the harbour wall where the usual gathering of fishermen was working at unloading their boats and mending nets while the seagulls circled and dived as they chased the scraps of food. Jamila enjoyed being down at the harbour; the quiet concentration of the fishermen stitching their nets put her in mind of 'Hammed working the leather, pressing in the patterns and stitching the seams on their foot treadled sewing machine. The love she had left behind was revealing itself now and then. She missed 'Hammed's ready smile. But she loved the sea, the busy harbour.

As Marie chattered, they shared a piping hot pizza and recalled Donald that afternoon. Marie mocked him playfully as she imitated his voice, its accent and pretended to be him, wrapping her scarf around her head like Donald wore his knitted hat, welcoming them and bowing low. 'Excuse me, girls…' It made them giggle but truth-to-tell both of them were flattered that he took them so seriously, spoke so willingly to them of what he was doing. And he was English into the bargain, thought Jamila with a smile. Marie wondered if she'd been hard on him.

'Well, Jamila. What shall we do? Go back on Monday like he said? We'll have to let the restaurant down.' Marie knew that Jamila would want to join the dig although for her the novelty was not quite so strong. She liked Pierre from the restaurant and was gradually letting him know. But she was pragmatic. Donald's offer was work, out in the fresh air and they seemed a decent bunch of people. Pierre would still be there in a few weeks' time. Donald and his archaeologists wouldn't. She knew Jamila well enough already to guess she would want to work on the dig.

'Yes, Marie,' said Jamila. 'I could never do it alone, but it would be fine with you. It's out in the open, they'll pay us and feed us, and we can sleep there. Why not? The work's interesting and Donald likes you anyway.'

'It's you he likes, Jamila.' The two girls laughed again. A group of boys walking along the quay, hearing their laughter, turned and blew them exaggerated kisses. Jamila was more than pleased to be with Marie as she'd not seen much openness like this in her village and watched for her reaction so she could copy whilst, in her heart, Jamila liked the attention. Marie just ignored them.

'So, why not give it a try?' said Jamila.

'We can look out for each other,' said Marie. 'It would be good to get out into the country for a while, time to think, a bit of peace and quiet, a chance to decide a few things. Shall we do it then?'

'Become anthropologists you mean?'

'Archaeologists.' said Marie, laughing. 'Posh either way. Why not? Let's join them.' Giggling and grinning Jamila and Marie jumped up and arm-in-arm strolled away from the harbourside, up the hill towards the city. 'It seems like a lot of fuss about some old bones but they seem like a pleasant bunch of people and it beats working in a café.'

As they skipped away Jamila was enjoying the liberation she experienced whilst also feeling slightly overwhelmed. Marie's easy acceptance of Donald's casual invitation to visit him shouldn't have taken her by surprise, but it did. For Marie's part she little realised how Jamila would be absorbed by this adventure.

3

'This feels more like a holiday than a job,' said Marie on Monday as they clambered down from the bus in the cool of the morning. They could see Donald in the distance and before long he was striding across the field to meet them again. He greeted them with a smile.

'Wonderful,' he said. 'I knew you'd come. Isn't it a beautiful day?' He winked. Both girls thought he'd winked at them. 'The team will be very pleased you are here.' He led them to a small tent on the edge of the field. 'This is yours,' he said, 'just leave your bags.' They glimpsed inside and saw two camp beds. Outside a small table and couple of chairs stood in the grass. 'It's not luxury but it's what we all have.'

The trio made their way across the field towards a figure, stooped on the ground, scraping dried earth with a small trowel who clearly felt awkward as he stood up to greet them, brushing the dust off his hands and rubbing his face with the sleeve of his shirt. They recognised David from their last visit. Donald was charming. 'David's a good fellow and will look after you so let's do the formal introductions. David, I want you to meet Jamila and Marie.' As they shook hands David dropped his trowel and Jamila without thinking bent to pick it up for him. As she handed it to him, she felt herself blush and had no idea why, but Marie noticed. 'I'll leave you with David,' said Donald. 'When you're finished, I'll be working over on the burials.'

'That sounds nasty,' said Marie.

David laughed. 'It's alright. They were buried a long time ago, Marie, so it's nothing to worry about.' As Donald strode away, David started to describe the broken pots and pieces of timber that lay partly uncovered where he had been working but within moments their concentration was disturbed by an excited call from across the field.

'It's here. I think I've found it. Donald, David. Come and look.'

'That's Connie,' said David and they all hurried towards her and huddled around where she knelt, brush in hand, blowing dust away from a piece of muddy coloured bone.

'Wow,' she said. 'It's like part of a human skull, a piece of jawbone with a few teeth still in place although most of the skull seems to be still buried.'

Donald, breathless after running, was delighted. 'Well done, Connie. You said it would be here, David, and you were right.' Donald knelt alongside Constance and was soon brushing dust away, stroking it into a small pan, gently uncovering an object which Marie was thinking resembled nothing she could recognise. Donald was instantly absorbed. Jamila looked on, noticing that he had knelt very close to Constance. 'If this is the burial, we think it is, we'll find more,' Donald said as he worked. 'Connie, love, make sure you have all the dust, all the fragments as we go. I think it's a jawbone. This is where the teeth grew. The smallest speck matters, Connie, and try to leave everything in place if there are fragments of teeth. If not make sure you match the specimen numbers.'

As they walked Constance was hanging on Donald's every word. As it came free Donald turned the piece of bone in the sunlight, deep in thought. 'It's beautiful, perfect. Make sure we have some photographs of the exact location so that if we need to, we should be able to put it back just as we found it. Connie, you need to work outwards from here and remember to board up where you are working so you don't tread the fully worked ground anymore.' Constance listened to every word, wide eyed, excited by her success, pleased to have impressed Donald.

'We will, Donald,' said David. 'Let's mark out the boarding now. Connie, grab the other end of this tape.' Marie and Jamila watched as they measured and marked out spaces.

'I'm sorry I've not said hello, Constance said as she worked. 'I seem a bit busy today.'

Jamila surprised herself as she answered, 'That's okay. I'm Jamila. My friend is Marie. We are both here to do some work. Can I help?' Within a few moments Jamila was on her knees, using a small brush to ease the dried earth from around another piece of bone a few metres away as she tried to absorb how it had come about that she was here, with Constance, who she hardly knew and with Marie, not so long ago a stranger as well, and yet how comfortable she felt to have put some of her fears and anxieties and self-doubt to one side. That feeling of being at ease was recurring. She watched Marie, stooping to her new work nearby. Jamila admired Marie, she had taken Jamila with her, and it was because of Marie that she was here. She liked all these people and that felt good. Once again, like yesterday, she had not thought about home. That felt good as well.

Later that afternoon Connie showed Marie and Jamila where to wash and to find food and chattering all the time about Donald she explained his routine at the dig. 'That's the way we'll have to do it,' she said. 'He's the boss.' The sparkle in her eyes when she talked about him was obvious to them both and it was clear to Jamila that she liked him as well as admiring his skills.

*

After a few days on the dig, the girls felt at home and useful. Jamila worked hard and loved to see everyone else working. Donald was meticulous as he explored the soil with small brushes and sometimes even tweezers, bending close to the surface, studying the debris around and ensuring that he missed nothing. Donald's intensity fascinated Jamila as he helped her to understand the significance of the history of the landscape and how over centuries 'artefacts', a word that was new to her, became buried and sometimes preserved and how when anyone disturbed where they rested, it was like folding back the history of the communities that had lived there as well as the objects themselves. Donald found her a willing student and helped her to understand that her life was part of history and that she left behind a footprint of herself wherever she settled. Leaving a footprint was a regular hook of Donald's and it caught Jamila. She liked that thought; she liked to feel a connection to the ground around her and she liked Donald. She already felt she wanted to please him. Sensing this Donald talked about his work with passion and drew her in so that soon she started to feel comfortable and confident. His warmth seemed to her to grow from his expertise and his willingness to share his skills.

'We are so fortunate,' he told Jamila. 'We can study the entire human past through its first toolmakers and hunter-gatherers, from farming, early cities, states, empires and their interconnections, right up to modern times.' Jamila felt this a fabulous notion. To know so much from a few bones and broken pots. 'Archaeological evidence holds the lion's share of global history, and it gives us a way of thinking through it, viewing through it, so we can see our old culture in its own landscape, the human factor in the long-term. It's a way of seeing how our minds and bodies have evolved physically and culturally and what fascinates me is that we can see how different societies are over time.' Nobody had spoken to Jamila like this before about her own world. She felt in awe of what Donald was telling her.

'And does this help us understand the present?' asked Jamila. She was regarding Donald almost as a magician.

'Good question. It does. Exactly.' These thoughts gave Jamila an energy and excitement that was altogether fresh and challenging for her.

'Is that why you do this, Donald? Is this a real job?'

'Of course.' Donald laughed. 'The whole point is to understand how and why human behaviour has changed over time. We search for patterns in the evolution of things like farming, the growth of cities, or the collapse of civilisations. We look for clues as to why these things happened.'

Jamila was captivated. By now she thought Donald was wonderful and she told him and he smiled to himself because he knew he was.

*

'I like it here, working with you and with Donald.' Jamila and David sat under a dark sky round a blazing wood fire later that day. Jamila felt more at peace with herself than she had done for months, her anger at Nadeem had abated even whilst it remained unspoken. David poked at the burning logs, turned them thoughtfully and she enjoyed his look of contentment.

'I like it here as well. It's good to have you two with us. Fresh faces are always welcome.'

'What is it you like about it, David?'

He gazed into the dark distance. 'The thinking, the teamwork, the way we solve problems together, the fresh air and I like all the analysis afterwards, when we get back to the laboratory in Edinburgh.'

'What's Edinburgh like, David? Donald never talks about the city. All I know is that it's in England.'

'Scotland,' said David. 'But you're right. It is part of England. Where do I start? It's a beautiful old country and Edinburgh is a lovely city. We have ancient churches, a castle, a palace and we are by a wide river. It's grand, but it's cold and dark in the winter. Not at all like Marseille where the sun always seems to shine. The University in Edinburgh is one of the best and oldest in the country and it's where we all do our studying when we're not away like this on archaeology trips digging up bones and teeth. I live there as well.'

'Would I like it there do you think?'

David looked at Jamila, a warm smile flickering around his eyes. 'You said you were born in Morocco, didn't you? I am sure Scotland is very different from Morocco.'

'Then I'd like it. I'm not ready to go back to Morocco.'

Marie, sitting quietly by the fire, had been listening and said nothing although she had started to wonder again why Jamila was against returning to Morocco. She knew she still needed to understand and promised herself she would find out soon. Then, as if reading her thoughts, David asked Jamila, 'Why did you leave Morocco?'

Jamila was quiet for a while. David could see her thinking and understood that his question was difficult. 'It wasn't kind to me.' She was quiet again for a while. David waited, listened, gave her space. 'I lost my mother and my family and then I just needed to escape. Things happened.' For Marie this confirmed what she had already surmised. There was a story here to be told.

David looked with kind eyes at Jamila, and she felt a warm heart. 'I am so sorry. I can feel that is a great weight for you. I know you met Marie in Marseille so have you come all the way from Morocco on your own?'

'We met on the boat but until then I'd come all the way on my own. By bus, by train, by boat. It's been the biggest adventure of my life.'

'I admire you, Jamila. That's been a brave journey. What next do you think?'

Jamila was looking slightly alarmed, and Marie was beginning to worry that David might accidently upset her so tried to steer the conversation. 'So many questions, David,' she said. 'We are not all as lucky as you with an interesting job and good friends.'

'I know, Marie, but what will you two do when we've gone from here do you think?'

'I don't know; we need to think about it,' said Marie. 'Back to being a waitress for me I guess.'

Jamila was still determined to open her thoughts. 'Yes, a waitress maybe, but perhaps I'll ask Donald if I can travel back with you to Edinburgh. Hearing you all talk about what you do sounds exciting.'

Marie looked at Jamila, astonished. 'What? Go to Edinburgh? What would you do?'

'I would like to go to your Edinburgh, David, to see your big river and your old university.'

'Does Donald know you think this?' asked David. He was surprised as well.

'No, I don't think so. Maybe you could ask him for me? He'll probably think I'm joking, but I'm not. I need to get away, right away and this feels like it could be a good chance.'

'One day maybe I might know why you so much need to get away?' said David.

'It's a long story,' said Jamila, and with a smile she added, 'but I'll tell you if I come to Edinburgh.'

'You'll have to work hard if you want me to ask Donald for you, Jamila, but we could do with the help. So, here's the deal. Work hard and I'll see what he says.'

4

Marie had been startled by Jamila's enthusiasm for Edinburgh and she could see that David's kindness had played its part. He seemed a good man. Later that evening the two girls lay in their camp-beds, surrounded by discarded clothes, going over the day's events. 'You're a dark horse, Jamila. Do you really want David to talk with Donald about taking you to Edinburgh?'

'Yes, Marie, I think I do. David told me this afternoon that Donald has a spare room in his apartment and that maybe if I work in the University for them, he'd lend me a room and not ask me to pay. Do you think that sounds a good idea? I like these people, Marie, they're kind to us and I think I'd like to go back with them and find a new life in Edinburgh.'

'But what do you really know about them, about Donald or even about Edinburgh? Isn't it all a bit sudden?'

'I love your questions, Marie, and the answers are, not much, and yes, it is a bit sudden.' When I was a girl, my mother, Habiba, used to tell me the story of Imran, the truth teller. He was the wise man of the village whom people turned to when they were in trouble. He might not have known the answers, but Habiba told me he helped them all to ask the right questions. I think David is a truth teller. He asked me what I planned to do. He says maybe Donald will pay my fare and maybe I will have somewhere to live. I have no money now and nowhere to call home, except your kindness, so what have I to lose by trying? I have left my family behind and only you know what it's been like for me. I guess he will ask me questions when he's ready and when he does they'll probably be good questions and I'll tell him the truth.'

'So, you'll have to leave Marseille and we've not known each other long Jamila but I'll miss you.'

'I'll miss you, Marie, but I'm not leaving you, we will always be friends and I'll be back? Thanks to you I feel I belong here, and I don't think that will change but to go to Edinburgh and work with these people just might be my chance. My papers have taken me this far and I believe they'll get me further and anyway David told us that people from other countries are welcomed at the University and I'll never know if I don't try. We have a saying in Arabic… "If the wind blows, ride it".' إذا هبت الرياح ، اركبها

Hearing Jamila speak Arabic, Marie was enchanted. It reminded her of being back with her brother in Algeria, sitting in the evening and listening to the chattering across the market square as the sun went down, but she was still worried for her friend although she had to agree that David might well be a truth teller. She felt the same about him but was less sure about Donald. 'How well does David know Donald do you think?'

'I don't know. It is a chance I will have to take. He's not like anybody I've known before but he's so keen on what he does and happy to share it and talk about it. I feel I could find out so much when I know so little. Why not?'

'But to travel so far with a man you hardly know. What do you think Habiba would say?'

'I don't know, Marie. Other than Zohra, my sister, you're the best friend I have ever had but I've decided, and all your questions make me even more determined. I haven't come here and found you and found this job without taking chances and it's all worked out so far, so I'll take some more chances.'

They heard laughter from other tents and voices in the distance. 'You hear that, Marie? I want to laugh. To wake up and know I belong somewhere, so if there's a chance, I'd be stupid to throw it away and I think you agree, don't you? If you really think I shouldn't do it I will listen to your reasons.'

Marie had enjoyed being with Jamila. She felt confident their trust was mutual and something told her that now was the right time to dig deeper. 'All right, Jamila, I'll tell you what I think, but first, why did you leave your village? Maybe I'd understand better when I know what drove you away; after all, whatever the reason was, it's why we are here now, outside Marseille, in this tent. It's why we met in the first place.'

Jamila felt herself pleased by Marie's question; she felt safe as they lay on their canvas beds in the comforting darkness of a warm night; she was ready. Marie was right; she might understand better if she knew the whole story. 'Do you remember when we were on the boat, I told you Habiba was not my real mother?' Marie smiled. 'Habiba never talked to me about my real mother and for me it is as if she never existed.'

'Did Habiba know who your real mother was do you think?'

'I'm sure she did, yes. I used to feel everybody knew except for me but it was only Nadeem who was unkind to me about it, who called me names. It was horrible, but nobody talked about it and only Habiba tried to stop him, but I've always been sure that everybody in the village knew Nadeem hated me. Coming away, travelling across Morocco I think I've realised they all knew more about me than I did.'

'From what you've said perhaps Nadeem resented you; he thought you'd taken his mother away from him maybe?' said Marie.

Jamila considered her friend, paused and drew breath as if gathering her strength. 'You understand so well, Marie. I think you're right about Nadeem; he was jealous, and the jealousy became hate. I was about ten when Habiba died and looking back, I think she was worn out, running around after us children and worrying about Ismail. Habiba once told me that Nadeem resented me; like you just said Marie. He was older than me, but I think we seemed closer in age than many people realised. Before Habiba died Nadeem always hurt me when he could, even though Zohra looked out for me, but he was crafty, so once his mother was dead, he went for me even more and even with Zohra's kindness I had to look after myself. She was a loving sister to me, but she had her own life to lead and I don't think she fully understood how angry I felt or how helpless.'

'What did Nadeem do? How did he hurt you?'

'He punched me, kicked me, knocked things out of my hands, tripped me up, spilt my food, hid my clothes and he bossed me about all the time. Habiba had always been angry with him for these things but not Ismail, whom I called papa. I knew Ismail loved me and he cared about me, but he was too busy to see what was really happening, so I just put up with it when Habiba was gone. Then when I was older Nadeem started to touch me. He'd catch me in corners, away from the rest of the family and try to brush my skin, rub up against my legs, even try to kiss me. He was clever. I tried but I couldn't escape him and if we were ever seen I knew I would get the blame because Nadeem could do no wrong and there was a lot of blame to be had because we were from the same family and I didn't want to bring shame on them. They were good to me. Looking back, I think I knew he wasn't my brother even though some people thought he was. I was sure when I was younger that my family loved him more than me, but I can never understand why I felt like that. More recently I've realised he'd known for a long time that he wasn't my brother. Maybe that was why he treated me like he did. Maybe Habiba had said something to him. I don't know.'

'So that was why you decided to run away?'

'No. Not that. That was bad enough. No, this was much worse.'

Jamila paused, shaping her memories and surprising herself with her own sense of being able to talk. She stretched her hand across to Marie in the dark and they held onto each other for a while.

'Can this be our secret, Marie? I want to tell you but please never tell anyone.' Marie squeezed Jamila's hand as she promised. 'I ran away on the night of my eighteenth birthday. The day before had been horrible. Ismail was planning a trip to the nearest town to buy supplies for the leather stall and Hammed, my best brother, wanted to go with him. I knew they'd have a good time and I knew Ismail would leave Nadeem in charge of the leather stall at home but he went a bit further and suggested they could spend all day at market planning the café we were going to open next to the stall, finding out prices, scouring the souk for the stuff we'd need, that kind of thing. Mohammed was excited and called over to me. "We're going to open the café, Ismail says so." The plan was that I was going to help with the café, but Nadeem didn't like that, he never had. He was angry, cursing that of course I was going to help. "It's always Jamila this and Jamila that," he said. Perhaps you can imagine Marie.'

'I can,' she said. 'You weren't his real sister, so by his reckoning it was none of your business.'

'Exactly. That's what it was. Whilst all this was going on Zohra and I were grinding corn and like we always did talking about getting married. Habiba had talked with Zohra about marrying and she promised me my turn would come. As we were working 'Hammed called across to me for some help so I went over but we started messing around like we often did and one thing led to another and he darted away from me laughing and calling me and we chased like kids around the leather stall, squealing and weaving in and out. Looking back, I suppose it was inevitable, but I tripped and crashed into the stall, leather goods went flying and of course 'Hammed just laughed all the more. I stopped and started to pick up the leather, but Nadeem was furious. His words are etched on my heart. It was the angriest he had ever been with me. "Bastard girl," he shouted. "Look at the mess you've made. I hate you, Jamila."

'He grabbed me, wrenched me around and slapped me across the face. It really hurt and as I stumbled Ismail stepped forward to steady me and I saw him scowl at Nadeem as I scurried away. But Nadeem was roused, anger in his eyes and heart, he tried to come back at me and as he did so Ismail stood between us, and Nadeem ran into his father. Ismail grabbed him by the arm. He'd spent his life working the fields. He had strong hands.

'"Leave your sister alone, Nadeem. You're a man now. Behave like one." I'd never heard Ismail talk to Nadeem like that before. "Leave her alone."

'"She's not my sister," Nadeem shouted at Ismail. "Everybody knows that."'

Jamila, laying on her camp bed felt the pain of these moments as if they had just occurred. She rolled over and sat up on the edge of the bed, her heart throbbing. Marie joined her friend and wrapped her arm around Jamila's shoulders. After a few moments of quietness, Jamila continued. 'Nadeem pushed Papa away and stood alone, clenching his fists, punching the air and scowling. "She's not my sister and I'm sick of you telling me she is," he shouted, jabbing his finger towards me, his bark echoing from the walls of the house; everybody must have heard. "You're the child of a whore, Jamila. That's what they all say but you never hear. You're a whore's bastard child! Jamila! A whore's bastard."

'I was horrified. Zohra tried to comfort me, but Nadeem's words stabbed at me, and Ismail said nothing. His silence almost hurt me more than Nadeem's fury had done and to top it all Nadeem strode away, kicking furiously at the stones and nobody cared to stop him, to challenge him, not even Zohra. He just walked away. I spoke to none of them for the rest of the day; I just had to carry the insults.

'The next day started like any other. Nothing was said about the day before and Ismail and Hammed left to go to market. I remember feeling shaken, especially as it was my birthday and since Habiba died only Zohra ever remembered. Habiba had always celebrated my birthday with me. Just the two of us. I never knew why it was like that, it just was, and I knew I would miss her that day. Nadeem hadn't spoken but I watched him looking at me and I knew his anger was unabated. For the first time I felt physically frightened of him; I felt sick; he knew it and, on that day, like all other days, he didn't care. Ismail wasn't there. I felt alone, and it was that day I decided I was going to have to get away, to leave home, but I little realised how soon that would have to be. I'd need papers and never had an ID card but I knew where Habiba had kept hers.'

Jamila paused, aware that the distant laughter had died away and occasional voices were the only thing she could hear. She gathered her thoughts, feeling calm as she chose her words. 'As I said, Marie, that day was my birthday. I walked away from the village and down to the river to be alone, in the cool where the trees come down to the water's edge. I was wanting to get away from everyone, even Zohra. The only person I had ever seen in this spot was Habiba, so it was a special place to us both, a good place to remember her on my birthday. I'd taken my book with me, settled down on the sand by a rock and I was lost in its story.'

Jamila felt her emotion grow again and she fell silent for a while. As she fled across Morocco, she had never imagined telling anyone all this, let alone someone who only a few days earlier had been a stranger and yet she felt safe with Marie, alone together in the darkness, and now she had started she wanted to go on, to unburden herself.

'I'd been reading for some time when I sensed a movement behind me and turned to see what it was and saw Nadeem and before I could do anything he threw himself at me, covered my mouth with one hand and pulled me back with the other onto the sandy bank. I tried to cry out for help, but it was useless. What frightened me the most was that I wasn't surprised. I was shocked, terrified but not surprised. I knew he hated me, and I'd always known that one day the hate would spill over but I never imagined being alone with him when it happened. He must have been hidden before I arrived, spied on me in the past maybe, taken his chance. I don't know.' Jamila paused, gathering her thoughts.

'Nadeem pushed me onto the sand and tore the shawl from my head and tried to stuff it into my mouth. His other hand was trying to pull up my clothes and rip them away and it was then that I realised that he was going to do more than attack me and I started to fight and kick to get him off me, scratching, biting, anything to escape. Despite all this he was ripping my clothes from below and was pushing down on me like an animal. His face was so close to mine. That was the worst thing, his rasping stale coffee scented breath so close to me, his eyes possessed by anger. In that moment, I realised I had clutched onto a stone wedged into the sand so without thinking I lifted it and brought it down on the back of his head. I don't remember how I did it but I'd hit him hard and his grip on the scarf around my mouth loosened for a moment and I was able to push up and turn him and hit him again so to protect himself he had to let go of me, swearing uncontrollably and in those few moments I pushed out from under him and ran like a mad thing back, up towards the village. Of course, he could not follow me for fear he would be seen. My clothes were ripped and torn and I had his blood on my face so I stopped at the well, washed myself down and managed to get back through a side way unnoticed.'

'God, Jamila. How could he have done that to you, his own family?'

Jamila paused, lost in her thoughts. 'I don't know, except to Nadeem I wasn't his family and telling you this, going over it again in my head, has made me understand that more strongly than ever before.' Jamila remembered the pain but now, from a safer distance, it was anger that coursed through her, a sense of being hollowed out, beaten by his sheer power and its injustice. It was anger that she was only just now beginning to understand. 'That was why I ran away,' she said. 'I felt I loathed them all. They had all endorsed Nadeem's behaviour; they had allowed him to hate me and then I had to escape to avoid being destroyed because if I stayed, I would be despised. Nobody would believe me if I told them it was nothing to do with me, and even if I did tell them I wasn't the same Jamila anymore and everyone would know.'

'What do you mean?' asked Marie. 'How were you not the same?'

'I felt I was broken, damaged, as if it was partly my fault, as if I might bring shame to the family and maybe I'd tempted him or made him think that it was okay and that when the village found out I would be blamed, marked out as a troublemaker, so I knew by the time I was back in the village that I would walk away that night. I gathered a few things together when they were all asleep. I knew where Ismail kept some money, so I took a little and I feel so guilty about that Marie, but it's all I could think of. I took Habiba's faded ID card and permits and a few of her clothes because

I knew nobody would notice. The photo on her ID card was scratched and tatty so even though she looked older than me my scarf hid my hair, which was darker than hers, so wearing her cloak wrapped around me and carrying a small bundle of things I slipped out and started to climb up the mountains, out over the plains and towards the sea.'

'Where did you plan to go?'

'I knew that Algiers was a long way, but I also knew that when I arrived, I could board a ferry to France, and that would get me as far away as possible. You know, I can speak good French and some English as well. I think I told you I'd learnt French and English from Zohra because there wasn't a place for me at school. Nadeem didn't like that either.'

'Why didn't you say something? Tell someone? Tell Zohra.'

'I think even Zohra would have thought it was my fault, but I wish I had told her. Ismail cared about me as well, but I knew Ismail wouldn't follow me. He had the family to consider. Zohra cared but she would not be able to follow. Along the way I begged a little and stole a little food so my money lasted until I met you.'

'And now you say you want to go to Edinburgh. What do you really want, Jamila?'

'A friend like you, Marie, with kindness like yours? I want to know who I am, to have someone to love, to love me. What would you want?'

'To find the man who attacked me and punish him I think.'

'But that would mean I would have to go back. I do want him to have to face me and hear me tell him what I think but I'm frightened of my anger.'

'You've been treated badly, Jamila; I can see that now very clearly. Nadeem should not be able to get away with it but you can only face him if you return with the truth.'

'The thing is, Marie, I would like to know who my real mother was, where she is now. I need to know her name, something about her, I need to know why I have never known anything. I cannot escape that feeling. I suppose my village is the only place I could find that out, but I am frightened to have to face Nadeem. I never used to think about it when I was at home in the village, but I do now. I need something else before I can face it all, but I don't know what it is.'

Marie was still holding Jamila by the hand. They looked at each other. 'Now you have told me all these things, Jamila, I understand why you left your village, and I can see why you want to take a chance and travel on to Edinburgh. You need the space, and you need to run everything through your mind over and over again. I might even have felt the same way if this had happened to me.'

'I wish it wasn't like this, but I can see a way to build myself a new life and it's a chance I need to take.' Jamila yawned. 'I'll never know if I don't try.'

Falling back onto their beds Jamila was soon asleep. Marie lay awake for a while going over Jamila's story, wishing they knew a little more about Donald, thinking that David was fine. That would have to do, she concluded as she fell asleep.

5

Donald gave Jamila a room in his flat in Edinburgh with no regard for the silent disapproval that met his decision. His own naturally casual demeanour was just that and so he saw nothing surprising in his own behaviour. Several vivacious and ambitious students anticipating his return from Marseille were startled to find he had brought back more than dusty archaeological artefacts, realising they would have to up their game to catch his eye. Only his own team of students, who had shared the journey back from Marseille, knew bits of the story and their sense of loyalty and self-protection meant that so far, they kept their views to themselves. Jamila's presence amongst them remained something of a mystery which pleased Donald as he was realising that to cultivate mystery, was to better impress his acolytes. He allowed himself to be smug that he had pleased himself whilst convincing himself that his behaviour only attracted envy from his colleagues. Insouciance was Donald's default position when faced with personal decisions that left him exposed to possible disapproval.

Jamila had no sense of anything inappropriate or otherwise, assuming David's assessment of Donald to be reliable. He gave her a room and she was free to use the rest of the flat. She couldn't have been more pleased. Her life had not prepared her for a moment like this and she felt neither excitement nor alarm. A few things pleased her and that was enough. Within a few days she was familiar with the local roads and walkways, had found a few shops and agreed to take a little cash from Donald to shop for food, which she cooked for them both as best she could. Her English was good and improved daily although she struggled for a while with the Gaelic tinges. To Jamila, Donald was kind, thoughtful and kept himself to himself. She soon settled into a routine which she thought of as a good beginning, despite remaining conscious of Marie's caution. She liked Donald. It helped that his house was a stone's throw from the Water of Leith, and he always seemed to relish walking by the river when he could. He enjoyed the chance to show off his local knowledge so it wasn't long before Jamila could confidently set out along the river path and divert to the Botanic Gardens, another favourite haunt, where Donald sometimes suggested meeting for lunch. In the first few weeks when he said he had time they had met at the South Gate. And so it was today. The inevitable rain had left the shades of autumn sparkling and given the squirrels an extra impetus to gather their winter food and bury it in apparently random places. Jamila loved watching their antics, skittering here and there, scratching as they travelled, stopping to sniff and quiver. Squirrels in her village at home were a rarity as they all ended up steaming in tasty tagines.

Even though she'd only been in Edinburgh a few weeks Jamila was already accustomed to Donald arriving late; not that this prevented her from being early; she was far too flattered by his attention to want to trouble him in any way and today was no exception. As she waited her eye was taken by a family walking by, two young children and a baby propped up in a pram. The mother smiled as Jamila stooped to admire the child. 'She's lovely,' Jamila said, almost to herself.

'This is Kirsty and she's six weeks today.' Kirsty's mother gazed down at the baby, delighted to share her pride.

'She's sweet and so tiny.' Jamila was pleased to be included.

'She may be tiny but that doesn't stop her making plenty of noise.' They both laughed. 'You'll find that out soon enough I expect.'

Jamila was startled by the comment but even so couldn't help wondering just what it would be like to have a baby, to feed, care for, keep safe and to love; she wanted so much to be able to love and to be loved. In these few moments with Kirsty her mind was filled with thoughts of Habiba, her gentleness and the love given to her by a woman who for reasons unknown to Jamila wasn't her mother. This mystery bothered Jamila but made little difference to how she felt about herself. She was where she had chosen to be. She was so absorbed in her thoughts that Donald's appearance before her was almost a shock.

'It's alright, Jamila. It's only me.' Donald's tone was reassuring, and he offered her his arm and she linked her own. She never considered any reasons why she shouldn't link his arm. He didn't ask. They strolled away from the gate and towards the Pavilion teashop nearby and chose a table in the sun where Donald ordered from the waitress.

'Good to see you again, sir,' she said. Jamila enjoyed lunch with Donald when she could, as already the days were lonely for her, although she would never have said so. She liked that he was recognised by the waitress; it seemed to her to give him weight and credibility.

Jamila didn't understand quite how their own relationship worked but that didn't matter, she'd taken a chance, and it was turning out fine. Only that morning she had posted a cheerful, newsy letter to Marie in one of those lovely red pillar-boxes and she'd already started to anticipate the reply. Lunch over with they walked out into the gardens. Passers-by wondered if they were a couple; Donald, self-assured and casually well dressed, tweed jacket and leather patches; Jamila, smiling, in a swaying pleated tartan skirt which Donald had bought for her within a few days of their arrival; maybe they are, maybe they aren't a couple, the passers-by pondered, with wry smiles and a vague thought along the lines that he seemed a bit old for her.

'I love these gardens, Donald. I love the deep colours of the trees and the winter flowers. They remind me of my home and the mountains in Morocco.'

'Do you wish you'd gone back to Morocco when we left Marseille?' Donald managed to subdue his testy feelings as he asked. He was insecure of course and wanted her to say that she certainly didn't wish she'd gone back to Morocco. Deep down he felt that he just might be getting too old to be desirable, so to feel better about himself, to reassure himself that he was still wanted, he liked to walk with Jamila on his arm, a token seen by others. He decided for himself that he'd planned it. For her part Jamila was already beginning to realise that he didn't like her talking about Morocco and wanting to please him she smiled, hardly aware of her own vulnerabilities or the downside of the slightly out-of-control feeling she was enjoying. After all, she chose this adventure. 'No, Donald. I'm glad I'm here and I'm looking forward to finding out more about what you're doing with all those old bones and teeth you've uncovered and brought back with us. I'd love to work with you on that. What do you do in the laboratory with all those things you've brought back?' Jamila had asked this question a few times and as yet had no answer.

'This is a complicated project, Jamila. David is still in France and we've stuff coming in from Marseille to be sorted and labelled and that's only the start before it's matched with artefacts from Genoa. We've been digging there, and the sites seem to have much in common. And then there's the dig in Dundee.' Jamila nodded and Donald went on. 'We analyse, sort out the samples, maybe do some restoration or find new ways of doing the work. That's exciting when someone has a bright idea, and we can improve what we do.' In as far as Donald had any specific plans for Jamila, working in the laboratory did not figure. Temporary work in admissions was high on his list. Not that they'd talked about it.

Jamila had noticed when they were in Marseille how Donald always warmed to any conversation about his subject. Most of the journey from Marseille back to Scotland was dominated by his mini lectures on all things archaeological, which she tried to understand but was struggling at times. Her problem was that she had little knowledge of her own to use when they talked, but she listened, and she remembered. Still arm-in-arm they had stopped on a bridge across a stream which flowed into a pond wriggling full of goldfish. Jamila was pleased for the diversion. 'Look!' she squealed. 'Aren't they lovely. It's a beautiful place for children here. I was talking to a lady before you came who had a tiny baby. What a great place to grow up.'

If Jamila had noticed the slight look of alarm on Donald's face, she didn't show it and she certainly had no idea what Donald might have been thinking. She just jumped from subject to subject.

'Do you have a laboratory in Dundee? Perhaps I could work there, Donald?'

'I don't think so, Jamila, it's just some other archaeologists like me and I need to visit as I have a project there that needs regular attention.'

'I see. One day maybe. It would be good to see David, Connie, and your other students again as well. David was good to me when I arrived at the dig. He told me you were a kind man. Connie seemed to be very proud of you.'

'Well then?' Donald laughed, self-consciously. 'There you go then. Ring-a-ding-ding.'

'Maybe I could work for you at the University, help with the sorting and organising all those bits and pieces you found in Marseille? That way I could learn some more.'

By now Donald was becoming impatient and replied almost sharply. 'I'm not sure about that, Jamila. You've seen what we do. I don't think you'd be able to pick it up so easily as you think.'

Jamila was hurt by his response. She was almost feeling as she had done when Nadeem put her down when she was younger, but she dismissed this concern, keen to move the conversation. 'Maybe I couldn't, but surely there is other work I could do?' On an instinct she didn't know she had, Jamila spun coquettishly towards Donald and as they walked forward, she pushed herself to her tiptoes, put her arms around him and kissed him. He looked a little alarmed but pleased.

'Jamila. Somebody might see us.'

'So what? I live with you, don't I? I'm interested in other things than old teeth.' She laughed.

In one movement Donald raised his eyebrows and drew Jamila towards him, kissed her lightly again and hugged her briefly before turning away. Making advances was normally his show but even so he wasn't disappointed and knew that this event would recur although he would rather initiate it himself. It was a series of actions that he fell into with ease. He was slightly startled and a little embarrassed by Jamila's flirtatiousness although pleased that she was onside. However, he needed to be in control. He needed to score a few singles before he hit a six.

'I need to get back,' he said.

'Oh, Donald, must you go?'

'I'll be back at the flat later this evening, enjoy the afternoon.' With that Donald turned and headed down the hill towards the city, leaving Jamila, a lonely figure, to turn back into the gardens, with several thoughts running. She walked towards Leith, pondering her temerity and searching for a better understanding of her motives. She wondered what Marie would have said if she had seen them in the Botanic Gardens. Would she have disapproved? Maybe she would have been surprised but not critical? 'You've got to start somewhere,' she might have said. Ismail would have been critical of course. Once he was round the corner Donald shrugged off his feelings, pleased to have had his ego boosted, keen to get back to the laboratory, keen to work, keen to see his team.

*

After the brisk walk Donald approached his laboratory, pausing to admire the nameplates before opening the door: Donald Lansdown PhD., engraved in red above another four plates; Fraser McBride, Alex Everette, David Cooke and Constance Fielding, all engraved in black and attached below his own. He knew his white lab coat would be hanging on the other side of the door, waiting for him, freshly laundered every week. His scholarship to Edinburgh University had been his greatest achievement after tedious years at Dundee Grammar School, mollycoddled by his mother and learning to imitate his father's egregious charm. All the doting domestic attention and flirtatious masculinity had left Donald with a fatal combination of indifference and arrogance. He was smart, fascinated by his work and seldom unsure of himself, unselfconsciously burdened with self-importance, which came across as charm, a characteristic he intuitively deployed in pursuit of his own interests, often female.

As he entered the laboratory, Fraser, Alex and Constance were beavering away at sorting and dusting bones. All was purposeful activity. He approached and there was a lull in conversation as Donald progressed between them, interested and intent. His laboratory was a place of learning, sacred and revered and he presided over it like a catholic vicar at communion. Like the same vicar admiring his pews, Donald found comfort in the dark oak benches, scratched with the names of patient students of science long departed and he basked in spiritual reassurance at the pervasive and familiar scent of dry earth that accompanies the archaeological artefacts whose silence he found enigmatic. Each piece was an irresistible anonymity. Once he was back in his laboratory his calm and apparent kindness on the dig was replaced by a perfidious impatience to catalogue and systematise.

'These pieces have just come in from David.' Fraser was opening a small package and moving its dusty contents onto a small tray.

'Ring-a-ding-ding, it's more teeth. I was at the Botanics just now and thinking that when we left Marseille there might have been more to find.' Donald swung all his attention to the tray of precious new pieces.

'There's a note from David as well,' said Fraser. 'He says there may be new finds in the other trenches so perhaps he should start a new search. What do you think, Donald?'

'Do you think we should give it a try, Fraser? You were right last time. It's a shame to waste the chance.' He called across the lab, 'What do you think, Connie? Shall we ask David to find us some more teeth? Come over and share your thoughts.' Donald, out of eyeline with the others, winked towards Constance as she skipped across to Donald's side keen to acquiesce with his signal and the three of them leant against the bench, vigilantly dusting and sketching what they were seeing in the trays. Donald, still absorbed, stooped over a fossil, his eyeglass feeding him a stream of information that he was calmly stashing away. He loved this feeling of being inside his own brain, sorting and filing, accepting and rejecting. Constance watched fascinated, following his moves, enjoying the warmth of his thigh against hers and trying to understand what he was seeing and what it meant. She, like so many others also admired Donald's tenacity and like Fraser and David needed his expertise for her own academic success. She also liked the man as a flirt but kept it to herself most of the time, or so she thought.

'We have a pack of teeth, Connie, and the soil you collected that goes with them, from the first burial. When we get the new radiocarbon decay measurement for dating samples, we can examine the timing of different cultural changes we might have uncovered. How long will we have to wait for the technical equipment to arrive do you think, Fraser?'

'A few months I would suppose. It's all very new stuff. I think we should carry on as we are for the moment.'

'Won't it be wonderful to be able to date all this accurately and work out its chronology?' Donald loved to conjecture what such information would tell them but only Fraser really understood what was going to be possible and how it would work. Donald just fed the narrative. He loved all the scraping and brushing, labelling and sorting but was less sure when Fraser was enthusing over the wires and switches of the new technologies and his mind tended to wander onto other things. 'How do you think we're getting on with the evidence we need? Shall we give David the go-ahead, Fraser?'

Before Fraser could answer Constance made her opinion clear. 'More, Donald. No question. If we doubled the evidence base, then our proposition would be even more powerful. Even in the last few days this is beginning to look like a strong case.' Fraser smiled to himself as he enjoyed Connie's charming keenness to please Donald whilst attempting to hide her self-seeking imperatives.

'You seem very sure, Connie,' said Donald, winking.

'I am. Female intuition!'

Donald chuckled. 'Whatever that might be. I'm told there's a lot of it about. But let's hear from Fraser, who's suddenly gone very quiet.' They laughed. Fraser was back at his microscope, ignoring them all but even so he instantly responded.

'Sorry. I was having to readjust, making way for Connie.' Fraser's slowly delivered sarcasm was lost on them both. 'I'm okay with that, Donald,' he continued. 'So we're all agreed.'

'Fraser, will you let David know that we'd like more if he can find more and tell him it needs to be before the end of next month because we need him back here well before the graduation day. That's only a couple of weeks.'

'Consider it done, Donald. By the way, how's our Moroccan friend getting on? Finding her way round Edinburgh?'

'It's funny you should mention her, she was asking me this morning if she could come and work here?'

Fraser liked Jamila and was wanting to be sure she was okay, but he knew that for her working here was a recipe for discontent. Certainly, Connie would struggle with the competition and Fraser liked to keep the peace. 'Trouble is we need someone experienced,' he replied, pragmatic as ever. 'Anyway, how are you both getting along? What's her story, Donald?'

'Why all these questions, Fraser?' Donald strung out his answer as he was preoccupied with studying the trays and felt a little under the microscope himself. He liked to avoid personal questions. 'She tells me she's eighteen, she was born in Morocco, she seems to like Edinburgh and she's quite comfortable in my flat. She is what she is,' he said enigmatically.

Fraser persisted though. 'Why don't you bring her to meet us again, after all she did well in Marseille, you said so yourself, better than that French girl, so it would be good to see her again. You're here working most of the time so she must be a bit lonely. Or even better bring her to the Union Bar.'

Donald didn't respond. Across the laboratory Connie was bent busy sorting her tray, listening to every word and doing her subtle best to attract Donald's attention by hanging over the microscope and shifting from foot to foot. Fraser was right that Jamila wasn't experienced, and Connie feared she would get in the way in several respects. She was unhappy that Jamila had somehow crept in and diverted Donald's attention away from her. Concentrating on her work seemed to her like the best way of staying onside with Donald, that and sharing an occasional drink together and she didn't want Jamila onside for either of those pastimes. She guessed that there was more to be shared with Donald than a drink and was preparing herself for that event, although Jamila's arrival had left her confused. For his part Donald was happy to play the innocent bachelor, arousing enough interest to satisfy needs but not too much as to make himself uncomfortable.

Donald picked up the conversation where he chose. 'Of course, Fraser, we need to have careful systems to separate the different remains of plants and animals so we can provide good evidence of past environments when the carbon dating arrives. Then we'll have much better records of diet, health and disease which is going to make what we do more helpful.'

'Yep. Everything will change.' Fraser couldn't help admiring the way Donald quietly made other people's knowledge his own but respected less Donald's skill at gaining the credit as well. For his part Donald was pleased to have batted away the subject of Jamila but to his surprise he was still thinking about her unexpected embrace at lunchtime. He knew she was naïve but that only added to the frisson.

6

The vaulted ceilings of the Union Bar, in Niddry Street, filled with cigarette smoke by lunchtime every day and on the rare days it shone, the afternoon sun sliced through the high arched windows, cutting the ashy air into horizontal stripes. On any day of the week a few dozen figures sat in combative conversation at the dozen or so round tables ranged across the dusty floor and as the day drew on, exchanges grew more excited and the opinions and the laughter louder, the scent of stale beer strengthened, and the sounds of scraping chairs intensified. Men argued. There were women, the Union Bar being progressive, although no more than one to every gaggle of men. Perhaps they were women tolerant of the acrid fumes that would cling to their clothes until the Monday wash came round; maybe women unusually determined to keep an eye on their men or equally unusual, women who could be bothered to keep up with the testosterone driven arguments.

Donald and his team loved this bar; maybe it was the bohemian atmosphere that contrasted to their precious and sometimes sterile laboratory or the acrimonious and refreshingly intolerant debate that characterised every table, but an hour in the Union Bar was all it took to shake away the pressures of the archaeologist's day. Today Donald was with Connie, deep in conversation, both sipping beer, a half-eaten cheese sandwich and a shared bowl of peanuts between them.

'I'm sorry you feel like that, Connie, but I don't see why you should be jealous of Jamila?'

'I didn't say that, Donald. Those are your words. But Fraser seems worried about Jamila, and I understand what he's saying. He feels sorry for her and says she left home because there was trouble. I'm thinking that he wants you to give her a job. My worry Donald is that maybe she was the trouble. Have you thought about that possibility? She may not be as naïve as she looks.'

Donald hadn't thought about that but even so he was surprised by Connie's vehemence and unsure why it mattered to her so much. For her part Connie was pleased with the way she had constructed her argument. Donald regarded Connie as a good colleague and knew she was keen to please, as well as fancying him, because he knew everyone fancied him. He liked that, preferring to avoid contrary opinions where possible and he also liked to have a woman on the team to keep everything shipshape and working well but he didn't admit to himself that what he wanted mostly was a woman to clear up after him and keep him distracted. He decided to test Connie. 'Come on, Connie. Jamila was hard working in Marseille and keen to learn. Fraser's right, I think she'd make a good member of the team. I thought you'd be pleased.'

'So, you care whether I'm pleased do you, Donald? I wonder why. It's not for me to be pleased or otherwise. It's your team, but it feels a little like she's someone for you to boss around. I can't say that I'd noticed but David seems to think you encouraged her with offers of a room.'

'So, what if I did. Why does it matter to you?'

'You did then, Donald. David was right. I can tell you that's raised a few eyebrows. You know what she's after, Donald. We all do. You, of course don't have the decency to think that I might feel upset with her all tucked up in your little flat. I bet it's better there for her than it was in Morocco.'

Donald felt under attack and didn't appreciate it. Added to which he was beginning to see that whichever way he turned he wouldn't win. Denial was his natural resting place, facing the issues his place of last resort. 'It's not like that, Connie. She just needed somewhere to live that's all.'

'Ha! I'm supposed to believe that am I? I sometimes wonder what drives you, Donald. Do you really take us all for fools, running round after you? And you need to watch that, Fraser. He may be good at what he does but he's a bit too free with his tongue in my opinion.'

'You've made your point, Connie.' Donald was starting to sound testy, and Constance saw that she needed to be careful. After all she worked for him as a student now and wanted to keep a university job if she could and was risking her arm by speaking out. Talking with Donald like this had also shown him that she was jealous of Jamila and Connie's instinct was to take care that she didn't get the blame. She sensed that a trap was being laid. For his part Donald was fine with the developing contest. 'Ring-a-ding-ding,' he might say. Donald loved the chase, the adrenalin rush of attraction and romance and he wouldn't recognise it, but the intimacy of attachment, commitment and honesty frightened him. As he has discovered, love confused him.

'Are you still planning on going to Dundee after your party on Tuesday?' Connie asked.

'Naturally. That work still needs to be done and I must keep up with progress. Dundee University expects me, birthday or otherwise.'

Constance laughed. 'I like you, Donald, in so many ways but you're a hard man to fathom.'

Donald ignored the laugh and the comment. He finished the sandwich, offered Connie the rest of the nuts, polished off his cup of tea and started to put on his coat. Once outside he put his arm around Constance and drew her towards him. 'Connie.' Donald addressed her as if taking her into his confidence. 'There's nothing between Jamila and me, you're perfectly safe, but I think I may want her to work with us. David is sending more material back from

Marseille, the work will need to be done and I might use Jamila to do some of it and I expect you to help her like you did in Marseille. I'll see you back at the lab.' Donald wrapped his arms around Connie, kissed her lightly on the lips and strode across the road leaving her to make her own way and deal with her own anxieties.

Constance was far sorer than she cared to admit. She thought she had made some headway with Donald before they left Marseille, that he had noticed her enough to begin to like her, to see her keenness, but she'd been proved wrong, or mostly wrong. Her limerence was getting the better of her. She also saw Donald as a route to her career. Jamila was now an unwelcome irritant to both ambitions.

7

In the few weeks she'd been in Edinburgh Jamila had begun to love the National Gallery on Princes Street. She delighted in its halls of grand paintings and best of all she enjoyed standing by a metal radiator warming her hands, superimposing her memories of home onto the dramatic Scottish landscapes around her, almost allowing herself to believe they were one and the same space, except that as she walked outside, she was cold and alone and although she had never considered it before, being alone in her home village had been a rare event. The Road to Loch Maree was her chosen painting today. Until she left Morocco, she hadn't realised how much she loved mountains, how it was mountains and not the village she missed and this vivid painting, with its startled deer and treeless hills, the stony track wandering into the distance, the lowering, wind whipped clouds; this bleak landscape felt close to her, close to what she was. It had taken her self-imposed flight from home to start to understand her attachment to the empty mountains she had left behind. She was startled by the control this sense of belonging had exerted over her as she absorbed the loneliness of this painting. It was as if the mountains gave her power.

It wasn't that the gardens below Princes Street weren't beautiful or that she didn't enjoy watching the flow of people and children along leaf strewn pathways, coursing down the slopes until they reached the platform below where a small military band was entertaining the crowd, it was just that today Jamila felt sad and quite alone. 'Am I in the right place?' she was asking herself and today it wasn't just the mountains. She missed the intense smell of the leather when it was being beaten with the flattening hammer by Ismail; she missed the crisp taste of the flatbreads she and Zohra rolled and baked on the hot stones of the wood oven. These were the things that made her wonder if she was right to be in Edinburgh, to have deserted what she was beginning again to think of as home. As these reflections occupied her, she felt anger returning at the injustice of her treatment by Nadeem and her self-imposed exile. His violence towards her cluttered her emotions and left her fearful of her home.

However, despite all this, today Jamila had a mission as she left the gallery. She walked up the way, crossed Princes Street and headed for Jenner's Department Store. The first time Jamila made acquaintance with Jenner's, accompanied by Donald, she had been overwhelmed. He seemed very 'at home' there. It compared to nothing she had ever seen; the commerce of the souks of Marrakech and the street markets of Marseille teemed with abundant, multifarious life; the commerce of Jenner's by contrast was quiet, tidy, well ordered, polite and deferential as she had never experienced before. But with encouragement from Donald, she had now become accustomed to the ways of Scottish shopping and now she was there again, on her own, in search of a hat.

Jamila found the right counter, put down her clutch bag, also bought at Jenner's, picked up a hat, turned it, looking without seeing and as she didn't know what she wanted, she put it down and picked up another and tried to put it on and true to the standards the store set itself, as she raised the hat to her head a bustling shop assistant approached her. 'That looks lovely on you miss. The style's all the fashion just now and the colour. It really suits your complexion.'

'Oh!' Jamila spluttered. 'Do you really think so? I've never had a hat. Just scarves.' Jamila was not at all sure how to react, so she took the hat off, turned it over in her hands, examined the label without reading it and put the hat back on the wrong display, an error corrected in moments by the assistant.

'Try this one, miss. Maybe a paler shade would suit you even better. You've beautiful, sunny skin. You look lovely in a hat. Here. Let me help you.'

The assistant moved nearer to Jamila showed her a mirror so she could look at herself from different angles and gently helped her arrange the hat. As Jamila saw herself reflected in the glass, wearing what she saw as a stupid hat, she was overwhelmed by a sense of loss, by soreness in her heart. What was she doing here, why was she here? She looked ridiculous in a hat, and she didn't want one, she didn't like it and she was only trying them on to please Donald. Inevitably the ever attentive assistant noticed Jamila was crying and seeing her customer's discomfort, transformed herself into a fairy godmother.

'Oh dear. Here, borrow my handkerchief. We don't want you being all sad when you look so lovely in that hat.'

'No! No! Please. I'm not used to people being so kind to me.'

'That's not to worry, sweetheart. You're a long way from home I expect.'

'Yes, you're right. I am. I have to go to a party tomorrow and I think I should wear a hat, but they all look so strange on me. I don't know anything about hats.'

Jamila was shocked at her own distress. She had accepted the handkerchief and wiped the tears from her cheeks and feeling agitated she took off the hat and put it down and dropped her bag as she did so. The assistant bent to pick it up and handed it to Jamila, who taking her bag found herself running for the door leaving the store clutching the bag in one hand with the shop assistant's handkerchief held to her eyes in the other.

'Oh dear! Oh dear! Such a pretty girl to be such a long way from home,' the assistant muttered to herself as she put the hats straight whilst another customer started to make her choice.

As she spilled out into the cold air Jamila looked at the handkerchief, wondering where it had come from, put two and two together, hesitated, turned as if to take it back and changed her mind as she couldn't face it. She walked up the street drying her eyes and a few passers-by turned towards her noticing her tears and her fluster, so sensing their disapproval Jamila turned up a side-street to escape the stares and gather her thinking before setting out once again for Donald's flat in Leith, which she did not think of as home.

*

A few streets away as the usual clusters of customers were passing the time of day in companionable banter, Fraser stood at the Union Bar placing an order. He was happy to see David back from Marseille. They were good friends, sharing their academic interest as well as a love of the Scottish hills, where they were often to be found hiking together in search of wild animal life. They laughed at how their pastime involved searching for evidence of the living and their work searching for evidence of the dead. Less interested in the living, Donald had joined them once for a trek but never stopped talking about archaeology. They avoided asking him again. For Fraser David's return was worth a celebratory drink. He walked to their table with a couple of pints. 'It's ages since we all met up at the Union. Cheers, David. Now you're here again do you think we'll be going back to Marseille?'

'Cheers, Fraser. No. We'll not be going back for the time being. I think we've found the main evidence and given the site a good going over and you've all the important finds in the laboratory now.'

'You've done a good job there, David.' Fraser was an expert when it came to kind words.

'Talking about finds,' continued David, 'how's that Moroccan girl getting on that Donald magicked out of nowhere? Jamila, is it? I'm not sure I trusted Donald's motives but she struck me as a nice girl, even if a bit naïve.'

'We've not seen that much of her, truth-to-tell. Donald doesn't seem keen on bringing her into the lab. He's ferreted her away and I don't know but I think he's getting worse and I'm not sure I like it.'

'Meaning what, Fraser?'

'All this success with the project is going to his head and he seems to think he can do just as he likes. He certainly managed to rub Alex up the wrong way; he'd tried so hard with Connie and then Donald just came along and swept her away and now Connie is starting to feel she's playing second fiddle to Jamila. It's quite sad really. Oh! Talk of the devil.' David was about to suggest that maybe the boot was on the other foot, and it was Connie who wanted to pursue Donald, but they were interrupted as Alex, drink in hand, strolled across and joined them at their table.

'Hello again, David. Glad you've had a safe trip. That's some good stuff you sent back.'

'Well,' said David. 'We all set it up together but it's certainly a good site.'

'True, but it's decent of you to say so. We don't always get the credit for our own work. Perfect timing as well, David, because you're just in time to win a prize.'

'What's that then?' said David.

'To help us organise Donald's party.'

'Thanks, Alex,' groaned David. 'My favourite thing! We were talking about Donald. How do you find him these days?'

'Work or play?'

'Does he work?' said Fraser. They laughed. Fraser had touched a nerve with them all.

'Ouch! Come on, Fraser. He does work and he keeps us all in work so we shouldn't complain,' said David.

'Yes. But there's some of us stay in jobs for different reasons than others. Mind you. I'm glad he doesn't fancy me,' said Alex.

'So are we!'

'He seems to have tucked that Moroccan girl away. Why do they all fall for him?'

'Books, bottles and beds Alex. That's Universities for you,' said David.

'Yes. I suppose so but it gets up my nose, all this staff and students stuff leaves us out in the cold.' Alex had pursued Connie but regardless of his failure he chose to believe that she preferred to try to get into Donald's trousers. 'Connie certainly tried her luck at the Christmas Party and Donald seemed happy enough to be draped all over her, although they were both bladdered.'

'Yes. Donald's hard to fathom,' said David. 'He likes to play the field but seems to fight shy of what he might call "Ring-a-ding-ding"! They laughed.

'What does that mean when it's at home? But from what you say I worry about our Moroccan friend. She's had a rough time and some bad trouble at home she told me and she didn't say what it was but apparently that's why she wanted to travel back with us. I think she deserves a new start and I hope Donald is treating her okay.'

'Well. She could make a new start with me any day.' Alex smiled wryly.

'I dare say but you don't have a flat, Alex,' Fraser quipped.

'Fair enough to give me a hard time, I know, but there's more to this than a bit of casual flirting in a free flat. Don't forget that Connie came into all this on the back of that lovely Welsh girl that Donald scared away.'

'Oh yes,' said David. 'I'd forgotten about her. Bethan, was it? We never did know why she disappeared.' David went silent realising that he'd not remembered Bethan when Jamila had asked him about Donald. He felt badly about that.

'No. But it was obvious Donald was to blame,' said Fraser. 'Do you remember her shouting at Donald in the lab that day when it all blew up?'

David did remember now. It was his first experience of Donald's penchant for pretty girls, but it seemed Bethan was having none of it. 'She said she was stupid to have trusted him and she never wanted to see him again.'

'She walked out there-and-then didn't she. In fact, she didn't walk, she sailed out of the lab leaving a trail of curses behind. Donald seemed to think she'd come back. He's always been arrogant. Just as well he's a good archaeologist.' Fraser wasn't bitter exactly, but he did resent Donald's cockiness. His life was modest whereas Donald tended to ooze entitlement and live without shame. 'The trouble was that ten minutes later Connie turned up and Donald started on her. Mind you she's feisty as well; a tough nut to crack.'

'You're right, Fraser. That's why I worry about Jamila,' added David, starting to worry about her even more. 'She's naïve, thinks Donald is a big name and probably assumes a gentleman as well. It's the impression he loves to create but I'm beginning to realise it's not really true.'

'Careful, David. Donald likes to be respected. Our jobs depend on him.'

'Whose jobs depend on what?' Connie had just appeared. Fraser, pleased by the diversion, jumped up and offered her a drink. 'Small sherry please, Fraser.'

'Where did you spring from, Connie? I thought you were working late.' David was glad of the diversion as well.

'Good to see you back, David. I was working late but I wanted to see you safe and sound and I wanted Donald out of the way as well, to sort out his party, but he was just being a bit, you know, a bit "Donald". Our Moroccan friend seems to have upset his balance. I like to keep my eye on everybody, you never know what you might miss.'

'You love to make things sound mysterious, Connie,' said David. 'I think we should look out for Jamila; she needs a bit of space I'd say, and I reckon she'd be able to handle Donald if she had to. When all's said and done, I think there's more to her than meets the eye.'

Constance couldn't help thinking that was just what she was bothered about, but she kept her counsel. She liked to share her opinions but only when the time was right; that wasn't now she judged. 'Anyway, David, tell us all about your prolonged stay in Marseille,' she said. 'It will give us something to talk about at Donald's party.'

'Yes. Come on, David. Spill the beans,' echoed Fraser. 'Another drink, anyone?'

8

A few hundred miles away Marie was working back at the café where Pierre was the boss, and they were getting on fine together. She liked him; he worked hard, was fair to his staff and treated the customers like friends. They'd started dating and after a couple of time-out breaks, it was working well. His kindness to others suited Marie; after all she'd always thought that caring about other people was what life was about. She'd lost close family in the war with Germany, and this had made her determined to avoid conflict and the grief of self-sacrifice. Thinking of the three million French dead brought tears to her eyes. This carnage had also shown her that small kindnesses mattered. She attributed to Pierre her friendship with Jamila; after all, they'd come together by chance at the café because both she and Jamila needed a job. Jamila had the drive that sometimes eluded Marie. She'd enjoyed their adventure into archaeology, even though they had to desert the café for a while and even though Marie never quite understood why old bones mattered. One evening she arrived home from work and was pleased to find a letter from Edinburgh in her mailbox and settled down with a coffee to read it.

> *How are you, Marie? I want you to know I often think of you and our conversations into the night. I have followed Donald, and he has taken me in and I have four walls, a room and food and clothes. He likes me to dress to suit his needs. He likes to buy me clothes. He's important here. His name is on his laboratory door in carved red letters, so he needs me to look smart. But that's not often. He says he prefers to be*

alone but I'm not sure I believe him although he's kind and good to me and I'm still interested in what he does but he doesn't want to talk about it yet. His students like him and he looks after them as well. So far, I have no other friends and no work yet. For Donald it's all work and I sometimes wonder why he has let me into his life but I'm lucky he has. So, you see, Marie, that's how it is.

Edinburgh is a great place to be. I love riding the city trams, sitting by the window and staring out as strange places and strange people pass by. To stop the trams, I must reach up and pull a string and the bell rings. You'd like it here, Marie. Sometimes it's like Marseille with the stony streets. They call them cobbles here and I love the Grassmarket, full of stalls laden with produce and teeming with people in dark coats and hats wrapped up warm. It's cold. I am often alone Marie and often cold. David told us Edinburgh was cold and he was right. We don't have a Cathedral on a hill like you do but we do have a castle on a hill which everyone says is a big hill, but they haven't been to my village. I wonder about my father and Zohra and how they are doing. I don't imagine they miss me like I miss them. Did I ever tell you about the leather stall? I even miss that and the café that Mohammed was supposed to be opening. Did I tell you that? I can't remember.

There are lovely gardens here, the Botanics, with plants from all over the world and I meet Donald there for lunch sometimes. It's special when we are alone together like that and he's kind and thoughtful and I see other girls look at him, all smart and well brushed, and look at me as if they are thinking, lucky her, he's alright, even though we're only friends.

Then I worry about what Habiba, my mother might have said and what you might think.

I love the art gallery in the city and the metal radiators that keep the building warm. You'd laugh to see me sitting on them. When people stand and look at the paintings, they sometimes look at me and I think they notice my skin colour. I heard someone say, 'she's foreign,' when I was standing by a large picture, like a whole wall wide, it was Scottish hills and mountains of heather, broom and deer with huge antlers. I've been back to see the paintings a few times because they remind me of the hills and mountains around my village and because it's warm in there.

I never talk about my life in Morocco to anyone and I don't know why but I'm frightened to share it. Donald wouldn't like it. It wouldn't fit. My life feels different here. He's posh and I'm foreign. But I like him. He kissed me the other day when we were in the park. I am still frightened of Nadeem, and only you would understand Marie. He'd never find me here I know but even so I worry he might try to and I cannot write to my family in case he works out where I am.

The dockyards are near to Donald's flat in the old city with tall ships coming up the river. It's a bit like Marseille. You'd like it Marie. I wander about in the City and I'm anxious of forgetting who I am, of not knowing what to do.

I'm going to stop now Marie. Write soon. Please come soon and stay x Jamila

Marie folded the letter. She thought Jamila sounded confused. She wanted to go and find her. She decided to talk about it with Pierre.

9

Alex did what he was told and brought his gramophone into the laboratory but when he played the first record he felt ill at ease. Despite the party hats and balloons, the wine and the meat pies, the sound of Scottish Dance music seemed not just unfamiliar in this hallowed place but odd in a serious room of study where light-heartedness seemed untidy. Would Donald rebuke him as frivolous? He reassured himself that the pies were Donald's choice but even so seeing Donald standing by his demonstration bench, underneath a painted sign; 'Donald's 30th!' was incongruous to say the least. To Alex he still looked like Donald the archaeologist, not renowned for his humour or lightness of touch but even so he loved meat pies and was even happier when they came with gravy. *Maybe*, thought Alex, *I'm being too critical*. Then he remembered that Donald had to be away by mid-afternoon to get the Dundee train, to work on his other project, and that maybe he was right to be sceptical. 'Frivolity doesn't fit,' Alex quipped to Connie, 'but then neither do my trousers.' Connie laughed, standing by the cake with matches at the ready. She was looking relieved as it was twelve-thirty, and everyone had turned up. The sooner it started the sooner it would finish. She wasn't a party girl.

Connie was avoiding eye contact with Jamila who sat discreetly behind a bench. David had been pleased to see her, drawing her in and fetching her a glass of wine, that she knew she wouldn't drink. She'd tried wine a few times at the flat with Donald but didn't like the taste. Jamila was watching Constance taking charge, fiddling with the cake, touching Donald from time-to-time and she also noticed

Donald seemed to like to be told what to do as if he was uneasy, not sure of himself. This was a side of Donald she had not seen before and to her surprise she found it reassuring. Even though this was his laboratory and she'd been kept away for most of the time since she'd arrived she wondered if perhaps he'd appreciate her being a little more organising when they were together in his flat and promised herself to give it a go.

Even though Jamila was trying to be invisible she'd not gone unnoticed. She knew Donald's team but there were a few other hangers-on who seemed to be surreptitiously observing her, in particular an elderly couple she took to be Donald's parents. Jamila's thoughts were interrupted as on a signal from Constance, Alex turned the gramophone down and she started to light the candles. At the same time everyone broke into song.

> 'Happy Birthday to you.
>   Happy Birthday to you.
>   Happy Birthday dear Donald
>   Happy Birthday to you!'

As the words died away, they were replaced by calls of 'Speech! Speech!' and chants of 'Don-ald, Don-ald'. Jamila observed as Donald drew himself up self-importantly until standing behind his bench, raised his hand for quiet and when silence descended, eyes looked his way and he cleared his throat. Jamila was quietly attracted by what she perceived as his importance and allured by his authority. 'Thanks to you, my friends, for friends you all are. Thank you to my parents, James and Elizabeth for being here today.' There were muffled cheers from everyone as his parents took a mock bow and smiled indulgently at Donald. Jamila's instinct had been right. James was solid, his face deep pitted with adolescent scars under a ruddy, puffy skin. His suit and tie gave him a formal air so as Jamila observed him from a safe distance, she saw little to comfort her, feeling in awe of his self-assured manner. Elizabeth looked even more daunting, complete with tight gloves and feathered hat to match. Jamila thought ruefully of her failed visit to Jenner's and how she accidently stole the sweet-scented handkerchief that she still had in her pocket.

Donald ground on. 'With our excavations in France nearly complete it is good to use my birthday to take a few minutes to remember how hard we have all worked. Thanks to David for leading the dig and for closing down once we had all gone. Thanks to Alex, Fraser and Constance who make all this possible by putting up with my demands and especially to Fraser who always seems to be around just when I need him.' The last comment drew mock applause and muffled mumbles of 'Hear! Hear!' 'Thanks to Jamila for joining us today for this celebration and of course, thank you to me for working so hard!' There was forced laughter all round. Jamila was embarrassed to have been pointed out and tried again to melt into the background, feeling herself blush as she tried to look inconspicuous. How she wished that Marie was with her today to lend her some confidence. 'You will all be pleased to know that Professor Macintyre told me today that he regards this as his number one research project. He'll be watching the outcomes of the carbon dating with interest, and I know we will not disappoint him with our findings.' Around the laboratory there were various mutterings of approval. 'So! Here's to the project, and of course, to my birthday.' More applause.

David stood up and there was quiet again. Seeing him standing there Jamila was surprised to feel a warmth. She wanted him to be okay, to be liked by everyone. David's words were calm and reassured. 'Before we move to the cake, I want to thank Donald for his skill and energy in bringing us all to this point. He has shown us all that archaeology embodies the lion's share of global history; his way of thinking about humanity is about comparing the lives of people across history, with archaeology as his starting point. Through our work he has displayed to us how our minds and bodies have evolved as they shed light on humankind's basic skills; he is working to explain the diverse shapes of human societies and social power. All this old stuff in our laboratory tells us so much about our lives today and it's Donald that drives that growth in knowledge. Happy birthday, Donald.'

'Hear, hear,' reverberated round the room and the clinking of glasses echoed as Jamila once more heard the Scottish Dance music above the general talking and chatter. Then to her horror Donald's mother was making a beeline for her, she couldn't escape and reaching her, this formidable woman was instantly in full flow. 'You must be Jamila. Donald mentioned you the last time he was with us. I'm Elizabeth, Donald's mother and this is James, his father. Donald was a naughty little boy you know. Never kept still. Then one day he started reading and never stopped.' Elizabeth laughed at her own wit and charm as she looked over in Donald's direction, where Connie was busily talking with him, her hand resting on his arm. Jamila was well cornered. 'Look at him,' Elizabeth gabbled. 'Our Donald is a one for the girls you know. Did he meet you in France? I guess he probably did. He said you followed him back. I know him better than that. I dare say he asked you back, pretty little thing like you. I hope he's being a good boy and not giving you a hard time. I don't suppose he's ever home is he. Does he still go to Dundee every week? He loves going on that train; always liked trains when he was a little boy. Trains and old rocks. I never could understand the rocks. He told me it was more work in Dundee. You'll need to keep an eye on him I expect. He likes collecting things.'

Elizabeth suddenly stopped and winked at Jamila who smiled uncomfortably and wished the floor would swallow her although she was surprised to find herself feeling quite angry. Elizabeth seemed to Jamila to be a most unpleasant woman. But she hadn't finished. 'He's not told us much about you. Where are you from? We assumed you are from France. Is that right?'

Jamila had already realised that to tell this woman the truth was not a good idea, so she decided to protect herself. 'Not really France,' she said. 'I was born in Morocco. In Algiers, in the Souk.'

'That's nice. I don't think we have those in Edinburgh, do we, James?' James was unresponsive. 'Is that where everybody washes?' asked Elizabeth.

Jamila nearly laughed at this stupid comment but was saved as Fraser came over to join them at that moment and stood politely listening. 'It's a market, isn't it, Jamila?' he said.

'That's right, Fraser,' said Jamila. 'It's the market, in the middle of the city. My father sells carpets and lives in a grand house, and he has servants and a cook, and my brother died when I was a baby, but I had several sisters.' Jamila was surprised at how creative she was being.

Elizabeth had no idea what to say on a subject so beyond her ken. 'Oh! I'm so sorry,' she managed. 'You must tell me some more sometime. You seem like a nice girl and your skin is a lovely light brown. Perhaps you might come to visit us. I'm sure Donald would like that. We've a beautiful estate in the Highlands.' Leaving no space for an answer, hoping that no such visit would ever happen, Elizabeth switched her attention to Fraser. 'Hello! So, you're Fraser. Donald's told me all about you as well. He says you always manage to find the right answers to solve his problems. You should have been around when he was a little boy.' More laughter at her own joke. Fraser was markedly silent.

'We've our fair share of problems, Elizabeth, that's for sure. I expect he's told you about the teeth. Do you know? Every tooth takes two months to study fully and everything must be noted and saved.'

As Fraser talked Jamila slipped away unnoticed, ducked out of the laboratory, walked down the corridor and with a sense of relief tarnished by her anger that such a stupid woman could leave her feeling so uncomfortable, she left the building. *His mother doesn't like me*, thought Jamila, *so why does she pretend to invite me to stay with her and keep asking me stupid questions?* Why did I lie to her as if she'd know how to check up on me? Only when outside in the sunshine did Jamila remember that she'd not even spoken to Donald. Walking by the river back to Donald's flat Jamila grasped that she was missing her village, her sister and the mountains of home. She was missing Marie as well, to talk with and to share her fears and although she would never admit it, she was also beginning to think about Marie's concerns about her. She went over the afternoon, especially Connie's behaviour and by the time she had arrived back at Donald's flat she had determined that she needed to start to be assertive with Donald and make herself important to him and it was Connie's boldness she would seek to imitate. She'd made her choice and taken her chance with Donald. *He's a little older than me*, she thought, *but maybe that's a good thing. He has an important job and people look up to him and there's plenty of students around in his life so why not me? He must like me, that's why I'm here.*

10

The evening after his party it wasn't until Donald was late back to the flat that Jamila put two and two together and realised that it was Tuesday and as usual he'd travelled to Dundee. She'd become used to Donald returning in a bad mood late on Tuesday, so she decided to learn a lesson from Connie right away and take matters into her own hands and despite Donald's mother, she'd come back from the party imagining being with him, properly living with him, having his children, standing by him. Only a few months ago she had never even thought of leaving her village: now she was in Edinburgh thinking about Donald and his birthday and wondering if she dared offer herself to him as his partner. She'd watched Connie sliding up to Donald and this had opened her eyes. It was far from anything she would have thought about back home yet now it seemed a practical way to secure herself; to commit and show her commitment. If it was okay for Connie to sidle up to Donald, why not her and why not now? She'd like to think that Marie would approve, she considered that Marie might be sceptical. But she was too far away to ask. Even if Jamila had been back in Morocco there would have been no Habiba to ask.

Habiba might have thought that Donald was a good catch. She'd always said that about Ismail. So, determined to be bold, realising Donald was going to be late, Jamila made herself ready for him. She had been there long enough to know what Donald liked to eat so she'd already brought back fruit cake and cheese from his favourite corner shop. She set to and tidied his flat, cleaned up his kitchen, changed into a cotton kaftan she'd carried in her travel bag and made sure there was a bottle of wine on his table. Then she settled down to read; she had recently found a copy of 'Little Dorrit' on Donald's shelves and when he told her the story started in Marseille, she knew she would read it. She hadn't been disappointed with the mysteries of Cavalletto and Rigaud, both entombed in the city's prison and she was longing to introduce Marie to the book when she came to visit. A whole new take on Marseille.

Jamila was deep into the story when she heard the usual Tuesday taxi pull up outside the flat and watched through the window as Donald emerged and paid his fare. She surprised him by opening the door to greet him and he was startled but happy to see her dressed casually in her kaftan gown. Within a few minutes they were sitting eating and talking about his mother and the party that afternoon and he was finding himself taken aback at how attentive Jamila was being whilst Jamila was pleased his usual foul mood on a Tuesday wasn't so foul today.

Jamila had talked with Zohra about men and sex and about the first time and what men and women did to each other and she thought she was ready for that experience. She was apprehensive but Donald had always been kind to her, even if his work took up almost all his time. She could allow for that because she believed he was important. Subconsciously that probably reassured her. She had decided he was a decent man. But she also knew that Donald wanted to sleep with her. She respected that he did not seem to have pushed himself. If asked she wouldn't have been certain as to why she knew, but she did. She knew when she had kissed him in the Botanic Gardens; he held her close, his hand across her back as he pressed into her. She was confident he was liked by his students and by now she'd convinced herself that he was far better than any man she would have met in her village. She had taken risks to get to where she was and for her, they seemed risks worth the taking. Offering herself to Donald seemed like the next risk.

Jamila continued to wonder what counsel Marie would have offered but she wasn't there so she had convinced herself that if he slept with her he would see her as his partner.

Donald had taken a little of his meal, conversation had run out and he had poured himself a second glass of wine. He knew Jamila's mood had changed and sensed her emerging openness. With nonchalant ease, he offered his hand as if inviting Jamila to touch him and the touch wandered, became two hands and they sat for a while. A gentle press to her hand invited her to stand and as they stood, he took her in his arms and they kissed, gently, like they had at the Botanic Gardens. He said he wanted to change out of his work clothes and whilst he did, she cleared the table and lit a candle. He was soon back wearing a dressing gown.

Donald wanted to sleep with Jamila. He'd wanted to sleep with her the first night they had met in Marseille; the customer and the waitress. His fantasies, always kept tucked away, were clichéd and he had always sought to make them his realities. His sense of entitlement was established by his parents and re-enforced by his privileged education. He smiled, they kissed again, and it felt quite natural that he should lead her into his bedroom where he held her soft cotton kaftan against his own flesh. Jamila felt apprehensive but calm. She had chosen to entice Donald and he had responded; she believed she had made these choices. She allowed her kaftan to drop, encouraged his kiss and enjoyed the warmth of his hands against her flesh. She had never known sexual desire but knew that was what she now felt and instinctively understood that he needed no encouragement. After all she'd watched the dogs in the village so she knew what would happen next.

Donald used women but was smart enough to know his pleasure was best served by subtle suggestibility. By such means they'd come back for more. He held her close, told her how warm she felt, that her skin felt beautiful. He knew to be gentle, and they slipped onto his bed, rolled over and he caressed her breasts with his lips and ran his hand along her waist. He guessed she was enjoying the feeling she had that she was a woman. He whispered, 'Are you okay?' and she could only incline her head in submission as in opening her body to the gentle touch of an older man she at least could feel secure that he knew where to go and where to touch her. She shook a little as he stroked her thighs and with slow, soft curves pressed her legs apart; she liked this intrusion, its tenderness, its warmth, its excitement. Neither of them hurried. When he judged the time was right Donald lifted himself above her, gently eased her legs further and pressed himself against her as she felt him warm and firm on her thighs, running up and through and into her as a small shred of pain interrupted her thoughts before he drew himself up and gently rocked into her again, along the soft mounds of her own moist sex. She consumed the sensation that ran through her, absorbed its essence and stored forever the intense closeness of this moment as they rose and fell together. Almost unnoticed by Jamila Donald released himself as she felt herself shrink and grow, shrink again and grow so she felt Donald shake above her, gently lower himself and slip away from her to rest his head awhile on her shoulder.

Jamila was surprised as she felt herself cry, soft tears rolling across her cheeks. She wondered at those tears, marking a disappointment she hadn't realised she felt. Or was it pleasure? Whatever the last few moments had been they were finished. Donald gently brushed the tears away, he had seen them before, shifted himself from her and stretched out on the bed beside her as she wrapped herself along his side and under his arm. He helped her to settle, to be comfortable and so sleep came easily to them both.

*

When she awoke, she was covered by a sheet and blanket and Donald was no longer there. For a while she lay in his bed, remembering the night, startled by her own temerity, already wanting to share her secret, check out its good points and the less good. She decided she would write to Marie today and urge her to visit Edinburgh soon, so they could talk, go over events and together better understand them. She put on her gown and found Donald dressed, in the kitchen, reading and making notes in the margins of his book as she had seen so often before. He turned, smiled, stretched out his hand to her. They held hands for a moment and he turned back to his book.

She sat with him and drank tea, ate toast and they talked about a ceremony to make him a professor that was due in a few weeks. Jamila had shared sex with Donald last night and was struck by how much this might have changed her and how little it felt as if it had changed him. He sat the same, said the same things in the same way, whereas she wanted to feel different but had no idea how to tell him and ended up feeling the same. In place of difference, she started to do again the things she had done the day before; to tidy, wash cups and make her bed. She didn't make his. She could feel herself sliding into a role that had been there before and available but was not what she expected. She had chosen to offer herself to Donald, he had accepted and for him that was what he expected, whilst she had not thought through what would happen next. This left her feeling uneasy but not knowing why.

'Are you okay?' he asked.

Jamila struggled with the question and even more with the answer.

'I'm okay, Donald,' she said.

'I hope I didn't hurt you.'

'No. You didn't.'

'I suppose I wasn't expecting that,' he said, telling the old lie with consummate ease. He would never have said it but he wasn't imagining Jamila would just offer herself to him. It felt too easy; he felt almost cheated of the chase, but that was fine. After all it's okay for me to have sex, he thought, to sow a few wild oats because it's what I need, and she'll be fine. She's no fool.

Jamila had cleared the breakfast, washed the cups and wiped the sink; she found these actions calming and their simplicity a foil for her emotional reaction to the night before and her realisation that the one thing she really wanted was to be needed, to matter and to help her work out what next. She sensed there was nothing more to say about the previous night, so she shared another thought. 'David suggested that I might be able to work in one of the offices if there's no space at the lab,' she said. 'He said there's an office near the laboratory that sorts out applications from students and that they often need extra staff. I need a job, Donald. I need to earn some money.'

Donald looked up from his book. 'You've been talking to David as well, have you? You're not daft, are you?' He sighed, shifted in his chair. 'I'll see what I can do.' He was annoyed that David had spoken to Jamila without his knowledge but tried to hide it. Such chatter didn't suit him. Saying no more he went back to his book, scribbled a few notes, finished his cup of tea, pulled on his coat and cheerily waved to Jamila as he left the flat more hastily than he had intended.

Alone again, Jamila regarded her body in the bathroom mirror and searched for any visible differences and found none except a small bruise on her neck which she assumed was something to do with Donald. She washed with more care than usual, chose her pretty clothes, dressed, picked up a letter pad and left the flat. As she walked, she felt as if she had parted ways with herself, lost touch with something and found a new sensation, intense, uneasy maybe and she smiled to herself and couldn't help feeling that others regarded her differently, that passers-by who knew her not at all, saw her changed even so. Jamila wondered if Donald was at the laboratory yet; she wondered how David and the others would be if they knew that he had slept with her in his bed last night; she wondered what it would be like tonight when they were both back at the flat, and what Marie would say, and how Zohra would be if she knew where Jamila was and what was happening now between her and Donald.

*

Burdened with these reflections and feeling less happy than she thought she might be, Jamila walked to the Central Library and found a corner to sit and write to Marie again. She'd written only days before but was pleased to do so again as if in writing she would preserve a chunk of the present for future reference. At the far end of the library several children perched on canvas chairs were listening to a story being read by a lady wearing a library badge, her tone hushed and the children attentive and absorbed. As Jamila watched them, she recalled storytelling around the village waterwell in the cool of the evening when Habiba and the other mothers took turns to share tales. Her favourite of many had been *'The King and the three thieves'*. She used to sit as close as she could to Habiba, and she knew every word by heart. She still did.

Several of the dark oak tables between the library shelves were occupied by women surrounded by piles of books, reading, writing into notebooks and pausing every so often to glance around them. Jamila supposed they were the mothers of the children and wondered what the fathers were doing just at this minute. She wrote to Marie, she pleaded with Marie to come to the city to visit her and to come soon. 'You can stay with me at Donald's flat,' she wrote. 'He will not mind. He is a good man, Marie.' She dared not write of what had happened last night, she did not have the words. She would have to tell Marie when they were both drinking tea in the Botanic Gardens. Marie would know the words.

As Jamila walked out of the library, she turned into George Street to find the Post Office and saw David coming out of a bank. Her instinct was to duck away but she thought better of it and continued towards him. He smiled as he recognised her.

'Jamila,' he said. 'What a nice surprise. What brings you to this part of town?'

'I've just been to the library. Not very interesting I'm afraid, David and now I am going in the Post Office.'

David looked admiringly at Jamila, as if seeing her for the first time. He was struck by her determination, by the deliberateness of her step, the grace of her movements. She'd come all this way, deserted her home and was making the best of things here in Edinburgh. 'I'm impressed how well you've found your way around. Donald's too bound up in his work to show you the sights I expect.' Jamila felt herself blush at the mention of his name. David couldn't help but notice but was too much the gentleman to say anything. They walked along together in silence for a few moments before David asked, 'Are you walking down to Leith? Can I walk a little way with you?'

'I'd like that very much,' said Jamila without hesitation. She liked David more and more; he was kind, thoughtful, interested in her. She went into the Post Office, posted her letter to Marie and when she came out there was David, waiting for her.

'What do you think of Edinburgh now you're here?' he asked as they walked. 'I guess you've been here quite a few months now. I remember you saying that you'd like it if it was different from Morocco. Is it?'

'Oh. Yes. It's different from Morocco. It's all a bit strange to me, not that I get to see much, but I like to be out and walking around. Donald's always working or out somewhere although we walk together in the Botanic Gardens. That seems to suit him.'

Jamila felt nervous. She was so far from talking about last night and that was what she was thinking about. Recounting her day-to-day habits, she found it hard not to tell David what she was thinking, it was all so near the surface, but she dared not, for why would he care, she wondered and how would he understand how she felt. Even so it was mainly Donald she talked about.

'He's a bit of a dark horse is Donald,' said David.

'I'm afraid I don't know that expression. Maria used it once and I forgot to ask her. 'Dark horse? What does that mean?'

'A dark horse has secrets; things we maybe don't know about. Like Donald. We all think he might be a dark horse. I think you might be as well, Jamila. Why was it you came here? You told me in Marseille that you might tell me one day. You told me a bit about your home but not why you left it.'

Jamila was relieved to be able to talk and even though she couldn't share with David an account of her night with Donald she was pleased to talk about herself. As they walked down the hill towards Leith, Jamila told David about Nadeem and how cruel he had been to her, but she didn't tell him about the attack by the river. It was too intimate. David listened intently, asking a few questions and taking it all in. Jamila was nearly back home by the time she had finished.

'Does Donald know all this?' asked David.

'No. He's never asked me, but I will tell him someday soon. I need to. Do you think I was right to run away, David?'

'Oh! Jamila, it's not for me to say. Like your own home, my family home was in the mountains here in Scotland. My dad died when I was a child and that's when I came to Edinburgh to boarding school. My mum came to live here with me a few years ago. I still miss the quietness and the open space of the mountains. Your reasons for leaving the mountains were very different from mine.'

'That's strange,' said Jamila. 'Habiba, who I called my mama died, and in some ways that's also why I left.'

'Are you happy staying with Donald?'

Jamila felt herself blush again. 'He's very kind, David. He gives me a room. I'm comfortable.' Something still held Jamila back from telling David everything although she suspected that he was guessing there was more to it than met the eye. They were near to Donald's flat, and Jamila was pleased to be back. She'd told David a great deal and wanted to have a chance to stop.

'It's lovely to have you here with us,' said David. 'Maybe some of your family will be missing you.'

'I'd like to see my sister, although she isn't really my sister. I'll tell you about all that one day, David. I'd like to.'

'Of course, Jamila. That would be good but now I need to get back to the labs. I'd like it very much if you told me the rest of your story one day, when there's a chance. Goodbye for now. See you at the lab sometime soon maybe. Make sure Donald brings you.'

'Thanks for walking with me, David.'

Jamila unlocked the door and as she walked in it was as if her world had altered since yesterday. She looked around her and noticed the flat felt smaller, she wondered where she would sleep tonight, and she looked forward to seeing Donald. She also felt more alone, despite the intimacy of the previous evening and that confused her because it was as if the importance of her home, her place in Morocco, had increased. There was so much about today that was unfamiliar and so familiar faces and places might be welcome. Jamila recalled a French word Marie had taught her, tristesse. Yes, she thought, I feel a sense of loss today. It was then she noticed that the letter on the floor was addressed to her. It was postmarked Marseille.

*

By the time Donald came home Jamila was very excited. She greeted him at the door. 'Marie is coming to see me. Can she stay here, please Donald. She'll be here next week.'

What Jamila didn't know was that Donald had been thinking about their night together, remembering that Jamila was the kind of girl he liked and how best to keep her happy. He'd been to the admissions office, and they'd told him they did have a temporary job. He had a copy of the details in his bag to show her when the time was right. Now there was Marie to add into the mix so maybe that might matter to her more than the job.

'How long do you want her to stay?' he asked.

'Just a few days. She says in her letter that she shouldn't be coming at all really because of her work. Please, Donald. Please can she come here and stay?'

'Yes,' Donald said, as he hung his coat on the back of the door. 'Yes, she can.' He was glad he could so easily please her.

Jamila hugged him and he looked embarrassed but still held her close, enjoying the warmth of the embrace. In those few moments he had decided not to mention the admissions office, thinking that she would be preoccupied with Marie's visit. He'd keep the job for later.

There was a routine they'd established since Jamila was there and it didn't change because of the previous night. Jamila put some food on the table, and they ate more-or-less in silence, Jamila thinking of Marie's visit and Donald his imminent investiture. Once they'd cleared away Donald took up his book and turned on his radio, listening to music on the BBC and Jamila took up her book, thinking that she needed to finish Little Dorrit before Marie arrived so she could tell her all about the story. Neither of them mentioned the night before. Neither of them talked.

As usual Donald fell asleep on the sofa. Jamila, with a sense of relief, resolved to write again to Marie the following day, took herself to her own bed and curled up. After a few minutes there was a knock on her door. 'Would you like to come in with me again tonight?' Jamila had hoped he would not ask. She opened her door, and he stood outside in his dressing gown. 'I'd like you to join me,' he said. Jamila had a clear sense that the words were more than a request. Even so she went along with him. He had been kind to her, he had given her a room, he'd agreed to Marie coming to stay. As she took his hand she wondered if it might be different from the night before.

11

Jamila was standing behind the passenger gates on Platform Five. She couldn't believe it was only a few months since she arrived here herself, looking in wonder out of the rain splattered window at the sign, Waverley Railway Station, Edinburgh; rattling into a destination that felt like a fantasy. As her train had pulled in, she had felt slightly sick, amazed that she was here and alarmed at what she had done, especially as Donald had provided her with no more than a one-way ticket. No turning back. That day they had arrived late in the evening on the train from London. Today she was meeting Marie on the morning train. Of course, Jamila was early: she was always early. All around her passengers hurried, dragging cases and bags, herding reluctant children, tottering along on walking sticks, everyone intent and determined, passing by her as she waited behind the ticket barrier whilst at other platforms trains hissed and clattered as they arrived and departed. Not so many months ago Jamila had rarely left her village and now she felt like a seasoned traveller.

She was excited as a child might be, her new friend coming to stay from so far away. She imagined Marie gathering up her bag in the carriage and seeing Edinburgh for the first time, just as she had done, looking out of the train window. The loudspeakers announced the arrival of the train from London on Platform Five and the black, shining engine inched its way towards them, folded in steam and far noisier than she expected. Before it stopped the doors started to open and within moments the platform before her was engulfed in passengers, heading for the ticket barrier. In no time at all Jamila spotted Marie jumping up and down, waving for all she was worth.

'Here, Marie! I'm over here. I'm here,' called Jamila, her words instantly absorbed into the communal noise. Marie had seen her, though. She ran and they embraced. After a few moments Jamila disengaged and starting to smile stood back, studying Marie, looking her up and down.

'Marie! she said. 'Are you pregnant? You never said. You are, aren't you? You're pregnant.'

Marie squealed with delight. 'I really am! Look!' Marie turned sideways and with a wicked smile on her face stuck out her tummy and giggled. 'That's why I came so quickly. I won't be able to travel soon.'

'Oh, Marie. I'm so pleased for you. So pleased.' Jamila was smiling, delighted, then she looked away, feeling imminent tears and she took Marie in her arms and cuddled her close as she steadied her emotions. 'You're so lucky Marie. So lucky. Why didn't you tell me? Why didn't you say? Oh! Come on. Let's get away from all these people.'

Jamila carried Marie's suitcase, and they skipped away down the platform arm-in-arm. 'We have so much to talk about Marie, so much to tell each other. So much to see. Where shall we start? Would you like a pot of Scottish tea?'

'Perfect. Show me the way!'

*

The next few days were a whirl accompanied by Scottish Dancing in every grassy square and bagpipers piping 'Scotland the Brave' on the corner of every street. Walking arm-in-arm, pointing at everything they noticed, toasting each other with cups of tea, imitating the grumpy faces of sad old women, laughing at men in dresses and sporrans, messing around, eating pie and chips, they left a trail of cheerful abandon behind them. They arrived back at the flat later every day and left earlier every morning. They hardly caught sight of Donald. They climbed Arthur's Seat and loved the view, the precipices and the wind. They pretended they were monkeys watching the other monkeys at the zoo and cried laughing at each other's silly faces. They had tea and cakes at the Caledonian Hotel, pretending to be posh and giggling at the waiters, who were glad when they left. They took a tram to Portobello, paddled in the freezing sea water, splashed each other and ate ice creams, whilst wearing scarves and woolly hats. They talked about their homes, their lives, and some of their secrets. Several times they rode the Hurdy Gurdy Carousel in Princes Street Gardens and climbed into the gondolas on the Big Wheel, driven by a mighty steam engine that hissed and blew fit to burst.

The few days raced by. 'I can't believe it's all over,' said Marie at the top of the big wheel. 'I'm going tomorrow. You haven't said a word about Donald yet. Come on, Jamila. You must tell me. We've been in the flat and hardly seen him. He goes early and comes back late. Where is he? What's it like living in his flat?'

Jamila and Marie talked as the wheel turned, looking down on Princes Street, across to Arthur's Street and up to the Castle. 'No. I know I've said nothing. I've so much enjoyed all this time together that I've hardly thought about Donald. That says it all doesn't it. I can't get it straight in my head, Marie. Do you remember when we were on the dig together that first time and you asked me about trusting Donald and seemed unsure yourself. I think I trust him. No. I've decided I trust him.' She found herself being more reassuring than she felt. Below them the flowerbeds were laden with spring roses and stiff, starched Nannies strolled with children in prams. Jamila and Marie sat side-by-side as the wind blew their hair whilst they hung onto the safety bars and the machinery of the big wheel clanked and grated.

'You asked me how I knew I could trust Donald and I said how do you know you can ever trust a man.'

'Yes. I remember,' said Marie.

'You're with Pierre now and you're pregnant already. How do you know you can trust him? Does he talk to you, do you always have him in your mind? Does he always think about you?'

'Yes. He does think about me. All those things. But that's not why I trust him. I know he's okay. I know he loves me. I know that if I was in trouble, he'd be there to help me.'

'That's just it, Marie. I live in Donald's flat; he sometimes talks to me when he's there but he's hardly ever there. Would he help me? Would he miss me if I wasn't there? He loves me in his own way maybe, but I don't think he loves just me; he's wrapped up in himself. I have slept with him in his bed, but we don't really talk. He's important. It's not for me to ask.'

'You'd never told me that, Jamila. I've always known you were a dark horse.' Marie was wide-eyed.

'It's funny. David called me a "dark horse" as well. He said he thought I might have secrets.'

'He's right,' said Marie. 'You do have secrets. You've slept with Donald. That's been a secret. Does David know?'

'Of course not.' Marie was startled by Jamila's sharp response, 'but I think he may have guessed. You trust Pierre because you know he's okay. You just said you know he loves you. I don't understand myself, Marie. Donald's own mother as good as told me Donald couldn't be trusted but I want to trust him. I want to believe he's a good man. I want him to love just me. He loves his work, that's for sure. But I know he doesn't love just me; over the last few weeks I've decided he just loves women, maybe just the idea of women and I don't want to face it. I still want him to love me. I think David understands and that makes me scared.'

'What was it like, Jamila, sleeping with Donald?'

'How can I say? I don't know. It was okay. He was kind, gentle, I wanted to sleep with him, and I thought he'd done it before so that meant he knew what he was doing, and it seemed okay, and it didn't hurt, and I feel different now. Do you remember Connie? I could see her touching Donald and trying to get him to notice her, and I thought that I might as well try the same thing. You must know what I mean. But I know he doesn't love just me; I'm not even sure he loves me at all.'

'You need to be careful. You sound a bit confused, Jamila.'

'You're right, Marie, I am. This is the first time I've talked about it. Do I have to love him do you think? I wanted to sleep with him, though, Marie. I'd seen how Constance was with him, a bit bossy, and I could see he liked that so I took it on and kind of tempted him.'

'He seemed close to her on the dig. Is she his girlfriend, was she his girlfriend do you think?'

'Connie? I can understand she needs him for her work, her career. She likes him, that's for sure. They like to touch each other but they all need him to keep their jobs. I like them, especially David, but I can't break in, be part of their world so I must fight for Donald on the outside, but now I am fighting for him I'm not sure I want him. But maybe I do love him, Marie. That's my problem; that's why I've slept with him. He doesn't know about my brother like you know and him attacking me, but I can't get that out of my head. I want to tell him why I ran away but I don't know how to and I don't think he'll be interested and I am beginning to feel that matters. It's safer not to tell him in case he doesn't care and then I don't know how to deal with it if he doesn't care because we have slept together and yet I don't know how he feels about anything, so I'd rather not know. I don't know how he feels about me because we never talk like that and in a way that's why I'm not sure I trust him. He seems a bit closed. Are you going to tell me I'm silly?'

Jamila began to break up a bit with the pain of talking like this. It hurt her and her eyes watered. Marie was quick to comfort her. 'It's okay, Jamila. It's okay for you to tell me. I think there's more isn't there and no, I'm not going to tell you you're silly. I thought he wanted you in his bed and I was right. He has his way.'

'It's about confidence. I wanted to come here, to be with him. He gives me a home; he says nice things to me sometimes. I am fascinated by what he does but he doesn't want me interfering. I can't just leave him now, can I? It was me that started it really. I didn't have to come and when I did come I trusted him.'

'Are you lonely, Jamila? Is that what it is?'

'Oh, Marie. You always get it, don't you? I'm not sure I have anyone apart from you and that's probably my fault. Habiba loved me, and she is dead. Why isn't my real mother here for me? I need her. And my father. I have no idea what it feels like to have a real father. Ismail was kind to me, good to me, but he didn't always look out for me, protect me. That's what I want Donald to do but I don't think he will as it's his work comes first.'

'That's why you left home isn't it, because you felt exposed?'

'Yes. Partly it is. I've had to fight for myself and yes, I feel a bit alone even though I've a fine place to live.'

'It sounds complicated to me. Do you always sleep together?'

'Just a couple of times, not long before you came. He is gentle but I don't want to force him, and he seems distracted. I've no idea what it should be like, Marie.'

'It's just men. They're all the same. Roll on, roll off. If you think he's not the right man just leave him and come back with me tomorrow. Come to Marseille. What's stopping you?'

'Go back with you? I can't Marie; I can't do that. What would I do? I'm not ready yet.'

'Shake all this away, Jamila. Break away from it. That's what you need to do. Go back to your home. Go back to Morocco, track down your birth mother and sort it out in your head.'

'No, Marie. No! I can't do that just now. I could never face Nadeem. I'm finished with all that. I'll have to find a way to win Donald over. I have no choice.'

'Well, Jamila. I think you always have a choice. If you change your mind, you can always come to Marseille and if you don't you must find someone here you can talk to, really talk to I mean, about what matters to you.'

'You're right. I'll try. I think I could talk to David. Thank you, Marie.'

The Carousel had slowed. Jamila and Marie embraced looking out across to the Castle. Marie put her hand to her own stomach, rubbed herself, stretched out to take Jamila's hand and placed it under her own on her bump.

'Can you feel it kicking?' asked Marie. 'It's only a few weeks and it has sea legs already.'

'Must be a boy if it's kicking,' Jamila said with a smile. The two looked at each other, laughed as their gondola stopped and they clambered out, back onto solid land. Jamila knew now that Marie was right; she did need to track down her mother, maybe even her father but first she needed to find the right place for her relationship with Donald.

12

The night after Marie returned to Marseille Jamila shared Donald's bed again. Things had not gone well for Donald that day and he believed he needed some comfort; as far as he was concerned, Jamila was there to provide it. For Jamila, Marie had gone and as in the ancient cliché she felt driven back into Donald's arms. Marie had been more than a diversion for Jamila; a life that felt quiet before she came, now felt empty so sharing a bed this time answered both their needs. Donald was again gentle with her, 'kind' was how she thought of it, but if she expected passion she found none, and any desire was too easily replaced by relief that this was all over without too much fuss. Jamila was left wondering why she felt less than excited, why she was left feeling frustrated but not knowing why any of that might be.

It was the same in the morning as well. She woke to find him in the kitchen, in his dressing gown, eating porridge. The only difference was that the kitchen was a mess. Jamila was conscious that this was partly down to her and mainly down to Marie, not the tidiest of people. The empty wine bottles were not their fault but the stack of dirty saucepans on the cooker were. Marie had promised to scrub them, but it never happened as they were away so early in the morning. The scene was set for a reproach and Donald was ready. 'It's a mess in here,' he said.

'I'm sorry,' said Jamila. 'That's our fault.'

'You were too wrapped up in your French friend to sort it out I suppose. It's my flat you know, Jamila.'

She felt stung by this comment although she knew Donald was right but something in his tone angered her. She felt as if he resented Marie simply because she was a friend.

'I said I'm sorry, Donald, and I mean it. I'll sort it out now.' Then there was silence between them. Jamila scrubbed out the pans, unable to talk about the previous night, unsure why she felt let down and resentful of her adopted role as housemaid. Donald read his book. He scribbled a few notes, folded back the cover and stood up to go. Jamila felt unsure of herself, uncomfortable and wanted to express her unhappiness but instead heard herself ask. 'Shall we meet for lunch today in the Botanics?' Not such a bad idea, she thought to herself as it might give them the chance to talk, and she wanted to talk and apart from last night hadn't seen Donald for days.

'No.' Donald's answer was immediate. 'I've far too much to do.'

Jamila already felt upset and this sharp answer hurt so much that she now felt she had suffered an injustice. Marie's caution about men in general had invaded Jamila's confidence where at the same time Donald had no concept of Jamila feeling vulnerable. It was only his feelings that mattered to him; the pedestal she was placing him on prevented her seeing that he had no idea of her feelings. It was probably inevitable that her anger escaped. 'You always have far too much to do to give me any time. What's wrong with me? Why do you want me to live with you and sleep in your bed when it suits you if you can never be bothered to spend time with me, to talk to me? It's as if you just want to pass me off. You just use me as diversion when you have a spare moment from your work and your students and those dusty old teeth.'

'Okay! Okay! I'm sorry. I don't want you to get upset. Here, have some porridge and calm down.'

'And don't tell me to calm down. It was lovely to have Marie staying because we could talk and laugh and cry together. I want to be with you, Donald, but talking with Marie has been so good. I've realised I'm lonely.' Donald was turning over a page of his book as she spoke. She slammed her fist on the table. Donald startled. 'You're not listening, Donald. You don't understand, do you? You just don't get it. Yes, I followed you here from France. Yes, I think I like you. I care about you, but I can't do it all on my own. I need you to care about me. And what is it I care about? Why do I care about you? You gave me a chance and I believed all you said, and I think you really cared. But maybe that wasn't it at all? It just made you feel good to give me a chance didn't it and now all you want is to have me in your bed when it suits you.'

'Okay. I'm sorry. I don't understand. But I have to get to work now.'

'Who do you talk to, Donald?' Jamila felt emboldened. 'Who knows what goes on inside your head? You wanted me here, "beside you," is what you said. But why? What am I worth to you? I don't think I know. Your mother was right, Donald. "Watch him," she said to me at your party. "He likes the women," she said.'

'Well! I'm glad you and she are friends,' said Donald smirking. 'What's that supposed to mean anyway? She doesn't know what she's talking about. Anyway, I am going to go now. I need to get dressed and I haven't time to talk. We have to put on an exhibition for my ceremony next week.'

Donald strode into his bedroom and threw on some clothes.

Jamila called across the hall. 'And you have this big event coming up and I've no idea what it's about because you can't be bothered to tell me. That's how much I matter to you. You always put it off don't you, Donald? You can't face talking because you don't want to know. You look as if you care but you pretend. David taught me an English phrase… "the penny's beginning to drop." That's how I feel.'

Jamila pushed her bowl of porridge away, unfinished, knocking her mug of tea which spilled on the table as she angrily wiped her tears away with her sleeve. Donald walked out, the front door closed with a bang, and she threw a tea-towel on the spilt tea and left it untouched. Donald had been kind to her and she did like him and she was confused as to why she was being so difficult. Maybe she regretted getting cross, but it was only 'maybe'. Marie had given her pause for thought, given her courage, that much was true, but even so she didn't have to be unpleasant, but she needed to tell him. Why shouldn't she?

Jamila resolved there and then to tidy the flat and as she couldn't meet Donald for lunch she would go and buy herself a hat to wear for this important ceremony that mattered so much to him. David had said it would be an idea to look good so she would try to look her best and a hat would be right, she thought. When the flat was tidy, she put on the dress that she had worn to Donald's party and gathering up her courage set out for Jenner's store again, determined not to make the same fuss she had on her last visit.

*

'That's a pretty dress and it looks lovely on you dear.' The assistant smiled. 'Oh! Hello, my dear, I didn't recognise you. Welcome back. I so hope you are feeling better.' Jamila recognised the same lady who had lent her the handkerchief.

'Thank you.' Jamila was flustered. She hoped the lady didn't remember the handkerchief. She blushed but gathered herself together. 'I'm fine, thank you. Do you think a hat would be a good idea with this dress?'

'Of course, my dear. We've just the thing. Try these straws. They came in this week from our supplier in France.'

Jamila looked up at the assistant when she heard her say 'France'. 'I stayed in France for a few weeks once and made a wonderful friend. I'd like to try one of these French hats, yes please. The trouble is I'm never sure what to do with the hat when I take it off. I think I might sit on it.'

'Leave it on my dear, I would. Don't take it off. That will keep it safe. Try this one. It matches your complexion beautifully. You might find a little clip will help keep it straight.'

Jamila put on the straw hat and the assistant fussed around her, pinning it in place. She looked good in the hat and unlike the last time was happy to look in the mirror.

'That looks grand, my dear. Very smart. You have such thick hair as well as beautiful skin. Perfect for hats. Are you going to a wedding?'

The question pricked Jamila's bubble. She lost her smile and almost visibly deflated.

'Are you feeling unwell, dear? You don't look very happy.'

'I wish I was going to a wedding. It's a University ceremony. I don't know what it's about and I don't know why I'm going. He doesn't love me.'

'Oh dear! Maybe he will when he sees you in this hat.'

'Maybe! But I doubt it but I'd like this one please.'

'Wonderful. It looks just right.'

'Well. We'll see, I guess.'

Jamila handed the assistant the hat and a ten-shilling note. She arranged the hat in a bag and gave Jamila her change. 'Thank you,' she said.

'My pleasure, dear, and best of luck with the man! I hope he knows how lucky he is.'

Jamila left the store with a heavy heart and lost in thought. Arguing with Donald that morning now seemed even more to be bearing down on her. Since she had first shared Donald's bed she felt less and less in control of herself. She knew what Marie thought but Marie was not in the same place so who could she talk with here, in Edinburgh? What was the answer to Marie's question? She had thought that the risks she had taken so far could somehow be revisited, she could go back, walk away, change direction. But now it was beginning to feel different. Was she trapping herself and did she know what the real risks were? *I feel proud of myself,* she thought. *I've asserted myself and proved to myself I can manage and so far, I've enjoyed the consequences, but will it last?* She was disconcerted that she could not answer that question, bothered that there was a question at all. She'd bought a hat to please a man whom she liked and wanted to be with, who gave her money, who was kind to her which was all fine but then she sensed that David doubted her wisdom and she knew that Marie felt it was unwise, yet despite her knowing so little of him, Jamila still tried to move herself closer. Perhaps I'm testing myself, she wondered. If this is only curiosity, can I get away with it?

*

Since lunch with Donald was not an option Jamila had decided to walk across to the National Gallery where she now felt at home in the dusty old building with the creaking floors. Across the grand canvasses of mountains and rivers, along the canyons and rocks of the Scottish landscape she searched for herself, for a clue to what made her. She peopled that landscape with her family in Morocco and imagined the circling vultures and condors above her village in the light of the evening sun. She fought against a feeling of regret that threatened to surface, telling herself not to be silly, to have confidence in her own choices but the regret was still there as she emerged an hour later into the cool sunlight of the afternoon. A brisk walk down the hill to Leith did a little to sharpen Jamila's mood. She reached Donald's flat, climbed the few steps to the door and was startled to find him there. He sat with a book open on his lap, a glass from a half-empty bottle of red wine on a messy side-table.

'Donald,' exclaimed Jamila. 'I thought you said you'd be at work.'

'We were going out for lunch, weren't we?' Donald was immediately angry.

Jamila responded, surprised by her own boldness. 'You said you were too busy so I assumed you'd be working.'

'Well, I'm not and I'm here. Where were you?'

'I've been to the National Gallery. How was I to know you'd changed your mind?'

'I changed my mind because I thought you'd be pleased but when I arrived here you were out.'

'I would have been pleased if I'd known and then I could have been here.' Jamila was upset and confused. 'It's like Marie said. You don't care enough about me to tell me things, you just care about yourself.'

'Marie again. Always bloody Marie.'

Jamila was feeling angry, and Donald was looking fierce, his cheeks red and sweat on his forehead. 'She's my friend, Donald, the only friend I have. Why do you feel you can criticise her just because I like her? You were happy enough to give her work in Marseille. You told me this morning that you didn't have time for lunch together so I went out and I assumed as anyone would that you weren't interested in lunch and now you're blaming me.'

'If Marie's so wonderful, why don't you go and live with her. You forget, Jamila, it was you wanted to be here. That's how it all came about.' He took a mouthful of wine as he built up his irritation at not being in control. 'And I've a bone to pick with you as well. What's so special about David that you can talk to him so much?'

'It's because he listens, Donald, like Marie listens. You can't take it can you, Donald? I realised today that you think you own me now I'm here. David's decent to me and he says you're a bit of a dark horse and he's right, isn't he?'

'I don't know what you're talking about. What's it to do with David anyway? Isn't it enough that you've a place to live for now and me to look after you?'

'No, Donald. You are kind to me and I like you but I thought you'd care about me, be interested in me, not just give me a room and expect me to look after myself and tell me you couldn't have lunch because you were working and then just turn up, expecting me to be here, waiting for you, hanging on every word.'

'What more do you want?' Donald stood, swung around on his heels as if he was thinking of walking out. Instead, it was Jamila who was ready to have the final word.

'I want to matter to you, but I don't do I, I'm just convenient, a distraction? I'm angry, Donald. I'm sorry. I wanted to share lunch and I'm angry that we haven't and it's your fault, not mine.'

'Well. It's too late now. When this ceremony is out of the way we'll have to get this straightened out, Jamila.'

'That's no use, Donald. I want you to say sorry, not just blame me.' Jamila looked at him, realised he would say nothing and strode out of the room, slamming the door. Donald went to finish his wine when she banged back through the door. 'I'm not sleeping in your bed tonight, Donald. Like you say when this ceremony is out of the way we'll straighten things up.'

Jamila was tense and petulant. Donald's indifference put down a marker for Jamila and helped her to realise why both

David and Marie had right on their side when they urged caution. She allowed herself to feel she had been let down by Donald and unfairly blamed; she felt used by him, that he didn't care and that was a shock. 'Perhaps I need to step back,' she said to herself. That night, after an almost silent evening, they each slept alone.

*

On the day before the ceremony everyone was preparing for the exhibition in the laboratory. Donald was less testy than he'd been in recent days as he paced between the benches in the lab offering a word of advice here and an instruction there, enjoying the sweep of his gown and the power that went with the attention. Constance was tidying, assembling displays of artefacts and microscopes and David sat bowed over a bench hand-writing labels. Donald admired David's perfect copperplate text, saying it lent an air of authority to their work. Who was David to disagree, especially as he felt as if Donald was regarding him less favourably in the last few days. Fraser was preparing microscope slides, taking great care as he manipulated tiny slices of bone between the slides and sealed them ready for insertion. He loved his work and its need for precision.

'This looks good, Fraser. What have we on that slide?' asked Donald.

'A slice through the latest tooth. It shows the scratch marks very clearly and there's some cross-sections of the grains we've been finding on the other slides in the carrier.'

'How about a few sample grains on the desk to link with the slide? They could be mounted and labelled. 'This is what they might have eaten.' Grains of wheat, barley, that sort of thing maybe?'

'And then it's like telling a story,' said Fraser.

'Exactly. I think some people like to see archaeology as a story, as chapters being uncovered and examined like layers of history. That's how I think of it anyway. Like those charts Bethan made.' At the mention of Bethan's name, a hush came over everyone in the lab, brief but unmistakable. Donald coloured, conscious of the awkward silence, his fair skin glowed around his neck, and he averted his eyes from Fraser. David continued working but felt disconcerted, sensing again that he hadn't remembered Donald's treatment of Bethan and nor had he included her in his thinking when talking with Jamila. His sense of Jamila's vulnerability was strengthened.

Meanwhile Constance ducked down behind the bench to sort out the refreshments. It pleased Donald that she was always ahead, knowing what he'd ask her to do and to hide his embarrassment he ducked down beside her. A kettle on a gas ring was steaming gently and teapot, teacups and saucers, tea strainer, milk jug and sugar bowl were all ready. Constance was wiping the cups with a cloth. 'These haven't been out for a while Donald. Would you like a cup of tea?'

'Perfect,' said Donald, winking. 'Sugar today, please.'

'Whatever happened to Bethan?' asked Connie. 'I never met her.'

'How am I supposed to know,' snapped Donald and Connie knew she'd chosen the wrong subject and immediately guessed why.

'How many people will come up tomorrow do you think?' she asked.

'No idea. A dozen maybe. It's mainly for the Prof that we're doing it.'

'I think he'll be impressed. I'll be glad when it's all over and we can get back to the real work. What time does it start?'

'Right after the ceremony. About 2 o' clock I expect.' Donald lowered his voice. 'How about a drink tomorrow,

Connie, when it's all over? Think about it!' He was still smarting from Jamila's reprimands and shamelessly sought alternative comfort, affirmation even, both guaranteed to come from Constance.

Her reply was swift. 'I have thought about it. Yes. Let's.' Constance smiled and blew Donald a kiss as he turned his back.

David noticed and frowned. 'Have you invited Jamila to the ceremony tomorrow, Donald?' he asked, making sure the others could hear.

'What's it to do with you? I think she's bought a new hat, so I expect so.'

David ignored Donald's testiness. 'We haven't seen her in the lab for weeks, more's the pity. Is she okay, Donald? Maybe she's missing her home?' David carried on with his questions, regardless of Donald's obvious displeasure.

'Homesick you mean? I don't think so, David. Some mountain village full of smoke and goats is where she came from, I'd guess, so I doubt she's missing it just now.'

'That's not what she told me, Donald,' said David with a sharp intake of breath. 'She told me she'd like to stay here but missed her home. I thought you were keen to have her working here?'

'You seem very interested, David.'

'Give her a chance, Donald. It's just like Fraser said once, you seem to think that women are here to serve just you. We could all do with a bit of help. Give her space and she'll be very useful to us in the lab and I for one am looking forward to seeing her tomorrow.'

Donald drew himself up, feeling threatened by David's reprimands. 'Jamila's not your business, David, she's my concern. She told me she'd been talking to you and I'm not sure I like that. About those slides, Fraser. Can we project one onto the wall above the bench there. That would look good.' Donald had abruptly changed the subject, cutting

David out. He thought that David would need to be spoken to after the ceremony as well as Jamila. He was uneasy that they'd talked together and bristled inside at the intrusion, the threat to his own control. 'Anyway, I need to be away soon, Fraser, so can you make sure everything is ship-shape please.' He walked over to Connie. 'I'll see you tomorrow at the Usher Hall Connie. Ring-a-ding-ding.'

'Looking forward to it,' she said, winking.

Donald hung his gown on the back of the door, gathered up a few papers and left them working.

David muttered to no one in particular. 'He's surely not going to Dundee today of all days?'

13

After a late night, Donald left the flat early the following morning. Jamila only knew he had been and gone because he left a dirty wine glass on the table and a cold cup of tea. She dressed with a heavy heart. Wearing her new straw hat, her pretty dress and enjoying the sunshine, Jamila took her time walking to the Usher Hall. Plenty of people had arrived before her so she soon melted into the crowd, which suited her well. She felt uncomfortable out in the open, like a startled animal on a mountainside. Until today she hadn't felt lost in Edinburgh, but this event was very new to her with its throng of the chattering and smartly dressed and in this crowd she felt conspicuous, where being alone in a crowd left her feeling even more so. Jamila, however, decided she preferred to feel alone than having to engage with the crowd. Everyone was talking, everyone was smiling, everyone seemed to think they were important and as she was jostled into the vast hall her nervousness mounted and she was relieved to be ushered into a seat near the back and close to the exit. Above the chattering she heard music, it sounded like the Cathedral organ she had heard many months before in Marseille.

She'd not been sitting long before she saw David coming towards her from the front of the hall, smiling and giving her a gentle wave. Typical of David, she thought, to be looking out for her. She noticed he looked unusually smart. 'Are you okay, Jamila?' he asked. He didn't expect to be reassured. She pulled a face. 'When it's all over, we'll be meeting up outside that door.' He pointed to the far side of the hall. 'Door 'C,' he said. 'Donald's parents are sitting with us. Elizabeth has been telling me she met you at Donald's party. They're joining us afterwards as well.'

Jamila was not delighted about that either. 'Will you be there, David?' she asked.

David's heart went out to her, she looked very much out of place. 'Yes. I'll be there. We'll all see you later.' David smiled as he spoke and touched her hand gently. 'I better get back.' Jamila felt a warmth towards him and was more than relieved they'd be able to talk afterwards. She wasn't expecting to see much of Donald who she spotted parading outside 'Door 'C' adorned in cloaks and scarves of brightly coloured cloth above his kilt, confident and important, talking to the admiring Fraser and Constance.

'It's beautiful to be surrounded by all you lovely people,' Donald said. 'I thought today would never come.'

'Your hard working and dedicated team of slaves you mean,' said Fraser to a round of laughter. 'When I first met you, Donald, I thought you were such a decent bloke! We all make mistakes.'

'I thought the same,' quipped Connie. 'Look at him. He looks decent enough. You're not, though, are you, Donald?' She winked and laughed at her own wit, clearly pleased with herself. David appeared through the crowd and jeered good naturedly, smiling at nothing in particular, negotiating with ease the social flexing of the home crowd.

'Careful all of you. I could always find myself a new set of lab assistants you know.' Donald as ever was enjoying self-congratulation and for once joining in the banter between them.

'You could, but they wouldn't be as good as us would they.' Fraser's quick repartee drew nods of approval.

'Nothing like as good as me!' said Constance to another chorus of light-hearted groans.

At that moment in the hall the ushers called the students to their seats and as they fought their way into the hall, the organ music rose to a grand processional and everyone struggled to their feet as the University Principal paced solemnly down the central aisle followed by dozens of staff, adorned in their gowns and hats.

Tucked in at the back of the hall Jamila craned her neck as the procession began to make its way down the central aisle and seeing Donald in its midst she realised with a degree of surprise, that she didn't really care. Surrounded by the paraphernalia of his University life, dressed in his robes, she understood with an unexpected sharpness that all this was not for her. She could have been fascinated by his work, but he had kept her at arm's length leaving her indifferent to its detail and cut off from what might have absorbed her interest. She cared about him, his kindness to her, his arresting passion for his work but she felt as if it was some other girl that had slept with him and sitting there absorbing the unfamiliar, she felt pleased to be detached from that other girl. She became aware in that moment that she was almost ready to put that other girl in a box. As the procession advanced before her she started to wonder why she had felt confident enough to become part of this ritual when she understood so little and then to wonder why Donald had been keen to take her on board. 'Why me,' she wondered, 'when there are so many others here who might fit the bill?' She began to perceive that question had bothered her for a while.

For the next hour Jamila sat through the endless line of students accepting a plethora of awards. Almost at the end Donald was called up and she understood from the words spoken to him that he had then been made a professor. He beamed out into the vast hall and Jamila felt unmoved, out of touch with what made him. *He's a decent man*, she said to herself. *At least I think he is*. But the ritual meant very little to her and no one had bothered to give her any leads. She thought Donald's hat looked a little on the large size, seeming to spill around the edges of his head, but everyone clapped, and she could see David and the others standing as they cheered for Donald. She also spotted Elizabeth on her feet, with what looked like a bunch of flowers on her head, presumably a hat. Jamila still dreaded meeting her again and as the ceremony ended and everyone fought to get out, she held back from 'Door C', preferring to wait inside until the excitement had played itself out. Meanwhile, outside in the sunshine, trays of wine were being proffered by waiters as the stream of staff and students emerged through the side doors from where Donald made his exit, blinking into the sunlight, straight into the arms of Fraser.

'Well done, Donald. Very gracefully accepted! I love your pancake hat.'

'You're a silly bugger, Fraser. Thank you.'

Fraser stood back as Constance threw herself around Donald's neck and kissed him. Even Donald was embarrassed by this, especially as just at this moment his parents cut through the throng. 'Donald. Sweetheart. Hello. Are we too late to congratulate you? Is there a space for us?' Elizabeth acidly addressed this comment to Constance, who faced with his mother, abandoned Donald, retreating to join Fraser. Undaunted Elizabeth still addressed Constance, wagging her finger like a school mistress. 'Sorry, dear. We didn't mean to disturb you, did we, James?'

James, so far staying inconspicuous, stepped forward, seized Donald by the hand and then threw an embrace around his shoulders. 'Well done, son! Great show in there today. Good to see you looking so smart and wearing that magnificent hat. Sorry it's not as obvious as your mother's.'

Donald, laughing with his father's jest, took off his feathered hat and handed it to him. 'Try it on if you like, Dad.'

James was about to try it on when Elizabeth sailed in again. 'Don't be ridiculous, James. You'll just look stupid.

Give it back to Donald. Where's that lovely Moroccan girl, Donald? Has she been allowed to be here as well? I'm sure I saw her in the hall, wearing a very nice hat. She brushes up quite well.'

'Yes, Mother. She's around here somewhere but I haven't seen her yet. I expect David knows where she is, he usually does these days. In fact, I was just going to look for her. Yes, that's right, I'll look for her.' Donald was pleased to have swiftly found an excuse to escape his mother.

Connie was now angry with Donald and David, so sensing danger Fraser interrupted, quick thinking as always. 'Would you like us to take Elizabeth and James up to the laboratory, Donald? I'll show them the exhibits while you find Jamila, then Connie can start the refreshments.'

'Good idea, Fraser. I'll be along shortly,' said Donald. 'David, do you mind hanging on a minute to check everybody knows where to go?' As Fraser took Donald's parents away it was almost as if Jamila had been watching for her chance. Elizabeth's chattering figure disappeared around the corner of the hall as Jamila appeared out of the crowd and walked towards Donald and David. Donald's customary nonchalance evaporated as Jamila appeared, his first instinct to try to escape, avoiding contact, unsure of his ground with David and wishing that the possibility of the three of them being together just didn't exist at this particular moment. David, always well-tuned to Donald's moods, sensed his unease and its potential to be uncomfortable for all three of them. 'Jamila,' Donald stuttered. 'I didn't expect to see you so soon. We need to be going up to the laboratory don't we, David?'

David had no chance to reply. At the same moment as Donald was speaking, two children broke through the crowd, brushed in front of Jamila and David and headed straight for Donald. 'Daddy, Daddy. We came on the train. It was great fun, Daddy,' called one of them, directly to

Donald. Before he'd finished speaking the other child chimed in, 'Look what I have, Daddy. Do you like my new dress? Mummy gave it to me especially for today. That's a funny hat, Daddy.'

Donald span in alarm as he heard the voices. Immediately behind the two children strode a tall woman, elegantly dressed in similar colours to the children, clearly their mother. Donald ignored the children, who looked crestfallen as they tried to cuddle him, and spoke to the woman with immediate ferocity. 'God, Sophia! What possessed you to come here? You've no right to come marching in and just presenting yourself. And the children for Christ's sake? What are you thinking of?'

Hearing Donald shout the children stepped back from greeting him and bolted to their mother, as if for protection. 'Mummy. Why is Daddy so cross?' Sophia wrapped her arm around the child. 'Don't worry, Sasha, sweetheart.' She laughed, unsmiling. 'Daddy will get over it.'

'Hello, Donald,' said Sophia, her tone ingratiating. 'Nice of you to be so pleased to see us. I telephoned the University last week and they gave me all the details of today.' She paused, studying Donald's dumbfounded expression and enjoying the impact she was making. 'You were certainly quick to tell me I've no right to be here, far quicker than you were to tell me it was happening today. But that's what you think isn't it? I've no right to come marching in here. That's not what the University said. They said I was very welcome and to bring your children.'

'You told the University you were bringing the children? You're joking.'

'Why must I be joking, Donald? I have your two children, but I have no right to be here today. Is that right, Donald? No, "Hello children, it's lovely to see you." Not sounding like the happy father now that you pretended to be yesterday afternoon when we were all safely tucked away together in Dundee. Mind you the University Office were surprised when I asked them about your children. They didn't seem to know about them.'

David standing by Jamila, wide eyed, was looking on with a growing sense of horror. 'My God, Donald. Your children?'

'Your children, Donald. These are your children?' Jamila seemed to mouth the words, feeling faint and looking as if the ground before her had melted away.

Donald turned to David and Jamila as if he'd only just remembered they were there. His face had drained of colour, and he looked as if he might topple and fall over. He rocked as he grasped his hands to his head and buried his face from view, rendered speechless.

Jamila was just beginning to grasp what she was hearing. 'Your children,' she repeated. 'These two children belong to you?'

'Yes,' said Sophia, addressing herself across Donald's silence directly to Jamila. 'Meet Sasha and Michael, and I am Sophia, their mother of course. Who am I speaking to? Another of Donald's conquests I dare say. Is he planning to marry you as well?'

Jamila was silent. She had no words. The children backed up to their mother and held her clothes.

'Well. You have all gone very quiet. Not such a jolly party after all, is it?'

'Why come today for God's sake, Sophia?' Donald spluttered.

'My little gift for Daddy's big day. That's why Donald. Michael and Sasha wanted to see you get your precious Professorship that we have all been slaves to for ever and a day, and I thought that was a good idea. After all, you kept talking about it as if it's all that ever mattered to you. And so. Now you're a Professor and we've seen the ceremony it's my turn for our own little ceremony. I'm here to tell you that I've decided that this is it. Here and now, Donald. Goodbye! Got it? My little gift. Goodbye for ever.'

'What are you talking about? You've only just arrived. You can't do that.' Donald blathered, ashen faced. Jamila and David stood on the edge of the tirade absorbing every stunning word.

'You just watch me! I can do it, Donald, and I am going to do it. I've been planning this moment for months. I should have done it years ago. I'm sick to death of hanging around waiting for you, Tuesday after Tuesday, waiting for you to come to Dundee to see us, to see the children, to frustrate us all with your selfish, conceited, arrogant assertion that you care. I don't love you, Donald, and you don't love me. I was sucked in by your chat and smiles and believed you would save the world. How wrong I was. You don't care. If you did, you'd change. You'd man up. Take responsibility. But you can't. You're incapable. You think that the world revolves around you. Donald in the middle, world around the edges. Well, it doesn't. And why would you care about me anyway? You have your fancy women lined up here, following your every move, hanging on your every word. That poor girl from Morocco or wherever it was. Is that you, poor thing?' Sophia pointed at Jamila and laughed bitterly. 'God, Donald, she's no more than a child. And Constance. She's certainly stuck around you, hasn't she? Swinging from your coat tails. I saw her hanging on your arm before you went in. I expect she's somewhere clearing the way for you even now.' Sophia paused for breath. 'Did you fuck them for the same reasons you fucked me?'

Donald gasped, drew in a deep breath and groaned. David looked on, aghast, astonished by what he was hearing, and Jamila stood by him, with each blast respecting more this woman, this stranger, for her directness, her courage and sheer determination. Jamila was alarmed to recognise in herself that same sense of inevitability that she had felt when Nadeem attacked her so many months ago; she had grasped then that she knew it would happen. Here she was again. She had wanted to believe that Donald cared about her, but she had known for a long time that he didn't, that Marie's scepticism was justified. She just hadn't admitted it to herself just like she hadn't admitted to herself that she didn't trust him and here, spread before her, was the evidence of her own stupidity.

'And don't pretend you don't play with us all, Donald,' continued Sophia. 'You play us like puppies and then we sniff around you like dogs on heat. I was stupid enough to be one of them. And I guess that was your senseless parents just walking away. I waited until they'd gone. Your absurd mother, doting on her "Oh, so clever" son. "He has a way with women," she proudly told me long ago. Too true. So, here's the rub, Donald, I have chosen today to tell you that we're going a long way. We're going to Australia. All three of us; Sasha, Michael, and Sophia. I've sorted out the immigration papers. Australia needs teachers and children so they can have us. We sail next week so you never need bother to come to Dundee again. We'll be on our way to Sydney.'

Donald was speechless. His mind was blank, sense-less-ness was seeping into him as he realised the power of the incontrovertible evidence of his deceit that stood before him.

'And I know you won't think about following us halfway around the world because your precious fossils will keep you here. That's all you really care about isn't it. I watched you walk up onto that stage to grasp your Professorship and I watched those self-seeking, self-opinionated, academic men sitting high and mighty on that stage with you stuck there and I sat there thinking, "This is the last time I shall have to see him. It's over!"'

'But, Sophia. What is it you want? What have I to do? How can I change? Come and live here in Edinburgh.'

'Drivel, Donald! That is surely a joke. Just tell me. Tell me how you might change. You're standing here, shocked by what I am saying with a new version of me standing over there. Look, Donald.' Sophia pointed at Jamila. 'Your fresh young escort waiting in the wings, staring at us both dumbfounded and you have the stupidity to suggest I could come to Edinburgh and you're arrogant enough to ask me what I want. Rid of you is what I want.'

'You could come to Edinburgh and bring the children,' yammered Donald.

'There you go again. Totally up your own. God, how I wish I'd been less naïve when this started. What you really mean is that I could change. I could come to you, change my life to suit you. After you've tied up your several affairs I dare say, Constance and your new girl and God knows who else. You idiot! You can't see, can you? Even when it's staring you in the face! You can't change, Donald. You just pass me aside onto another sample tray like you cast a fossil away when you've examined it through your bloody microscope. You might be smart in the University, all brains and artefacts but out here in the big, bad world you've no bloody common sense, you can't see what's in front of your nose, that's you Donald. And we've all fallen for it, that's what's so absurd. You only care about yourself, your fossils and the chance to seduce another and another and another woman witless enough, like me, to be trapped by your insidious charm.' Sophia paused, looked around. 'Come on, you two. Enough. We've seen Daddy, now we're going.'

'But, Mummy, we haven't had tea with Daddy yet,' pleaded Sasha.

Sophia laughed. 'You see, Donald. That's as good as it gets for the children. Tea with Daddy! Once in a blue moon. That's all you are to them.' Donald stood, looking on speechless. 'We'll have tea on the train today, Sasha love! I've booked us a table. Three for tea on the train. By the window whilst we're speeding along.'

'Tea on the train. That's great. Thank you, Mummy,' said Michael.

'But can't Daddy come?' said Sasha. 'Daddy, can't you come with us? Mummy won't mind will you, Mummy?'

'Mummy does mind, Sasha. Come on. We're going now, so say your goodbyes.'

Sasha edged towards Donald who stooped down and kissed her on the top of her head. She stood back a little, 'Goodbye, Daddy,' then turned towards her mother grasping her hand as they walked away. Michael turned, waved to Donald and blew him a kiss. Donald, silent and close to tears, looked on as all three strode into the chattering crowd and disappeared.

Now left alone, Donald hardly noticed that David and Jamila had vanished as well.

14

David was rendered incredulous by the events he had witnessed that afternoon. Donald Lansdown, the academic archaeologist, just today, made Professor Lansdown, had managed to bury, unseen, a lover and two children in plain sight of all. David had known Donald as a philanderer, but today's revelation left him stunned. He was not an expert on children's ages but could see that the children were around six or seven years old, leaving him further astonished not just at the deception but also at how long it had lasted. David had been Donald's student for several years and not just an ordinary run of the mill student; they had travelled together, stayed away on archaeological digs together as well as studied together and David was perplexed that he had no idea that underneath this apparently innocent relationship Donald had kept a secret profound enough to change the lives of the whole team.

And what kind of man was Donald? David had needed to believe Donald was an okay guy, honourable, reliable, honest. He trusted him and he now discovered he'd been deceived. David's perspective had shifted irrevocably, and he saw with an unexpected clarity that Donald had behaved as if women didn't matter; they were there just for him; it was his right to seduce them because he's Donald, top of the food chain. David was shocked to realise that in a stroke Donald had lost any integrity, ripped up the rule book. 'Donald's a liar,' he heard himself say and I've been fooled all this time. Then David started to wonder. Surely somebody must have known, guessed, suspected? Why did Sophia play along with it for so long? Years? How did Donald stay undetected for all that time?

Despite his own feelings and thoughts David's first instinct as they walked away from the Usher Hall was to help Jamila. 'I'll walk with you back to Donald's flat if you like, Jamila.' They had not talked but David assumed that Jamila would be as incredulous as he was. 'You'll need to get yourself sorted out I expect. I'm worried that you're going to be okay. I live with my mother not very far from here. Would you like to come and stay with us for a few days? I'm sure my mother would be happy to have you if I asked her.'

'Oh yes, please,' she said with an immediacy that relieved David. 'I would like that very much if your mother doesn't mind.' David's warmth had presented her with a solution to a problem she had not yet been able to identify. 'I'd like that very much.'

They walked in silence both lost in their own thoughts. When they reached Leith, they sat on the harbour wall looking out across the shipyards, watching the inevitable seagulls as they squabbled and squawked around them. Jamila thought of Marseille, of Marie. As they had walked, she knew that was where she needed to go, back to Marseille and then back to Morocco to her village. She had run away from Nadeem but now Jamila had resolved that she had to stand up to Donald so if she could find her way back to her village, she would stand up to her brother. She felt the shock passing and a new anger rise up within her, anger with Donald but also her as yet unresolved fury with Nadeem, the author of her own foolishness.

As they sat looking out across the water, David told her a little about his mother, described her small house not far from Leith where the back garden looked out across the broad reach of the Firth of Forth to the mountains beyond. David felt he needed to talk, to reassure Jamila, reassure himself. He was an only child and he liked to see his mother happy just as he was pleased to see Jamila able to sort herself out. David admired them both and found himself deeply antagonistic towards Donald, astonished by his deceitfulness, and already growing ashamed not to have understood his duplicity.

15

When Donald went back over the events of that afternoon, he couldn't remember how he reached the Union Bar. He recalled he should have returned to the lab, that he should have met his parents and that he was supposed to be meeting Connie at six. It was too late for the first two, but meeting Connie was still possible. He arrived at the bar, shortly after six o'clock and paced back and forth up the street, looking at his watch and waiting in vain. He expected Connie to be angry because he had failed to get to the lab. He did not expect she would know about the events of the afternoon. He had concluded that David would not have returned to the lab. He hadn't even considered Jamila. Fraser wasn't on his list so when Donald saw him approach, he would have disappeared around the corner if he'd had the chance, but it was too late. Fraser carried a folded note which he gave to Donald, avoiding eye contact.

'Where have you been this afternoon?' Fraser asked as casually as he could muster.

'Not well,' said Donald. Fraser knew that was a lie as he walked away.

As Donald read the note his expression remained impassive. He folded it, placed it in his pocket and turned, walked across the street and set out up the hill. After few paces he slowed, spun back on his heels and shambled back into the bar. He took a stool alone, bought himself a pint of strong bitter and a whisky chaser and with his back to the doorway, downed the chaser, started to sip the beer and then drank the whole pint. 'Here, barman. I'll have another please, the same. And the whisky.' He slapped a five-pound note on the bar and left it there, whilst he continued to drink.

The barman was used to the waifs and strays of the university fetching up there, the worse for wear, gowns akimbo and hair frowzy. Donald was ignored, left to drink himself into a stupor.

Later that evening, much the worse for wear, Donald staggered home and fell up his front steps. He struggled to find his key, rummaged through his pockets and as he did so the folded note handed to him by Fraser dropped to the ground. Bending over to try to pick it up he lurched down a few steps, managed to hang onto the railing and lurched back up to his door, forgetting why he'd gone. He couldn't locate his hands or his key and decided to kick the door. Loudly. There was no answer. He kicked again just as his neighbour appeared on his stairs.

'Lost your key, have you, Donald? She's locked you out. Silly son-of-a-bitch. That girl needs to work out which side her bread's buttered.'

'Who's that? Thank God you're here. I can't find my key. I had it before I went out to school but it's not here now you see, look, look.' Donald turned out his pockets and shook them. His key fell out. 'Oh. That's for my door but I can't find it, I meant to open it and I think I might be as drunk as a skunk.'

'Do you want me to do it?' Donald's neighbour asked.

'No. Not now. No. That's fine I can do it I just need to get a bit closer.' His neighbour gave up and turned away. Donald leant forward with the key in his mouth just as the door swung open and Jamila appeared in a dressing gown.

'You're drunk,' Jamila said as Donald lurched through the door. She stood to one side. 'You stink.' Jamila pushed him through the door, and he sprawled into his flat cracking his head on the wall as he did so.

'Fuck. My head. Jesus Christ.'

As he swayed Jamila shoved him towards the bedroom, through the half open door, aimed him at his bed, shoved him again and he collapsed across the sheets. She turned, slammed his door, went into her bedroom and locked her own door.

*

In the morning, Jamila pulled on her clothes and found Donald in the kitchen, drinking hot tea and nursing a large bruise on his forehead. She assaulted him with her questions to which of course he had no answers.

'Why are you so angry?' Donald asked in a pause to the onslaught.

'Angry? You have no idea, Donald. You're right. I am angry. Angry with myself for being so stupid as to fall for your sly charm and to think your posh job made you a decent man. I, Donald, can do what I like. You, Jamila, must just put up with it. My God, Donald. I've done a lot of thinking since yesterday. So, come on, tell me, who was the woman with those two children? Their mother it seemed, with her two children, your children Donald. David was right, wasn't he? You're a dark horse. She knew you'd be there, didn't she, except you didn't invite her, did you? Whoever she was, she came with those children, her two children, your two children to see you, their Daddy, get his professorship, but you didn't want them there did you, you didn't know they were coming did you, because they're supposed to be your secret aren't they, Donald? I'm not supposed to know about them, am I? Nobody was supposed to know about them, were they?'

Donald stayed silent.

'No. Of course not. They're your secret, aren't they? No one in your so-called lab knows about them, do they? And she is one of your women isn't she and you can't speak about it can you but it's true. You're a liar aren't you, Donald? A massive liar! And do you know what? I don't hate you. I feel sorry for you because you are such a pathetic, useless waste of space and I thought you were so important?'

'I can explain, Jamila. Let me explain.'

'You're joking. Why would I want to listen to your stupid excuses for using me? It's those poor kids you need to explain it to, those two children whose lives you have messed up with your selfish, self-satisfied stupidity. I'm right, aren't I? Don't bother to answer, Donald. I know I'm right. We'll come to that later. I'm going out.'

'But, Jamila!'

Jamila took her coat and made for the door and as she opened it, she saw a folded note on the doorstep. She picked it up, read it and then in a mocking voice, still standing on the doorstep, she read it to Donald. *Sorry, Donald sweetie. I'm not feeling very well just now and don't think I can make dinner tonight. You'll just have to put up with your boring friend from Morocco instead. Sorry. Lots of love. Connie.*

Jamila folded the note, put it in her pocket, looked straight at Donald, slapped him across the face and exited the flat, slamming the door behind her.

*

With the exhibition out of the way, Fraser and Constance were working on clearing away the displays. They had been surprised and concerned that Donald hadn't come up after the ceremony the previous afternoon and mystified as to where David was. Prof McIntyre showed up and seemed annoyed that Donald wasn't there, but he said nothing. Elizabeth and James had stayed a while but needed to get home and seemed pretty fed up not to have seen their son. Half a dozen other visitors came and went and although interested in what they saw, with no Donald the whole thing fell flat. Then, to add to the mystery, there was no David or

Donald this morning. Constance was beginning to worry. 'Do you know what Donald did after you gave him my message, Fraser?'

'Well. We both can guess.'

'True. That'll be why he's not here I suppose. Too hung over! Doesn't account for David, though. He never drinks too much.'

At that moment the lab door opened, and Jamila appeared, taking Fraser and Constance very much by surprise. Connie was quick to greet Jamila despite her apprehension. 'Jamila. It's good to see you. Have you brought Donald with you?'

'Good morning, Constance. You could answer that question better than me, I'm sure. After all, you've nothing better to do than write him notes about me, have you? When it comes to being a good morning, we have something in common don't we?'

'I've no idea what you are talking about.'

'Do you expect me to believe that, Constance. "No idea" you say. That's very unlikely.'

'Hang on, Jamila. You can't come barging in here and just start ranting at me. If you don't like the way it is with us and Donald you can always clear off back to Marseille or Morocco or wherever it is he found you.'

'Well! That would suit you nicely wouldn't it, Constance? There's nothing you'd like better than to get rid of me because you think you'd have him all to yourself then wouldn't you. You've always thought yourself better than me.'

'That's just not true, Jamila, but I did get there first.'

'Not true, as you'll see. So, I guess this isn't true either then, is it?' Jamila took the note from her pocket she'd found on Donald's doorstep and read it back to Constance, her tone mocking. 'So here I am. '*Your* boring friend from Morocco.'

'Give that here. Where the hell did you get it from?'

Jamila avoided a lunge from Constance as she tried to grab the note. Fraser looked on astonished, as having taken Constance off balance, Jamila simply handed her the note.

'There you are, Constance. No need to struggle. That's not why I'm here. Oh no, not one little bit. I have far, far more to be angry about, mainly with myself. You're not the only stupid one here are you, Constance? You think you found Donald first, but you're so wrong.'

Constance snatched the note, her note, screwed it up and threw it on the bench. She peered at Jamila, sneered and laughed. 'So, what does our friend from Morocco know I wonder that will make us both angry. What do you think, Fraser?'

Fraser looked uncomfortable, caught in the headlights and was frantically searching his brain for what might be coming next, although he could find nothing. Jamila remained silent.

'Well then, Jamila,' said Constance. 'We're not here to talk about Fraser. Say what you need to and then maybe we can get on with our work.'

'Good luck with that. You like to work with Donald, don't you? Does he share all his secrets with you?' Jamila looked to Constance for a reaction. Now it was her turn to be silent. Jamila raised her voice, found her words and began to feel in control. 'Do you trust him, Constance, and does he make you feel important and that you matter to him?'

Constance stayed silent and glared at Jamila, whilst wishing the floor would open and swallow her.

'Does he treat you well, share lunch with you, make you feel wanted?'

Constance was seeing a Jamila she had not seen before and didn't like it.

'Can I suggest that you ask Donald about his children, his two children? You might ask him as well, Fraser?'

Constance looked at Jamila as if she was coloured green and had sprouted wings. 'You don't know what you're talking about. I've known Donald since I came here, and he has no children. You're out of your mind.' She knew Jamila was just being stupid. Fraser nodded agreement with Constance but never-the-less stayed silent.

'You're so smart, Constance. So clever with all your fossils and microscopes and your wonderful University but you haven't seen what's been under your own nose all this time. Ask Donald yourself, Constance, if he ever has the gall to walk in here again. Two children who call Donald "Daddy"! And ask him about their mother, a mother of two children who seems very unhappy with Donald and very angry with him; ask him about this mistress and the two children that he has kept secret from all of us I suspect for as long as they've been born and before that as well. Ask him, Constance, and listen to the answer if you dare.'

Constance glared at Jamila; her eyes flashed. 'You're lying, Jamila, this is all some fantastic invention and for Christ's sake what makes you think that I'll believe all this? You must be pretty desperate to make up all this trash.'

'Well, ask him, Constance. Ask him if they were in the hall yesterday to watch him walk up, so important, on the stage? Didn't you see them, Constance? You slipped up there. Perhaps you'd gone before they appeared. Ask him the children's names and what they call him! It's Sasha and Michael and they call him "Daddy". "Daddy"! Ask him where they live? Dundee? Have you heard him mention Dundee? Ask him if you have the guts!'

Constance stayed silent and wide eyed.

'Dundee you say, Jamila?' Fraser said cautiously.

'Dundee, yes. Ring any bells. He'll deny it, Constance, of course, he will. But how will you explain that I've seen them, spoken to their mother, Sophia, listened as Donald and Sophia argued outside the hall yesterday with David there as well, listening like me, watching like me, seeing the children and their mother like me. Ask David when you can find him. Yes, Constance, David heard and saw it all. Then you will have to decide for yourself if you want to carry on flattering this self-satisfied and deceiving man by believing whatever sad story he creates for you to cover up his lies and deceptions. He has seduced us all by deception, by his snivelling false virtue, and I thought he was so important. Will you have the guts to face it when you know it's true. I wonder what the University will make of it now they know that their blue-eyed boy isn't all he cracks himself up to be?'

During these words Constance sat down, shrunk, bowed and deflated. She looked at Jamila with a fleeting sense of admiration.

'Okay. I'll ask him, Jamila. And if it's not true I'll find you and tear you limb from limb. Get it. Limb from bloody limb.'

'Don't waste time then, Constance, because I won't be here much longer. Donald is a lying parasite. If you don't believe that you're an idiot. Oh. And find David before you decide, Constance. He will fill you in on the details, all the details. He's the only one amongst you that has any common sense.'

Jamila turned and left the room, strutting down the corridor and away. As she reached the outside door, she came face-to-face with Donald coming the other way. He swerved against the wall, and she swept straight past him and went on her way. Horrified to realise where she was coming from, his red eyes and unshaven face swivelled to follow her walking into the distance.

16

Shamelessness oozed from Donald that evening. Jamila said nothing to him of her arrangement with David. She just kept asking, 'What's going to happen next then, Donald? Now you've lied to us all.'

'All right Jamila. Alright! Don't keep saying that. I hate you saying it like you do.'

'Oh! You hate it do you Donald,' she said. 'Well. That's too bad. How do you think I feel? What did Constance say? How was she this afternoon when you finally turned up at your laboratory? I bet she wasn't pleased to see you, was she?'

'How have you the gall to go to the lab and upset my team? Don't you realise I could lose my job? What then? Constance works for me. She's on my payroll. She could report me.'

'Report you! Why? What have you done? You haven't done anything you keep saying. What can she report? If you've done nothing wrong, why would you lose your job?'

'What makes you think you're so smart, Jamila?'

'Well! There's a thing, Donald. I think I'm smart, do I? I think I'm stupid. Constance works for you; you flirt with her when it suits you, you invite me into your bed, you lie to all of us and none of us deserve to hear the truth. Constance doesn't deserve to know that you're a two-timing, deceitful man – because she works for you! So, you just do what you please and she's no right to know. But then of course it's your precious work. That's all that matters, isn't it? I'm the stupid one.'

'That's not what I said.'

'Oh! Isn't it, Donald? You help me come here with promises of a place to live and food to eat and you're full of kindness and want me to be interested in your bloody archaeology and everything I think about you I find out is a lie. I'm just your hobby and Constance, she's just another bit on the side; and as for Sophia and those two poor children, what are they, Donald? We've all been stupid enough to let you wrap us in rings with your lies and deceptions and now it's all out in the open you've no idea where to turn have you? I felt sorry for myself yesterday but today I just feel angry. Even more furious for that poor woman and those children. I'm even furious for Constance who has been lied to by a man she was stupid enough to trust, just like me.'

'You don't have to keep saying it.'

'Why shouldn't I keep saying it? You're a good liar, Donald, I'll give you that. But I knew there was something up and Marie certainly did. How can that be? Somehow, she just knew, and I was too clever to take any notice of her thoughts. She just sensed it, Donald which makes her way smarter than me. But you'll never get what you want because you're totally found out now and the pain will be yours and you certainly deserve it. You're a cheat and a liar. Okay! You're a disgrace, Donald.'

Donald was silent and visibly shrank as the onslaught continued.

'I know about secrets, Donald. I have my own. I was attacked when I was eighteen by my stepbrother. I was never going to tell you Donald, because I felt so bad, so guilty. He cornered me out in the mountains and set about me and I've never dealt with it, never cornered him, shouted at him. I hate him but it was me that was ashamed. I never wanted you to know because I believed you were a decent man with your posh airs and graces and smart Scottish upbringing, an honest man to be with and to love and I'd be safe and respected, and I was totally wrong. I didn't tell you because I thought my past would stop you liking me. I didn't know who my mother was, Donald, or my real father. I understand how Sophia feels for her poor children. But you're as bad as my stepbrother, you just have a smart gown and a posh hat to cover you up so we can't see the pile of shit you really are.'

'I didn't know. How the hell was I to know all that? I wouldn't have left you alone whilst I was working if I'd known.'

'While you were working. Don't make me laugh, Donald. You were with Constance or your precious Sophia half the time. You went to see Sophia, didn't you? Week after week but you just never said. Well, I never, she lives in Dundee. There's a surprise. Even your mother had worked that out! What a bunch of fools we've all been. You don't love me, or Constance or Sophia or those two children. You love yourself and your dry, dusty boxes of old teeth and you deserve each other. I know what I must do now, Donald. The penny has finally dropped.'

'I appeal to you, Jamila. Let me make it okay to you; give me a final chance.'

Jamila found she was drawing herself up to her full height, proud of her defiance and feeling adrenalin strengthen her resolve. 'For what, you stupid fool? You're going to tell me you've been unkind and selfish and thoughtless, aren't you? You're joking. Do we all have to give you one final chance? Which one of us will you choose? You tried that yesterday with Sophia. "Daddy wants a final chance!" Is that what you said? Did it do any good? A mistress, deception, babies, Tuesdays in Dundee. And where's she going? Australia. Good luck to her I say. She's made a good decision there. And now you think that's good for you, don't you? Your cowardice, her courage. Your selfishness has driven her away and all you do is appeal to me to fill in the space. You were arrogant enough to think that's great, Sophia has solved my problem for me. She's gone. Now all I have to do is enjoy my new freedom and because my life is a lie and so is mine in its own way, you get to appeal to me. Big bloody deal. I've run away, Donald, just like Sophia is running, except she is taking your children with her. I ran away because I just couldn't carry on dealing with what happened to me, just like Sophia and you with all your smart hats and cloaks and gowns and professorships. Wring us out and toss us away. Now everybody knows about you, so best of luck with that. I'm going. I came here to escape my own home, my past and what do I find? It's worse here. Here there's endless lies where I was stupid enough to think I'd find honesty and warmth. Thank you, Donald, and thank you, Sophia. You've both shown me that I must face my own life in my own way and in my own place. I am going.'

'When?' asked Donald, tears in his eyes. 'When are you going?'

'Tomorrow morning, I'm walking, Donald.'

Silence. Donald stood alone, in the middle of his flat, unable to move, his brows furrowed and his eyes wet with self-pity. For the first time in his life he was not sure how to deal with the realities that faced him.

*

The following day Donald was working in silence at his bench at the front of his empty laboratory. He wore his academic gown and his Doctoral hat lay on the seat beside him. He hadn't shaved.

He was comforting himself, peering into a microscope, adjusting its focus and fiddling with the slide. He had no idea what he was looking at or why he was looking. Outside children's voices echoed. Inside the clock by the chalk board ticked. Donald sighed, uncurled, stretched his back, took the slide out of the microscope, examined it, cleaned it on his gown, replaced it, looked up, sighed, walked over to the window, gazed out across the playground where the children played, wandered back and looked down his microscope. Fraser, wearing a white lab coat, appeared at the open door. He stood there silent, observing Donald, but they did not communicate. After a few moments Fraser took a screwdriver from his coat pocket and unscrewed David's name tab from the door. He replaced 'Doctor Donald Lansdown' with a new tab reading 'Professor Donald Lansdown, PhD'. Fraser watched Donald for a few moments, slipped David's door tab into his pocket and took out his tray of samples and started to work on them.

Donald stood alone, gazing at his slides, seeing nothing, eyes downcast, oblivious to Fraser, considering which of the others if any would join David and resign their posts and abandon their studies. It seemed hardly any time at all since he'd set up this research facility but already David was a significant loss. Donald walked back to the window, distracted, uneasy. Hearing the voices of the children again in the playground below the window, the unwelcome echo of yesterday's encounters washed over him. 'Daddy! Daddy!' his children had called. Only now, now that they were lost to him, did Donald comprehend they were his children and even though for years they had been no more than a weekly diversion, often inconvenient, today they were lost to him, and the loss was beginning to penetrate. He stared out of the window wishing his two children were playing on the grass below, bitterly realising his abject failure to love them. 'Sow a few wild oats,' his mother advised as she pushed Donald out the door to take up his scholarship at Edinburgh University. 'There's plenty of fish in the sea.'

'Mixed metaphors mother. Your speciality,' he said as he hugged her goodbye. The oats would get soggy in the sea.' His mother laughed, for ever indulgent.

Donald remembered himself as he had breezed into Fresher's Week, a smiling young man just out of school, with what he'd cheerfully taken as his mother's instructions still ringing in his ears. He'd relished the week, and this was the last night. The coconut shy was set up a stone's throw from the beer tent ensuring plenty of testosterone on display. Donald stood at the centre of two new pals who regardless of their unsteady balance were eager to outshine each other but it was Donald the cricketer who took down three coconuts, gave one to each of his pals to carry and offered the other to the girl in the admiring crowd who most took his fancy. With an exaggerated bow he presented her with his prize. Giggling, she turned away. Later that same evening they bumped into each other by the big wheel. She still held the coconut. They briefly introduced themselves. Sophia was coy but never-the-less his so easy invitation to her to join him in a gondola was eagerly accepted and they swung up into the night sky, his two male companions abandoned. That was to become a familiar pattern.

A few days later Donald was sauntering by the Water of Leith enjoying the sunshine. Best enjoy it while it lasted. Everyone in Scotland knew that summer was a rare event in Edinburgh. Sophia held his hand. Her breezy cotton skirt swayed in the sunshine, and he couldn't help smiling when other men walking towards them noticed him. Donald liked to be noticed, making Sophia an attractive proposition. For her part Sophia couldn't believe her luck. She'd enjoyed the gondola ride and the few friends she'd made reckoned that Donald was quite a catch. He was suave, self-assured, shaped by fresh mountain air. They had no notion that his confidence needed more than a little attention or that he was yet to taste the bitterness of rejection. Unfortunately, it wasn't only his mother that had doted on him when he progressed from short to long trousers.

As they walked, he weighed up his chances. Donald was never given to excess conversation and Sophia found him a wee bit quiet. She'd grown up with big brothers, club rugby and beer nights. Donald was cricket and cricket was posh, white wine and canapes. Strange that Donald talks so little, she thought, when he seems so alive. For his part he cared little for what she thought or liked or disliked; she was attached to him for now and that was enough. His latest male mates had noted her 'classy chassis' and that was all that engaged his interest. Never mind conversation, he was enjoying the feel of her thighs as they brushed against his own whilst they walked. 'Ring-a-ding-ding'.

That morning he'd collected a filled picnic basket from Jenner's store, complete with wine and glasses. He had plans for Sophia today; he had plans to end the week with a bang. There were several places along the river where the grassy banks dropped away from the path, and they all made perfect, discreet picnic spots. As they walked hand-in-hand, he held in his other hand the picnic basket and a folded rug ready to be thrown on the grass. Kicking through the autumn leaves Sophia felt that she could not be happier.

'Don't you just love Edinburgh, Donald?' she said.

'It beats Dundee, that's for sure,' he replied. She smarted a little at his criticism of Dundee. She loved her home city.

Sophia skipped around to face him on tiptoe. 'Maybe you're right,' she teased as she kissed both his cheeks. With his free hand he embraced her for a few moments before they walked on in silence. He liked the kisses, so reaching a bend in the path Donald stopped, bent to put the basket down on the path, reached around Sophia's waist with both his hands and pulled her towards him, almost roughly. He then kissed her, firm and lingering on the lips. The embrace lasted long enough for an old couple to walk by, look with disapproval at the two students and mutter 'disgusting young people,' as they passed.

Donald pulled away and smiled at his own bravado. Sophia appeared surprised, almost shocked. Gathering up the picnic basket Donald led them on, and they walked for a while in silence. As they walked Sophia processed her growing realisation that Donald's impatient behaviour might be more ambitious than she expected, as well as subject to the disapproval of passing locals.

It wasn't long before they stopped again. 'How about just here for lunch?' he said putting the blanket on the grass. Sophia acquiesced with a smile that needed preparation. The picnic spot he had selected was shaded in part and a few strides from the path. Below them the river glistened on the rocks whilst above them willow trees rustled. Not many minutes before, Sophia had felt happy and excited; now she had become apprehensive. Donald, guessing at her caution, spread the blanket, placed the basket in the centre, and sat carefully to one side, leaving space on the other side for Sophia. With the basket between them Sophia felt some calm returning to her, although Donald's lingering kiss still lived in her lips. He'd kissed her several times that week but the intensity she had just experienced was unsettling.

He opened out the Jenner's picnic. 'Smoked salmon,' he said. 'It's the best in Edinburgh. Shall we drink sparkling white?'

'That's nice,' she said, dreading the need to consume more wine in a Fresher's week already littered with empty bottles. Sophia's parents were Scottish Presbyterian and teetotal to boot. Alcohol had never been allowed in the house and her two brothers' love of beer frowned upon despite the good quality of their rugby. Sophia had probably drunk more since Fresher's Week started than during the rest of her life, but she didn't like to say. She didn't want her new friends and especially Donald to think her a killjoy.

She didn't like smoked salmon either, since her grandmother described it as slimy shoe leather, but like her taste for wine, she didn't want to offend Donald by telling him. If Donald had known all this, he would been indifferent and he'd no more thought of asking what she liked than he could fly to the moon. As far as he was concerned this was all just fair game and why he was here.

The cork flew skywards, Sophia's glass was filled, and Donald held his own. 'Cheers!' he said. 'Bottoms Up.'

Sophia took a sip and managed a smile. 'That's lovely,' she said. She felt uneasy, as if she was part of something but didn't quite know what. Were they celebrating? If so, she had no idea what the celebration might be. Did Donald know something she didn't? He passed her a plate and offered her a sandwich which she accepted taking her place in a ritual she didn't understand. Her acquiescence, she thought, seemed to help Donald relax. Was this a good thing, though? Sophia was feeling unprepared, hesitant, while she sensed Donald's spirits were rising. It was then she realised that he had already drunk a glass of wine and poured himself another.

'Drink up,' he said. She took another sip of her glass. 'Another sandwich?'

Sophia didn't want another. 'Yes,' she said. He pushed the sandwiches towards her.

'No,' she said flustered. 'Sorry. I think I've changed my mind.'

'Ah! You think. So, you're not sure really.' Donald's verbal prod disconcerted Sophia further and she began to sense an edge to his charm. She had begun to feel herself slipping out of control. He took another sandwich and consumed it in silence, drained his glass and poured himself another. The trouble is, she thought, he is quite good looking, and I need to hang onto him. Sophia looked out across the water and sipped at her wine, hoping that soon they would move on, and she could get back to her room in Hall, where there was safety in numbers. She liked her room, its airy sparseness and view of the hills to the north of the River Forth. After working hard in school here was her chance; more than anything she had wanted to study Scottish History but however much fun it seemed she wanted next week to come, lectures to start and parties to end. Her thoughts were broken when she noticed that Donald was moving the picnic basket away and had rolled himself over and stretched himself beside her.

'I'd like some more of that kiss,' he said and before she had been able to gather her thoughts or to answer, there he was, back on her lips. She never knew whether it was intentional or not, but his weight pushed her back and she found herself lying on the blanket. Her memory is that she submitted to him; it was only her willingness that she came to doubt. Thus, the kiss continued, and all might have been well except that Donald moved one hand down through her lustrous hair and across her neck, gently and surely towards her breasts. For Sophia this was a step too far. Hardly knowing what she was doing she gathered her strength, threw him back and as he fell, she slapped him, hard, across the face. He laughed, grabbed her hand and pushed her away. This time it was Sophia who rolled, sprang to her feet shouting, 'You're beastly, Donald. I never want to see you again.'

Donald lifted himself up from the blanket, propped onto his arms and watched her stride away, her skirt swinging and cutting a fine figure. 'That's what they all say,' he muttered to himself and smiled. Turning away he tossed several stones into the river where the ducks scattered and squawked. He poured himself another glass of wine. A careful observer would have seen him grin. 'She'll be back,' he muttered to the ducks.

17

It was two days after the drama of the Usher Hall ceremony. Donald scurried out of his flat in the morning, only too pleased to get away and with him gone it hadn't taken Jamila many minutes to put her things in her bag. Even with his usual nonchalance, Donald wanted no 'goodbyes'. His cast iron ego had taken a hammering that even he would struggle to overcome. Jamila wore most of her clothes so there wasn't much to carry, and she put 'Little Dorrit' in the bag as she hadn't finished reading and planned to give the book to Marie when she arrived in Marseille. She left her hat on the bed as it was only bought to please Donald but kept the dress as she thought she might wear it again, although she couldn't imagine where. David had offered to meet her that morning and walk with her to his mother's house. Before he did, he cycled to the University to resign his studies and so arrived on his bike to collect her. He found Jamila sat on the steps; her bag draped by her side. He was not surprised she was forlorn. They exchanged smiles. David put her bag on the saddle, and he pushed the bike as Jamila walked along beside him. After a few moments she turned and looked back at Donald's flat. 'That's done then,' she said and turned back to David.

Jamila was already unhappy and even more so when David told her he'd given up his studies; she felt he deserved to study and to abandon his work seemed hasty. But he was clearly determined. 'I couldn't work for a man who had treated us all so badly,' he said. 'He's lied about his children and to his children so why wouldn't he lie again.' She admired him for his sacrifice and his directness. 'I expect the others will resign, as well,' he said. 'It will only be a matter of time.' David said he had decided to get another paid job and maybe re-enrol at the University next year, but he wasn't sure. 'What do you think you'll do now?' he asked Jamila as they walked.

'I need to think for a few days,' she said. In her heart she knew she would have to return to Morocco, but she wasn't ready yet to say the words. Jamila grasped that she had tripped past a childhood she barely understood and that she needed to return, to unpick, to understand and to relearn. Marie had always said that standing and fighting is the best way. Jamila had been wrong about Donald, but her mistake had shown her that running from her home to escape trouble had helped her to see things differently. She wasn't quite ready to tell David because she was still unsure whether she wanted to face Nadeem, and she knew David might ask her, so she changed the subject. 'I'm looking forward to meeting your Mum, David. What shall I call her?'

'Moira,' said David. Jamila soon discovered that everybody around her home seemed to know Moira and that Moira had told everybody that Jamila was coming to stay and that she'd come all the way from Morocco. Jamila was to remember her few weeks with David and his Mum with great relief and affection, recalling Moira's laugh, her sunny smile, her wisdom and most of all her cooking. Haggis and neeps was a taste she would never forget.

Jamila discovered David to be unfailingly kind so that with his help she was able to shake off the despondency that Donald's behaviour had left in her. David told her a little about himself, his mother and their life in the mountains. He told her his father's story, of working in the last of the Niddry coal mines, how he used to cough up blood when he'd been down the mine and how he died painfully unable to breath. David explained that his mother wanted something better for him and made sure he worked hard at school. Jamila could see how proud she was of David. He had told his mother about Donald and his secret children, and she was pleased David had turned his back on him, although worried that this might upset her plans for him to have a good job. David promised her he would be fine although Donald's bombshell had rocked his self-assurance. 'How could I have been so wrong?' David wondered during those few days.

'I feel stupid,' Jamila said to Moira when they were talking one morning. 'I trusted Donald when I should not have done. It's a mistake I must not repeat.'

'Perhaps you'll find Jamila that your heart needs more time to accept what your mind already knows.' Moira's thoughtfulness warmed Jamila's heart. 'Donald is a bad man and that's tough for you because you trusted him. So did David. You've both drawn lines between good and bad and those lines have been kicked and blurred so what made a good man for you both doesn't make a good man anymore. You must both walk to that line, redraw it and understand again what makes a man good.'

'But how do I know if a man is good?' Jamila asked. 'How did you know, Moira?'

'My mother used to say, "A good man gone wrong is usually a bad man found out," and I think she was wise. There's a bit of bad in many of us but a little good in all of us. A man might be smart, make you laugh, support you, like your friends and family, understand your feelings, respect you. He might listen to you, celebrate with you – but then babies are born, children are made, and men can change. Or other things can shift, and the good man might shift as well. We must all work at it if we want a relationship to last, unless like Donald, the man is a liar. We just have to spot that and walk away from it. And some men are liars, Jamila, and have no idea and no care about how much impact their badness has on the lives of their partners. But I think Sophia did the right thing in the end, walking away from him and taking her children with her. It was bound to happen in the end so the sooner the better. You certainly did the right thing, Jamila.'

Jamila loved Moira for her plain common sense. It wasn't many days before she was thinking she'd miss her when she left. A few days later David asked Jamila again. 'What are you going to do next? Have you decided yet?' She had and it was then that Jamila told David about Nadeem's attack and why she had left her village. David took in every word. He was troubled to hear her story and pleased to have so many questions answered as the story unravelled. His admiration for Jamila was growing. 'I have decided I will go back and face up to Nadeem if needs be,' she said. 'I have only myself to please so I will go from here to Marseille, see Marie and then take the ferry back to Algiers. My family won't know I am coming but I think they will be pleased I have returned. As for Nadeem he will hear my anger.' David was beginning to feel sadness. He had grown fond of Jamila, Moira's affection for her pleased him and her departure would leave a gap in his life that he might not have known was there.

That afternoon Jamila found herself a job on the docks in Leith, working in the kitchen of a works café. She would have to leave Moira's home early but would be back for tea. She went to the railway station and found out how much it would cost to go by train to Marseille. She knew how much the ferry was and the price of trains from Algiers. She calculated that it would take her six weeks to earn sixty pounds, enough to pay her way back to her mountains. Moira was delighted she would stay that long, and she told everyone how much she liked 'my visitor', as she always called Jamila, and it wasn't many days before Moira was thinking that David and Jamila would make a 'lovely couple.' Moira wouldn't take any money from Jamila. She'd been wanting to pair David off with a 'good girl' for some time and Jamila seemed just the ticket. David knew his Mum and knew what she was thinking.

David's kindness had kept Jamila going when she most needed it and he had always been good to her. 'Will you come and visit me in Morocco, David, so you can meet my family? I'd love to show you my village and you'd enjoy walking in the hills.'

'That would be wonderful, I'd like it very much. When I have saved the money, I will, Jamila.' David was delighted she'd asked him; Moira was thrilled.

18

'Oh, Marie. This is a fabulous smell. I'm so hungry.' Jamila took a bite from the baguette. 'Better than anything I ate in Edinburgh, apart from Haggis and neeps.' Laughing, she reached into her travel bag. 'This book is for you, Marie. Little Dorrit. I borrowed it from Donald, but he'll never get it back. It's all about England but the whole tale starts in Marseille in an old prison which is a dreadful place and there's lots of travelling. I know you'll enjoy it even if it is hard work but if I can read it you can. Something for you to do while you're waiting for the baby to come.'

'A good book's a great idea,' said Marie. 'Thank you, Jamila.'

'It's so good to sit here again with you. It seems an age ago that we said goodbye in Edinburgh, and you look so well. Being pregnant suits you.'

'That may be,' said Marie. 'Pierre says I've become obsessed with tidying up the apartment. I think he's right. I've been pretty grumpy with him as well, especially when he leaves his clothes scattered around. But we'll get there. He's very attentive and I like that.'

'Have I been a fool, Marie? You think I have, don't you?'

'No. Jamila, you're no fool but I was surprised about Donald. Are you sure he was good to you; he didn't force you did he?'

'No, he didn't, Marie, but there is something about him that made me feel it was kind of inevitable and that might have been to do with me. He was never unkind to me but after we had slept together nothing changed, he didn't seem that bothered or pleased. It almost felt like he assumed I would sleep with him because he was Donald and Donald usually had what he wanted, but when it all fell apart, it felt as if I knew it was going to happen. I've thought about that and it worries me.'

'Tell me more about Donald's family. Did you meet his children? Speak to them maybe?'

'No. Not at all. It was just as I said. I only saw Donald and Sophia together after the ceremony where he was made a professor. I'd kept out of the way when it was all over because I didn't want to have to meet everybody, especially Donald's mother, and when I came out, I thought Donald and David were on their own. That was when Sophia appeared with the children. She just jumped out of the crowd. The children hardly spoke. It must have been horrible for them. It was all arguing and shouting. That night Donald and I had an argument as well. He didn't want to admit they were his children, even though they'd called him 'Daddy' and their mother was there. Nobody knew, Marie. None of his team that we met at the dig knew. You wouldn't believe it. I couldn't believe it, but you were right to warn me not to trust him.'

'Why were you all taken in?'

'I've asked myself that over and again in the last few days and I don't know.' Jamila felt guilt although she was ashamed to admit it, even to Marie. 'I suppose it was there for me to see but I just didn't want to see it. That's made me doubt myself again. It's horrible. I really don't want to tell you this but that is what it was like with Nadeem? Afterwards I felt guilty. Did I just miss the signs, whatever they may have been? Was it my fault?'

'For God's sake, Jamila. It can hardly have been your fault. Why do you blame yourself?'

'But all that time with Donald and now I ask myself why I slept with him, why I trusted him, and you saw it, Marie. You saw it coming, didn't you?' Jamila was finding it hard to face herself with the truth and increasingly sure that Marie had been right all along.

'Not exactly, no. I just don't trust anybody much I suppose, but we only believe things when we know them for ourselves. Anyway. You look at bit better today. Pierre was worried about you yesterday.'

'He's so kind to me. I'm just tired, Marie, it's all that travelling.'

'What do you think you will do now?'

'Well, finally I've taken your advice. I've decided I'm going back to Morocco, to my village to find my family.' Jamila was confident of her plan as she told Marie and she spoke easily and felt happy to be saying it. It felt right.

Marie looked hard at Jamila and broke into a smile. 'That is the best possible thing for you to do and I am so pleased. Stay with us for a few days, get your strength back and then go.' Marie stretched out her arms and embraced Jamila, pleased in so many ways and certainly believing it was the best thing for her.

'Of course, I'll stay with you. I'd like that very much.' Jamila still felt troubled. 'I wonder about Nadeem, though, Marie. Do you think it could have been my fault?'

'Oh, come on, Jamila. Did you ask him to search you out?'

'No.'

'Did you tempt him in any way?'

'That's the trouble, Marie. Did I? Maybe he just saw me and was tempted.'

'Does that make it your fault?'

'No. I suppose not. You're right. I'll try thinking like that and see how I get on, but I'm still frightened of seeing him again, of his anger. I could be lucky I suppose, maybe he will have left the village.'

'Maybe? Come on. Let's walk down to the harbour. By the time we get there it will be time to have one of those delicious pizzas for lunch.'

*

A few days later Marie and Pierre said goodbye to Jamila as she boarded the ferry to cross to Algiers. Marie asked Jamila to come and see her once her baby was born. 'You have never told me the name of your village, Jamila.'

'Sidi Sayfa. How can I never have told you before? I haven't said it for a long time. The name feels warm inside. I'm pleased I'm going back, Marie.'

So now Marie had a name to add to her picture of Jamila's home as she and Pierre waved from the noisy quayside and Jamila walked up the gangplank, wearing her old scarf and carrying the same bag as her last visit to Marseille. Halfway she turned, put her bag down and raised her arms to wave. From the quay Marie waved back. Even at that distance the quizzical expression on Jamila's face was obvious, feeding Marie's recurrent concern for her. She seems wise, thought Marie but is she as strong as she seems? 'I wonder what she will face when she gets back to her village. It sounds beautiful but they may not be pleased to see her. Do you know, Pierre, I still worry about her?'

Pierre nodded. 'I know, but I suspect she'll be fine. She's a way to go yet but she'll get there.'

*

Jamila watched the coast of France recede from the stern of the ferry, confronted by the reality of her return, not so many months since her departure. She stretched out on the deck to rest with her head on her bag. After a breezy, cold journey, alone with her thoughts she gazed at the emerging coast of North Africa exploring and re-exploring the events of the last few months, searching for an understanding of herself and the consequences of her travels. It was a rough journey, so she was more than relieved as the boat approached Algiers and warm air returned. From Algiers she took several changes of train and nearly three days to reach Oujan, on the Moroccan border. It was heavy travelling. She climbed onto a bus at the border, tired and dusty, but curiously elated, fearful as to what awaited her and yet excited, but even so as she rested her head on her dirty scarf against the half-open window, she was able to sleep, waking with a start when they reached Marrakech. With the help of a hawker, she found a truck to Sidi Sayfa and climbed on board to await its departure.

*

A couple of hours later, rattling along the rutted tracks Jamila saw her village on the other side of the valley, her place, her home, hewn out of the stone and built onto the rocks, strewn with the evening sun, a proud and ancient settlement stretched out above the terraces of green leading up the sharp mountainside, staring strong and confident across the harsh and relentless landscape. She thought of the paintings she so much loved in Edinburgh and how they had shown her what it was she missed about home and here were her own mountains stretched out before her again, welcoming her, despite Nadeem. She recalled how she and Zohra used to smile to themselves at the travellers looking for 'peace' and couldn't help but wonder at the irony as she was now returning, searching for her own peace.

Jamila wrapped her scarf around her as she climbed down from the bus on the edge of the village. She drank in the familiar chill of the evening mountain air. Nothing had changed that she could see. As she reconnected with the red dust of the landscape, she felt an intense introspection; the truck rumbled away and she put down her bag and gazed around her, bemused and close to tears. Her thoughts surprised her as she reflected on the paradox that she had gone because she felt defenceless, yet in returning, she felt safe. Painfully she relived how she'd left on foot, in the dark, with no firm idea of where she would go, her sole purpose to escape. Today, she'd returned by choice, returned to try to find some harmony within herself and discover and devise ways of untangling the knots that defined her origin. Only as she stood in the dust where the driver had deposited her did she begin to understand the demands she would be making on her family, the shock they would feel and the chance she was taking. She had never considered that they might reject her. She closed her eyes tight and wished it not to be so.

Despite this apprehension, familiarity assaulted her; as she walked up the slope towards the centre of the village squealing children chased and skittered, chickens foraged, women worked at grinding grain, chattering, kneading dough, and everywhere the warm air was steeped in the familiar sweet scent of flatbreads baking in smoking charcoal ovens. Squatting in the village square, next to the tiled Mosque, a cluster of men were talking, where others sat, cross-legged on the red stones, hands resting on their laps. Several looked up inquisitive, regarding Jamila with care, a woman alone, strange and yet familiar. Then, as she turned the corner into the accustomed street of her childhood, she saw the family leather stall displaying its wares and next to it a small café, tagines steaming, with fruits and flatbreads served to a few benches where several travellers sat eating whilst a couple of hikers picked over the leather goods on the stall where she had tripped over with 'Hammed in pursuit on the fateful day that preceded her travels not so many months ago.

Jamila saw Hammed behind the stall and in the sunlight that glowed through the tagines steaming on the charcoal fire, standing beside the tables of the café, a so recognisable figure shielding her eyes against the glowing light, who studied Jamila as she approached. Jamila saw her put down her ladle and start to walk and then to run towards her calling, 'Can it be you? Jamila? Is it you?' The customers in the café turned to watch as this event unfolded, along with several villagers who until that moment had been going about their business. 'Jamila,' called Zohra again. 'Jamila.'

As they met, the two women stood for a moment to regard each other and then they moved together scarcely believing this new possibility. Closer together they studied each other and as if for the first time, fell silent as they embraced and Jamila felt herself flow across the miracle of love and friendship where this moment felt for her, as if her soul smiled and lingered between them, enriched, renewed, held tight again. Neither of them noticed that as they remained in their rekindling, those around them resumed their day, settled back into their tasks and thoughts and the commerce of the time continued almost uninterrupted. Arm-in-arm, filling with happiness, Jamila and Zohra walked silent towards Habiba's home by the road, each in unequal measures burdened with history and alteration.

*

'Why did you want Donald so much, Jamila? Why did you need him in your life?'

'That's a question I keep asking myself. That's what Marie always asks me. "Why?" she says. It's always "Why?"' Jamila and Zohra were sitting in the morning sun, continuing from where they had stopped the night before. They had talked into the night and after a few hours' sleep they were together again to talk some more. Zohra already knew about Moira and David and just a little about Donald. Nearby at the stall 'Hammed sat working the leather, listening where he could to their conversation and occasionally advising another villager, new to the job but now looking after the café. This was where Jamila had been expected to fit in, her place in the order of things, a place she had abandoned. 'It's a *why* I am beginning to understand, that I'm beginning to unpick,' said Jamila. 'Donald was just a means of sealing my escape. I guess I saw him leading me to another life in another place and I now see that I hadn't resolved the old life and to try to escape without resolution was a mistake. But, Zohra. Let's stop talking about me for a while. Tell me about papa. How is he really?'

'You have seen this morning, Jamila. He is sick. Worn out, I think. Worn old. I look after him, but even so I don't think he will last long. The doctor is no use. He comes twice a week, scratches his beard, tells papa to rest, gives him some useless medicine. Rest is all papa does except that he grieves for Nadeem, always Nadeem. It is this grief that is killing him, the loss of his precious first son.'

'Ah! Nadeem. I feared Nadeem and now I find he has gone but Zohra, I cannot grieve his departure. It was him more than anything that forced me to go and stopped me coming back. I feared him, dreaded facing him again, allowed him to decide my actions.'

'I know. But, Jamila, after you left, Nadeem never seemed the same. It was as if he carried a burden when we all thought he would be pleased you'd gone. After all it was no secret that he never liked you.'

'You're right, Zohra. He never liked me, but with me gone, why did he go? Please tell me now.'

'I think I can tell you, although it might upset me. You don't know, Jamila, but we all missed you so much and

Ismail missed you also. He fretted and Nadeem was angry, complaining that even though you'd gone his father still seemed not to be pleased. Nadeem told everyone that he was glad you had gone because you were a burden to us all and he demanded to know why Ismail was angry with him when he should be pleased. Ismail simply accused Nadeem of driving you away and Nadeem hated that. But there was also a mystery because at the same time as you went Nadeem injured his head and he could never explain how it happened. He told a story about falling on some steps by the Mosque, but it never seemed quite right. No one believed him and because he was always unkind about you, he gradually became disliked for his callousness. It was as if his dislike of you became a reason to criticise him when he expected us all to like him more.'

'Are you saying Ismail was sad I had gone? I have felt so guilty that I took some money from his purse the night I left the village.'

'Ismail was sad that you had gone although he never mentioned any money. It all came to a head when Nadeem lost his temper with Ismail over something to do with the leather stall. It was a petty matter that Ismail had complained about. He had said something like, "Jamila would never have done that, would she?" to Nadeem, when something had been damaged, I think. It was the straw that broke the camel's back.'

'What do you mean?' asked Jamila.

'I'll tell you. It was then that Nadeem started to claim that he was the reason you'd gone. He said he knew that day was your birthday and that you would go down to the river. "She always went on her own with Habiba on her birthday," he told us all. We never knew that but then realised that Nadeem had been spying on you.' Zohra was upset and Jamila took hold of her hand. 'He said that Ismail was planning the café and it was wrong that you were going to be in charge of it and he wanted to pay you back so he said that he watched you walk alone to the river with your book, that he followed you and waited and that all he wanted was to frighten you but that you'd hit him with a rock and you'd run away because you were frightened of getting into trouble.' Zohra paused, tears in her eyes.

'That was part of the truth, yes, but not all the truth. He did attack me, Zohra. He hurt me terribly. He tried to rape me, ripped my clothes, forced himself on top of me but I got the better of him by hitting him with a stone from the riverbed. I somehow knew he'd planned to corner me. I don't think I'd realised how much he hated me, and I never imagined he would attack me somewhere isolated like that. That night all I could think to do was to leave you all. What else was I to do? I would not have been believed so what he told you in the end was almost true.'

'That's so terrible for you, Jamila, that my own brother would do such a thing. I worked it out for myself really, but he didn't help himself and, in the end, the whole village turned against him and said it was terrible, that he was an evil man, so much so that even Ismail was angry.'

'What happened to Nadeem then?'

'Soon after you left, he started going to Friday prayers.'

'No. Surely not? He'd never done that. He had always ignored the Mosque unless he had no choice,' said Jamila.

'Exactly. We asked ourselves why this happened and could find no answers because he always seemed to have so little faith but that changed after you left us. He started to go to prayers and became very committed; he joined the discussion groups about politics and faith, and he often came away from Friday Prayers distracted and deep in thought. I could tell he was troubled. Then he volunteered to join the rebel forces fighting against the government in Chad and like I said, he has never come back. The last we heard was that he was in the Tibetsi mountains. The French were fighting there as well on behalf of the government. It must have been very dangerous.'

'Do you know what happened to him?'

'No. We have never found out. We were not surprised he didn't return because hardly any of the rebels ever did but we don't think he was killed because there were lists of casualties and he was never on it. They were only boys really. Ismail was devasted and he has never recovered; for him it was as if he'd lost you both.'

'So, you don't know if Nadeem died.'

'No. We don't know for certain, and we all struggled to understand why he went to fight but now you have told me all this I understand. What he said he'd done was almost true, but it was even worse than he said, and he knew, and he was seeking forgiveness for his terrible treatment of you, Jamila. I can see now that is why he started to go to Friday Prayers after you left and why he joined the rebels. He left it in the hands of Allah to decide his fate.'

'And now I have come back, and Nadeem has been punished. I almost feel cheated, deprived of the chance to face him with his evil actions.'

'I can see why you'd think that. But that's all the story that I know. I have missed my brother but now I have been blessed that you've returned, Jamila. What will you do now?'

'May I stay with you for a while?'

'Of course, Jamila. This is your home.'

'Will Ismail mind me being back?'

'No. I think he will be pleased. I will ask him but do you want to tell him about Nadeem?'

'No. It would do no good. Let it be something that only you and I know.'

*

Just as Zohra had predicted 'Hammed was pleased that Jamila had come to stay. He had missed her when she disappeared, and he felt more complete again. Hammed always enjoyed Jamila's laughter and spirit. It wasn't very long before everybody knew that Jamila was back and, in a few days, Zohra and Jamila had become inseparable and both were now helping to care for Ismail, who could only be pleased. When they had time together, they had taken to walking down to the river, picking their way carefully down the track, caught up in animated conversation.

'I feel as if I have never been away,' said Jamila as they trekked by the river one day. 'And yet I have been here only a couple of weeks. I love this walk.'

'Mama loved this walk as well,' said Zohra. 'If she disappeared, we always knew where to find her.'

As they walked and chattered Jamila had started to find out what she could from Zohra about her real mother. She had decided that Marie had been right to encourage her, and this question was always at the back her mind as she talked with Zohra. She had decided that today she would ask. 'Do you know who my mother was? My real mother? I wish I knew. I would like to know her story and my story.'

Zohra took Jamila's hand, wrapping an arm around her as she did. 'I wondered when you would ask. Habiba wanted me to promise never to tell you. We sometimes wondered if you would return one day, and I knew you might start to be unhappy if you did not know the truth.'

'Did you promise Habiba?' asked Jamila. 'I so hope you didn't.'

'No. I didn't. I was never sure that it would be right to keep such a promise.'

'So, you do know, Zohra? Please, will you tell me?'

Zohra was quiet for a few minutes, deep in thought, looking across the valley to the hills beyond. Since Jamila had returned, she had been thinking about this moment, knowing that Jamila would ask. Not long before she died Habiba had told Zohra that her cousin, Nada had been there when Jamila was born. The cousins had been good friends and Nada had always lived nearby and had helped lay out Habiba before her burial. Zohra had grown to love Nada even more since her own mother died and they talked a great deal so she wanted Nada to tell Jamila the story of her birth. After all, she had been there.

'Your real mother came from this village. Her name was Latifa,' said Zohra.

Jamila smiled. 'That is a beautiful name. Latifa. Why didn't I stay with her, what happened to her? Did she die when I was born?'

'Habiba told me some of the story and because Nada was there, she knew it all as well,' said Zohra. 'Please can we ask her to tell you?'

Jamila smiled. 'Of course, Zohra. I'd like that very much.'

19

From time-to-time, when Jamila was a child, especially in the winter when it was harder to find fuel, she would take Nada some warm food, prepared by Habiba. Nada lived with her own mother, the two of them in a couple of rooms, away from the main street down a steep slope in a tight alley and whenever Jamila came calling Nada always asked a few questions, about school or Ismail or politics and Jamila would stay a while chatting and sipping sweet, mint tea. After Habiba died, Jamila often spent time with Nada. When Jamila disappeared, Nada had missed her company and was delighted that she had returned to the village.

Many years before when Nada's own mother died and after the prayers, Jamila followed the procession and watched as the body was lowered and Nada dropped a little dry soil into the burial place. Habiba cried that day and held tight to Jamila's hand whilst Zohra helped Nada. 'You have been a good daughter to me, Jamila,' said Habiba as they both walked back up the hill towards the village, 'and Nada a good friend.' Jamila remembered Habiba's tears that day. She had never seen Habiba cry with such intensity and was surprised to discover the closeness of the relationship.

'Your mother was always kind to me,' Nada explained to Jamila. They were sitting together beneath a scented rose that grew around the window of Nada's room. 'I promised her I would say nothing to you of your birth. There were four of us there that day and we all respected Habiba for her generosity and goodness. But now she is gone I think she would want you to know the truth, how it all happened, why she became your mother.'

Nada leant towards Jamila and took her by the hand. 'As Zohra has told you, your real mother's name was Latifa. Her family lived in the village for generations, and everybody respected them. They were good Muslims and never missed prayers and their children were obedient and hard working. Latifa was their first daughter and like all that generation the children grew up during the war with Germany. That was a terrible time.'

Nada paused, her voice cracking slightly and Jamila sensed that this story was seldom told. 'When the Germans invaded and Morocco became involved in the Second World War, there was fighting all the way down the western side of the country and into the mountains. The English were here, the British helped us, but the French were with Germany. When the war ended the soldiers left. But not quite all of them. A few stayed, many wandering around the country, not knowing where to go or what to do. Some of the village men, Ismail was always one, would argue that we could have done it without the Allies and they should never have come, but there were few who agreed. Even so the troops were often unpopular. They seemed unfriendly and we felt they thought they were smart and we were stupid. No one noticed at the time, but a stray soldier wandered into the area and somehow Latifa met up with him and they started to see each other secretly. It must have been going for several weeks but then of course Latifa's father found out. He was furious and the men tracked down the soldier and threw him out of the village, even though he fought for us in the war. He was from England. But that wasn't the end.

'Not long afterwards the family discovered that Latifa was pregnant. I guess the soldier never knew. There was a great deal of fuss, her family being so proud, and the Imam decided she had to be punished so Latifa was banned from the village and made to live in the hills, depending on charity for food and shelter. If the baby survived it was to be allowed to stay in the village, but Latifa would be banished. She had let us all down, brought her family into disrepute and had to be punished. When the time came for the baby to be born a few of us women were expected to find her and take the child. I was one and Habiba another. By then the disgrace of their daughter's actions proved too much for her family and they had moved elsewhere to escape the shame. We now know that they went to Marrakech. I think her brother was a clothier. At the time Habiba was still nursing baby Mohammed and so Habiba felt it her duty to nurse Latifa's child. We climbed above the river and left food in a cave in the hillside for Latifa and that was how we knew when the baby was due to be born. It was hard, though, because it was a long climb, and we couldn't go every day.'

Nada paused again, leaning towards Jamila. 'I've never told this whole story before,' she said. 'It must be hard for you to hear it.'

'Yes, Nada. It is. But I want to hear it because knowing will help me to understand so much. Did you talk to Latifa?'

'We weren't supposed to, but we did. We weren't allowed to stay when she collected the food but we knew when the baby was coming because Latifa didn't collect the food so we set out to the cave where we knew she was living.'

'You're saying my mother was alone when I was born,' said Jamila.

'Yes. She was. We found the cave,' continued Nada. 'When you are down by the river you can see it. It's the cave above the Yellow Rock, once the home of a Berber family, now living in the village up the valley, a family Latifa knew well and loved well. The sun shines on that mountainside almost all day.' Jamila was shocked. She already knew and loved that place with no sense of its significance to her. *It is the mountains have made me*, she thought. *This is why I came back home.*

'On the day you were born Habiba and I climbed to the cave with two other women from the village. Habiba called into the cave to attract Latifa's attention and we could hear movement and feel the cool of the air in the cave. We could just see into the grey darkness. Latifa made her way towards us, picked her steps across the rubble, shrouded her child and endured her pain. We heard her rod tapping against the cave wall, then she emerged, unbent herself, and the dusty sunlight flashed on her blood smudged cheeks. I can remember so well the fear in her eyes. "We don't want to hurt the child," Habiba said and the four of us stood silent, frightened, in awe of your mother. At that moment there seemed no sign of the child, but we soon noticed the unfamiliar mound across Latifa's chest, her hand hidden, the child so still, so quiet. It was a terrible thing, Jamila, and yet it seemed like a miracle that you could be there and Latifa seeming so calm.'

Jamila was subdued by what she was hearing from Nada. This child was her, new-born. This woman to whom Nada reached out her hand was her real mother whom she had never known. What it had been like for her within that cave she found painful to imagine. The courage she required beyond measure.

'I remember I reached out, took Latifa by the hand and guided her across the threshold of the cave into the fullness of the morning. The sun illuminated her bloody shawl and tear-stained face.' Nada slowed and her eyes watered as she was speaking. 'We were humbled in that moment faced with the burden of our duty and the sadness of our hearts as we began the descent. Latifa repeatedly stumbled and Habiba helped her to right herself as she struggled on the steep slopes. Ismail told us that evening that he had watched from the village as we twisted slowly downward towards the river, and he also told us that he had cried. He was to become the father, your father, Jamila, and the duty lay heavily upon him.'

*

'As we stumbled down the hill, we could see a small party of men walking down from the village towards the river. We were to meet them. Latifa struggled as she clung to her baby, and we steadied her when we could. I remember well that she never fell, she was far too proud.' Nada took Jamila's hand. 'Your mother was courageous, Jamila. Before we reached the river we slowed and gathered around Latifa. I watched her with a heavy heart knowing the price she was about to pay for her soldier, your father. All of us were crying as Habiba stretched out her arms to Latifa.

'"You must give me the child now, Latifa," she said. "I will protect her, love her and keep her safe. What is to be her name?" Jamila was transfixed as Nada spoke, holding her breath for fear of interruption. "Jamila." Latifa's reply was almost inaudible. Her voice was broken, and surely her heart in torment. "Jamila," she repeated. "The beautiful one."

'She drew the child, you, Jamila, out from the warmth of her breast, turned back the shawl that wrapped her and softly kissed your forehead. Latifa's tears fell as she repeated your name, several times. Afterwards, when we were talking, we all said we thought that moment was like a prayer, a blessing. Habiba stretched out her hands, caressed your tiny head as Latifa pushed you towards her and then she took you in her arms, lifted you towards her own face and kissed you, wiping a little mucus from your forehead and whispering "Jamila, Jamila," as she slipped open her own cloak and took you down to her own warmth, her own safety. For you there could have been no notion of change, no sense of difference; warmth to warmth, love to love.'

Jamila attended to every breath from Nada, stretched out her arms and embraced her as tears gathered and rolled down her face. She had never fixed a view as to who her real mother had been and why her past was shrouded in mystery; but what she was hearing now established beyond doubt the virtue of her mother and transformed her view of herself and Habiba. She felt she was deep in a well swollen with the love of both her mothers, sustained by the gentleness of their hearts despite having been created by a mother who until this moment had not existed for her.

'As Habiba held you, Latifa cried out and wrapped her arms around you both and sobbed. Habiba held you close, cradling you with one arm and comforting your mother with the other. "We must go now," Habiba spoke to Latifa. "We must go, and I will leave you with the women of the village." Habiba walked quietly away and as she went Latifa stretched out and we clasped her arms, held her, restrained her convulsed as she was in sorrow. When Habiba had passed by us we each hugged her and sat with her, crumpled against a rock as we watched Habiba walk away. When Habiba had crossed the river and disappeared into the side streets of the village, one by one we crossed the water, a wretched procession. Latifa remained, motionless, sobbing.

'As we struggled up the slopes towards the village, I turned and saw Latifa stretched on the sand, looking towards the sky. A small group of men approached the river. Ismail was one of them and still on the river's edge he shouted, "No. No more. She has been punished enough. Go, Latifa. Go and never return. Do you understand, Latifa? Never." We had stopped as Ismail's words echoed around the valley. "Go, Latifa. Never return."

'Latifa stumbled to her feet took a few steps, fell, stumbled again, and fell again. I saw Ismail, tears spilling down his cheeks, turn back towards the village and so one-by-one did the other men. As the men went past me, I could see Latifa as she lay there, still and silent, stretched on the stones. Later on I returned with Ismail, searched the shores of the river, behind rocks and trees but there was no trace of Latifa except for a shawl, which I washed out in the river and carried back to the village. We would never see her again.'

Jamila felt the burden of her own ignorance lifting but the weight of the truth starting to accumulate. Nadeem, whom she had cursed since childhood, she now knew was cruelly right when he called her a 'bastard child' and the only person who had spoken the truth. It was he who had ridiculed her lighter than brown skin and he was right again. She was the child of a stray English soldier who had taken advantage of her mother.

Since she left Scotland Jamila had not reflected long on her relationship with Donald, scalded as she had been by his temerity but now his behaviour was brought into a new perspective for her as she sat with Nada in the afternoon sun streaming into her room.

*

Nada took a faded piece of cloth from a box under her window. 'Here. Take this please, Jamila. It is the shawl we found by the river, your real mother's shawl.'

'That is a beautiful gift,' said Jamila. She held the scarf to her cheeks and brushed it against her skin, shuddering with a new closeness to her real mother. There was more that Jamila wanted to understand. 'Why was Habiba asked to be my mother, to care for me? Why was she my mother?'

'Mohammed,' Nada said immediately. 'Your mother was nearly finished with nursing Mohammed and so if she took you to her breast, she could feed you also. She was your wet nurse. It was 'Hammed who had a cause to be jealous but it turned out to be Nadeem, who had less reason.'

'Can you tell me more, Nada? What did everyone think about me do you suppose?'

'You were the centre of attention in those early days. The fate of Latifa had saddened many of us so you seemed like a blessing, a way for us to channel our sense of guilt that Latifa had been able to let us all down so badly. I remember hearing the Muezzin call for Friday Prayers as Habiba walked back into the village that afternoon, carrying you in her arms and I watched as she walked on to her own home passing the men gathering outside the Mosque. Many had their eyes downcast, sad at how events had turned out. Everyone in the village knew of Latifa's fate but none talked of it. Habiba's own children knew. Seeing Habiba carrying you the boys abandoned their football, the girls left their chores, and they ran to her, chattering, excited, curious. The women knew that now Habiba would take you as her own, nurture and sustain you. We hoped she would love you but who could tell. We knew the burden Habiba was carrying, recognising the sacrifice that she would be making to fulfil the decision of the Imam.

'I remember so well the other children running round Habiba that afternoon. "Can we see the baby? Please, mama." Several children were jumping up-and-down, excited. Zohra, your lovely sister, was calmer. "Please show us, mama. We would like to see the new baby." Nada smiled as she played with these words. She loved all of Habiba's children, even Nadeem.

'Habiba was always worried about Nadeem. She told me he was jealous of his younger brother Mohammed even before you joined the family. I can recall Nadeem stood facing away, kicking his ball against a wall, backwards and forwards, wanting to be noticed. He was so often like this. Even Ismail struggled to keep the boy contented. Habiba always knew Nadeem would not like you because he didn't seem to like anybody. That day in the village square, when Nadeem came over, he stood close to you and poked you. I remember it all so well. "It's still dirty," I heard him say to Habiba. "Why don't you clean it properly. Why is it so bloody? What is its name?"

'He fired questions at your mother, calling you "it" with a mean rasp in his voice. The other children were wide mouthed, peering at you, gentle and kind. Your mother was a good woman, Jamila. "The baby is called Jamila," she said to them all. "Zohra, Nadeem, say *hello* to your new sister."

'"Jamila," the children chorused as she held you to them. Other village children had come over to Habiba. They all wanted to talk to you. "Hello, little sister, hello, Jamila. Can she talk, mama? Where has she come from? Can I hold her? Please." But not Nadeem. "I don't want a new sister, mama," he said. I remember Ismail as well. "That's the bastard child, is it?" Ismail said. "The child we must rear just because 'Hammed is weened."'

'Was it Ismail who called me "the bastard child"?' Jamila almost whispered.

'That was tradition speaking,' said Nada. 'Ismail grunted like he always did when he saw you were sleeping but despite his fierce manner he reached out and softly touched you. I can see him now; he tenderly removed an obstinate clot of blood from your chin. At the same time, he stroked your forehead and sung in his husky way a few lines of his favourite lullaby and as he sang the children joined in.'

As Nada began to sing Jamila joined in:
    'Sleep my baby, sleep.

Until the meal is ready
And if it isn't made just yet
The neighbour's meal will be.
Sleep my baby sleep
Until your mommy's home
The bread is on the table
The sweets are on the tray.'

'We were sitting in the square and as the men heard the call to prayer, they walked across to the Mosque watching Ismail cradle you, now his new child to care for, he went back to the bloody marks on your face, licked his fingers to dislodge them, wiped them away and tidied your shawl. To have lost Latifa was a burden to him, where his heart and his faith had collided, and his grief had to become his comfort. He looked down at you and I knew he would love you for Habiba and for Latifa. I recall Habiba held her 'Hammed close and I guessed she was thinking he would have to make do without her milk now. Then Ismail took Mohammed back in his arms, kissed him, laid him on his mat and strode across to the Mosque. That was 'Hammed weaned I guess.'

'Ismail tried hard to be a good father to me, didn't he, but he faced a great deal of conflict,' said Jamila. 'Of course, I never knew.'

'He did,' said Nada. 'And he was always good to me and to my mother. He is a good man.'

'Do you know what happened to Latifa?' asked Jamila.

'Not really. We think she made it to another village where they took her in and she lived, isolated, on the edge. But we don't know. Some say she joined her family in Marrakech.'

Jamila was silent. 'Your questions are answered then Jamila,' said Zohra.

'They are. Yes. Nada, you are a miracle to have been so kind and so sure.' Jamila held Nada close for many minutes, drawing on her strength, soaking up her wisdom and as she did so she felt suddenly tired, enriched by a better understanding of herself, anxious to find a way to restart her life. 'One day soon I would like to walk to the Yellow Rock and find for myself where I was born. When I am there, I will say, "thank you" to Latifa, my mother and "thank you" to you Nada. Then I will search for my mother so that if she is still alive, I can forgive her. But first I shall have to work to better understand myself. Now I know where I have come from I must decide where I want to be going.'

20

After a few weeks Jamila had settled back into the rhythm of her home and ran Nada's story many times in her heart, gradually reshaping herself to a new understanding. Within a few days she was working the stall and the café with Zohra. Jamila felt that to be paying her way made her less guilty for stealing from Ismail's purse, although he had still said nothing to her. Mohammed was delighted Jamila had returned, especially as it gave him some relief from manning the leather stall. All this helped to settle Ismail. He liked to rest outside and frail though he was he enjoyed watching the passing trade of the leather stall and café – although he often slept, especially in the afternoon. In his heart he was glad that Jamila had returned, even though he was gruff to her. He needed time as well; time to re-find the place in his heart that Jamila had always occupied.

When they weren't working the stall, Jamila helped Zohra look after Ismail and within a couple of weeks he began to show signs of rallying. Jamila liked to sit with him. Thanks to Nada she better knew she owed him her love and was pleased to share it with him. Ismail, eyes often closed, still spent a long time every morning in bed but his breathing was improving, and he seemed to have a little strength in his legs. Next to his chair stood a small table with leather goods from their stall and next to the bed on another table rested an enamel mug of water and a screw top bottle of cloudy medicine. It was Zohra who told Jamila that the pieces of leather, chosen by Ismail, had been fashioned by Nadeem. This is the best of Nadeem, Jamila thought when she was sitting there admiring the leather, crafted by the closeness of the same hands that had so much damaged her.

Jamila enjoyed a black-and-white photo of Habiba pinned to the wall above Ismail's bed. Other than the picture on her travel pass it was the only image she knew of her mother. Next to the picture of Habiba a likeness of Nadeem looked down at her, a constant reminder of his place in Ismail's heart. At the same time the truth of her own birth did much to ease her mind about Nadeem. She understood his behaviour towards her better now she knew more about herself, although forgiveness remained hard to find.

*

Jamila had been feeling tired for a few days and mentioned to Zohra that she felt a little unwell. Zohra laughed. 'You look the picture of good health. I'd assumed it was the fresh mountain air after your foggy city adventures in Marseille and Edinburgh.' Jamila's smile was tempered by a growing realisation of her problem. She suspected she might be pregnant, a complication halfway between the unexpected and the expected and complicated by regulation as she knew if she was right, that her illegitimate child would be denied any official papers. Jamila decided to mention this to no one and hope she was mistaken.

However, Jamila's growing sense that she was carrying a child reignited her self-doubt. Despite the shock of Donald's revelations, she had left Edinburgh glowing with the warmth of David and Moira and since she arrived back in her village, she often thought she would write to them but lost courage when she judged the moment had come to do the writing. She craved the chance to let David know she was back in her village and that she was okay and that she missed him, missed Moira and her cooking. She wanted to tell him that her family were well, that her brother Nadeem had disappeared, and that Zohra and she were still good friends and spending time together, working together and making sure Ismail was fine as well. She knew she would never write it in a letter, but she would have liked to tell David that she now knew about her own mother. Jamila knew David would be pleased she was well, and she would like to tell him again that he was welcome to come to Morocco to visit her and they could walk in the hills and along by the river and it would be like the beautiful paintings of the Scottish Landscape in the National Gallery on Princes Street. She knew David would enjoy watching the birds spiralling above the valleys and the smoke drifting across the villages in the distance and that he would appreciate the scent of the wild roses and acacia scattered in the sheltered nooks and crannies of the rocks. There was so much that she wanted to tell David but the one thing she was frightened to tell him was that she might be pregnant. She thought he might disapprove, that Moira might be unhappy and maybe not want to see her anymore. Worse still she worried that David might tell Donald if they saw each other and she did not know how to ask David to keep it a secret.

Jamila had told no one that she might be with child and yet she knew. In this regard she was alone. Eventually, certain she was pregnant and despite her misgivings she wrote to David but did not tell him about her baby and then, if she was right, when he visited, he would find out as a surprise. She still worried he would be cross or offended although her brighter side thought he would not, and she knew she was silly to be concerned but that didn't stop her worrying. Jamila did wonder what Moira would think if she knew about the baby but as she reflected, she decided Moira would find a way to reconcile her surprise with a pragmatic view of the nature of men and their regard for women. As for David, Jamila concluded he was a practical man and this would see him through. She told herself she needed to stop worrying but then there was Zohra and the rest of her family to be considered.

*

Jamila's journey to Edinburgh had taught her the extent of her love for Zohra and her return had reignited her respect for Nada and more than anything, she wished to share with them both her possible pregnancy and her child. Her instinct told her that both would be sympathetic, and both would be forgiving so whilst she began by considering the importance of speaking with Zohra, she gradually came to realise that she also wanted Nada to know. It was thinking through this intention that led Jamila to understand that she would need to leave her village quite soon. *Perhaps*, she thought, *I could have my baby in Marseille*. Marie would help me and that would give my child the possibility of French papers. There were many Moroccans with French papers, why should her child not be one of them? Jamila also realised that it would be wise for her to leave the village before her pregnancy became obvious. In that way she could reduce the possibility of the community resenting her profligacy and rightfully judging her morality. What use the explanation that she hadn't realised Donald was a father of two children; that if she had understood this she would never have gone to his bed. That would do nothing to improve the morality of her situation.

These thoughts were still spinning around in Jamila's mind the following day when she joined Zohra walking by the river. They'd been walking a while talking of this and that when Jamila found herself saying, 'I need to tell you something. It's quite difficult.' She paused, choosing her words with care. 'I'm going to have a baby, I think. I'm not sure but I'd be surprised if I am wrong.'

Zohra regarded Jamila almost with a smile. 'I think I knew,' she said. 'I don't know why.'

Jamila was reassured by Zohra's calm response. 'How do you feel about that possibility?' she asked. 'My wonder is, do you know the father?'

'I do, yes. It is Donald. The man I told you about.'

'Does he know?'

'No. I don't want him ever to know.'

To Zohra this was unexpected. She didn't understand and wanted to. 'Why not?'

'I've thought about that a great deal. I've started to understand that he used me. It was Marie who first told me to be careful, but I did not take her seriously enough. Now I am sure that Donald pretended to like me to get from me what he wanted. He gave me somewhere to live and I stupidly thought it would be a job as well so I felt obliged to him.'

'I don't understand that, Jamila.' Zohra was struggling, quite expecting Jamila to say she would want to marry him; instead, the child would be fatherless, like Jamila.

'He was good to me. He seemed kind to me. I thought he was charming, decent. He had a senior place at Edinburgh University and I thought that made him important and if he was important, I could trust him. Other people trusted him. People I liked. I thought I liked him. When we were still in France he explained archaeology to me and encouraged me to be interested, but now I see it was him he wanted me to be interested in. I'd left home when I met him and I felt he was rescuing me but what was really happening was that he took advantage of me and once we arrived in Edinburgh he gave me a room in his flat and just waited. Once he was ready, he kind of seduced me, although I was willing and I went along with it even though I knew I wasn't the first but that didn't seem to matter to me. In fact, I thought it was a good thing. Even his ghastly mother more-or-less told me he was dishonest. How wrong I was not to take her seriously?' Jamila stopped walking, rested against a boulder and looked straight at Zohra. 'Please will you help me, Zohra. I've been naïve.'

'Yes, Jamila. I will help you. Will you tell Nada? She will know what to do.'

'Yes, Zohra. I will. But I only want the two of you to know. I will have to leave the village again to have this baby. My child will not be entitled to papers.'

'I understand that, Jamila. Where will you go. If you don't want the man to know you can't go back to Edinburgh?'

Jamila told Zohra that she might ask Marie to let her travel to Marseille and have the baby there. Zohra listened carefully and agreed that France would be a good idea, but she was thinking that it would be wonderful if Jamila could return to her family once the birth was registered and settle down in the village with her child. She felt sure the whole family would be pleased. 'Maybe I could come and find you in Marseille, Jamila. What do you think?'

'I think I would like that very much,' said Jamila. 'That would be wonderful. I'll ask Marie. But what about Ismail? Will he be okay if you leave for a while?'

'Maybe Nada might help there?' Zohra hadn't been away from the village for several years and the chance of a break was attractive to her, even though there would be work to do. She'd square it with Ismail. 'There's something else as well I think Jamila. You have no papers of your own, do you? You told me you had managed with Habiba's. Perhaps you could apply for French papers as well.'

'Of course. That's such a good idea Zohra. I will apply and Marie would be pleased if I had French papers.'

During the coming few days Jamila spoke with Nada and wrote to Marie. Like Zohra, Nada was not surprised. Marie on the other hand read Jamila's letter with alarm unsure how much time she would be able to give to Jamila as well as hang onto her own job at Pierre's restaurant and help her have her baby. However, her alarm subsided when she read that Zohra could also come if Marie thought there was room. Marie was even less surprised than Zohra that Jamila was pregnant but even so was set to wondering if this might not be the best thing to have happened. She guessed that Jamila's inclination might well be to return to her own village, rebuild her life there with her family and find that suited her very well. So, in the end Marie was pleased Jamila wanted to come to her and relieved that she might have some company as she travelled. She was also delighted to know that through her close involvement in this unexpected event she could become a part of the family about which Jamila had told her so much.

Armed with Marie's enthusiasm, Zohra's support and reassured by Nada, Jamila began to see the last few months in a new perspective and to feel her burden was manageable. She wrote to David, a letter he was to keep for the rest of his life. It was the pencilled kiss that drew him in. Since they had first met when he was on his hands and knees in the middle of a field with a dustpan and brush, Jamila had respected David. These days, when she thought of Donald, she understood that she had found a man probably ruined by his doting mother. She was right to think he had felt entitled to seduce her on a slow burn, storing her for his spare bedroom in Edinburgh. Donald had seen her vulnerability to his philosophical ramblings as he dangled archaeology before her like a sticky flypaper and rolled her in. She only understood that now she was pregnant, but at least she did understand. At the messy end of it was David who had rescued her, a service that Jamila would never forget.

> *Dear David,*
> *I am back in Morocco, in my village, with my family.*
> *Thank you for your kindness and good sense David.*

You more than anyone listened to my story, and I want you to know part of my search is complete; I know about my real mother and how things were when I was born. Please will you come to see me. You will be welcomed by us all.
Jamila. X

David delighted and excited immediately replied.
I'll be there at the end of next month.
David x

21

A few weeks later, from the vantage point of the leather stall, Jamila had been watching the jeeps and trucks arriving in the village square knowing that sooner or later David would appear. The family stall and its little café stood to the edge of the square and usually the first place any travellers stopped was under the shade of their awning, amongst the prayer mats and leather sandals, so it was easy for her to keep her eyes on arrivals as she warmed the tagines and turned the flat breads. David and his backpack arrived in a dilapidated army jeep. Having taken the ferry from Marseille he had found the cheapest transport from Tangier. He was crammed in amongst the half dozen or so others. Since Jamila had last seen him in Edinburgh his beard and his hair had grown, so had his smile breaking out all over as he climbed onto the dusty square. They embraced. Back in Edinburgh they had never touched each other, David careful to respect Donald's ownership and Jamila denying of her own feelings, and so today, after a long trip to find each other, they understood that their relationship had shifted in a direction they both welcomed.

David found himself genially hosted by Jamila's family just as she had been in Edinburgh by his mother, Moira, in the days after her connections with Donald fell apart. With David's cheery face reminding her of a chequered history, Jamila found it hard to connect her baby with that time even though there was no possibility Donald was not the father. It felt like an age ago and yet the seasons had hardly changed, although the location surely had. And now she needed to tell David, whose smiling face was like a tonic to her. That left her feeling disconnected to those moments of her past as she realised how comfortable she was in her village and asked herself, as so often recently, why she had embarked on that expedition in the first place. She had escaped Nadeem in Marseille, so she had hardly needed to attach herself to Donald's team of archaeologists and its journey back to Scotland. She was surprised when David shared with her his own conviction that her decision was unexpected to him as well. He said he put it down to Donald's behaviour, leaving Jamila with little chance but to agree to his opinions: She resented the implication that she had been used, but recognised the accuracy of the assertion. She was starting to see Donald as the serial philanderer she now knew him to be and realised the justification of both Marie's and David's original counsel of caution.

David was hungry when he climbed down from his jeep and was soon enjoying a tagine at the family café table. Jamila was attentive and nervous. David recounted his journey, which had gone well. Jamila recounted parts of her story but she knew she must tell him of her pregnancy before Zohra or Nada had a chance to meet him, so she lost no time. 'Since I wrote to you, David, I have discovered I am pregnant. You need to know. I'm sorry to tell you this way.'

'Is Donald the father?' asked David looking shocked. Jamila was surprised that his question was the same as Zohra had asked. The possibility had passed through David's mind when they were together in Leith because he knew Donald too well to expect anything else but he needed to be sure.

Jamila nodded. 'Yes. Donald is the father. I have only told Zohra and our friend Nada. You will meet them both today.'

'I had imagined that it might be possible,' said David, almost to himself. 'Are you okay?' This kindness brought tears to Jamila's eye. How could this man be so thoughtful and how could she have been so careless of him? He'd travelled across Europe to find her and now could only think of her. If she didn't love him before she loved him at that moment. Her tears surprised her. David reached across and took her hand, smiled and said nothing. His silence comforted Jamila as she could never have imagined and it wasn't long before she had introduced David to Zohra, whose curiosity was finally sated and then to Nada, who promptly found herself loving him.

Nada was torn between wanting to pick him up and cuddle him and admiring him for his common sense and plain talking. Then there was the twinkle in his eyes. It wasn't just that she respected Jamila's view of the world and her own obvious admiration and respect for David; it was also the contrast between the mild disdain and inflated self-belief of the average traveller passing through the villages searching for 'peace', and the gentle warmth and the regard David showed for others in everything he said and did. David was able to acknowledge Nada's commitment to Jamila as a part of the natural course of events where others might find her overbearing. David was a gentleman, schooled in respect by his mother and trained in self-sufficiency by his father. He was pleased to have Nada as a friend, even at three times his age.

'How did you two come to meet?' asked Nada.

They both started to answer at once, but David naturally gave way. 'In a café in Marseille,' replied Jamila. 'I was the waitress and David the customer. He was talking with his friends about buying floor brushes and dust pans as I fussed around them; I couldn't help but overhear and thought that dustpans were strange things for a group of men to be discussing. That's right, isn't it, David?'

Through his smile David chatted. 'I suppose it seemed strange to you but to me it seemed natural. That's what we needed to help us clean up the old bones and pots we found in the ground. You helped us well when you came to join us, Jamila.'

'True. You were a good teacher, though, David. So was Donald at that stage.'

'So,' said Nada, her interest taken. 'You know this Donald do you, David? Is he interested in old bones as well?'

'I do know him, yes, and I am often ashamed of what I know, although his skills as an archaeologist are considerable.'

'What does an archaeologist do?'

'Oh!' said Jamila, 'David, please can I tell Nada.'

'Of course, Jamila. I'd love to hear you explain.'

'It's often about old bones. Archaeologists study what extinct groups of human beings left behind them as they died out. If they're lucky they find the remains of communities, pots, bones, bits of walls and fences, where they lived, usually under the remains of more recent communities, including our own. Layers upon layers of muddled and incomplete stories. Isn't that right, David?'

'It is, yes. Hundreds of thousands of years ago, people probably lived here, Nada, around what's now the village square, and if we dug deep, maybe even under this floor, we might find their bones, bits of buildings or pots or tools. Where archaeologists have the chance, we study those remains and try to understand something of how those ancient humans might have lived.'

'That seems a bit strange, David, to think they might be under this floor. How do you know if you're right?'

'That's a good question, Nada, and we don't know but sometimes we can compare findings from all around the world and patterns emerge.'

And Nada gradually came to know, began to understand and so started to see even more what it was Jamila liked about David and she also enjoyed his reflections and his sensitivity to the sanctity of lives lived, those completed and those in progress. It was curious to her and to Zohra that Donald's skills in archaeology left him disrespectful of people, where David's interest seemed to revolve around respect for everyone. A few days later Nada reminded David that he'd said he was ashamed of Donald. 'Why are you ashamed?' she asked.

'Perhaps Jamila might answer that question, Nada. She knows better than me.'

'David and I are probably ashamed of the same thing, Nada; not seeing what was staring us in the face.' said Jamila. 'How could we have been fooled into thinking well of such a selfish man?'

'You are both so young, though, Jamila. How could you be expected to know?' Nada's love for Jamila and growing respect for David led her to want to avoid them sensing any blame.

'That's true, Nada, but it doesn't make it any easier. You know all about Marie, how we met on the ferry across to Marseille and ended up working with David and Donald and his team digging up old bones. I liked that, Nada, it was amazing to see them at work and Donald seemed such an enthusiast and spoke about it all with such passion, or so I thought. I felt as though it was me that wanted to follow him, but Marie and David think he simply tempted me. Don't you, David?'

David nodded and smiled. 'Yes. You're right, Jamila, but he is good at his job. After all he tempted me as well, so much so that I came to rely on him for work and friendship. It's easy to be wise after the event but I think he needed to control both of us.'

'That's true, David, but my mistake was to think he was going to give me a route to a new life, an escape from my fear of Nadeem when what he had in mind was that I'd need to rely on him. I thought I was special as well and that was a massive mistake.'

'This all sounds very mysterious,' said Nada.

'I wasn't the first Nada, and I was naïve not to understand that. He told me when we were on the dig that I could work at the University in Edinburgh. It was me that imagined he meant in the team, working with the others on the dig. But that's not what he meant. When it was time to leave, Marie had already gone back to Marseille. He bought me a ticket to Edinburgh, and it was one-way, so I imagined that he was going to pay me to work for him, so I'd have the money to get back. But that didn't happen. It was my fault I suppose because he never said that; it was just my assumption. When we were in Edinburgh, he showed me the spare room in his flat, which was fine, but I soon realised there was no job and I had to find my own way around and borrow his books to read. We muddled along, walked out together and he gave me money for clothes and to buy us food, but no job. And I still thought I was special. More fool me. I enjoyed going to the National Gallery, full of pictures of mountains, but I always went alone. He said he didn't like pictures. Donald was always working at the laboratory, except every Tuesday, when he went to Dundee where he said he had another project. The truth turned out to be a very different thing.'

'So, he wasn't a good man?' Nada was struggling to understand why Jamila didn't see what seemed obvious to her.

'You wonder why we felt ashamed, Nada,' said David. 'We sometimes talked about Donald in the team and thought he seemed a bit distant, but he was an expert in his field and that's what mattered to us. We needed that and we needed our jobs. I suppose we wondered why Jamila had joined us and we did try to befriend her, but Donald was possessive, and we were wary of contradicting him, so he had his way. We had no idea what was really happening.'

'What was happening?' asked Nada.

Nada poured more mint tea into their earthenware beakers. David was enchanted by this golden green liquid as it twisted from the pot, steaming and lemon scented. His pleasure delighted Nada.

Jamila took up the story, trying as she talked to help herself to understand how things had worked out. 'I slept with Donald. I don't know why. Perhaps it felt expected; perhaps I was curious. I had talked with Zohra about sleeping with men and Habiba had said she would tell me about being married, but she died before that happened. I trusted Donald. He was older than me and felt wiser and he had a posh job in the University and he gave me a space and some clothes and food. He treated me well up to then. I watched him with one of his students, Connie, and she flirted with him, and he seemed to like it so I thought I'd try to be sweeter to him and we ended up sleeping together. During those days I decided that if he was going to choose between Connie and me, I wanted him to choose me. It never crossed my mind he would choose us both. We didn't sleep together much but it was enough.'

'Why did you decide to come back to us?'

'I decided to return to Morocco on the day that Donald was made a professor during a graduation ceremony for hundreds of students and families. I didn't want to be there because I was daft enough to believe all these people were better than me but David helped me out and we were standing outside afterwards talking to Donald when two children ran out of the crowd towards him calling, "Daddy, Daddy!" and with them was their mother. Donald shouted at them. He knew their names!

Nada looked perplexed. 'You mean they really were his children? How long had you known about that?'

'Not at all,' said David. 'We had no idea. None of us had any idea. The children ran out of the crowd, right out of the blue and their mother followed. Sophia is her name and she had come to tell Donald that they were leaving Scotland to travel to Australia. The children and Sophia were Donald's secret and had been for years. He tucked them away miles from Edinburgh. When he shouted, clearly shocked, the children cowered behind their mother while a fierce argument developed. We heard it all. Donald had visited them every week, in Dundee and we all believed it was a work project he went to. We still have no idea who she was or how they knew each other but the children were six or seven at least so they'd been there a long time. How did we all miss it?'

'I had been stupid,' said Jamila. 'I was shocked. Sophia treated Donald like an idiot and calmly informed him she was going to Australia with the two children and had the tickets already. Donald pleaded with her to stay, to give him another chance but when she'd had her say Sophia turned and with Donald's two children at her side, strode away. We were astonished.'

'Donald was an expert on extinct humans but useless with the current version,' David said. Jamila was surprised. She had never heard David sound bitter before.

22

The sun and the mountains framed the glistening water surging through the valley reminding David of his home and its familiar landscapes. 'This is why you loved the paintings in the National Gallery,' he said, smiling at Jamila by his side as they walked by the river. David had promised to share what he knew of Donald and the rest of his team so there were no questions that needed to be asked and they both knew instinctively why they walked alone. Jamila listened as David talked about the day she had left him in Edinburgh and how he had been feeling. She was surprised that he was so angry with Donald for his deception and selfishness. She found it hard to imagine such a gentle friend as David confronting Donald. David described how a few days later he had arranged to meet Fraser in the union bar and Fraser had told him that Donald was now virtually alone other than Connie and they all thought the research project would fall apart as Donald's isolation increased.

As he talked David almost began to admit to himself that he felt a sense of shame that he had failed to see what now seemed so obvious. News of Donald's deception had circulated around the University and both Fraser and David had found themselves answering questions from students and researchers they had never really come across before and some people seemed to David to be critical of them for not noticing, not realising that all was not well. 'It's strange how you fail to see what is staring you in the face,' said David. Jamila detected a sense of guilt. 'There was nobody who knew about Sophia and Donald's children,' said David. 'Nobody.' As Jamila listened and took herself back into those weeks, she wondered at how simple minded she had been. Did she feel guilt, shame even? David recounted how in the weeks that followed it seemed that Donald often had too much to drink, and this increasingly happened during the day. She could only imagine that he had been unhappy. With his deceptions uncovered few people were willing to give Donald the benefit of the doubt. 'In fact,' said David, 'there was no doubt.'

There was a sense of regret in his voice Jamila thought as David described how Connie had tried to hang onto Donald and take advantage of the situation that she found herself in. But it wasn't just Donald's team that was the problem. Old Professor McKenzie had taken a dim view of his behaviour and had talked to David and Fraser in order to try to establish the truth. Once Mackenzie realised what Donald had been doing his research grants had been cut so within a few days of Sophie revealing herself outside the Usher Hall, Donald's world was effectively falling apart. Jamila was discovering horrors about Donald even as David talked. In so many ways there was so little that she understood and this made her even more angry with Donald, who she saw ever more clearly had taken advantage, used her and tricked her. David became the most emotional as he recounted how his own mother had been upset at Jamila's departure. She had never had a daughter and missed having Jamila around the house, but Moira thought Jamila had done the right thing. Jamila wanted David to reassure her that his mother would not be too shocked that she was carrying a baby. David was less sure about that but promised he would break it to his mother gently.

'I wanted to see good in Donald,' said David. 'I wanted to believe he had good intentions and successes.'

'But I never knew how he thought about himself,' said Jamila. 'I never saw him as he saw himself. He kept himself secret and not knowing who he really was ended up mattering.'

'And the real Donald is a liar,' said David. 'That's tough. He seemed confident and right but he was a lie and that hurts because I was stupid enough to believe the lie.'

'Me, too,' said Jamila.

'He only ever wanted to be praised and if I tried to criticise him, he closed up, tightened, defended himself but there were always others who would say good things. He wanted it all one way. Looking back, we never had conversations, he always just told me.' David was relieved to be able to talk about these feelings with Jamila. She understood as no one else had seemed able to. They felt between them a warmth that was ever more tangible.

'I'm blaming myself,' said Jamila. 'I should be blaming Donald.'

David agreed.

*

David would only be staying a few days before he needed to return home. Directly he arrived Jamila knew she would not want him to go. With him she felt less vulnerable; without him less confident. For David, he had arrived in a swirl of dust and drama and within days he knew that he had to leave this place but that it could only ever call him back. Jamila's family drew him into their lives. He had been fond of Jamila from the first day they met, as she stooped to pick up his trowel on the dig in Marseille and he saw her blush lightly around the neck as she handed it to him. He was seduced by her courage and made better when he was with her. He had a sense that his lonely days in Leith might soon be over. With Donald's misogyny now exposed he saw Jamila as a victim. Her pregnancy, however unfortunate, arose from her naivety more than her foolishness. He was already making the words to ask her, but he believed he could offer her marriage if it were possible and that he would treat the child as his own if Jamila would accept him. His own deterioration would render Donald unlikely to care very much, even if he knew and David had no plans to tell him. David could not prevent the wry thought that he would curate the child on Donald's behalf, just as he had curated the artefacts. When Jamila asked David if he would consider being with her when the child came his answer was immediate. She already told him that Zohra would be there and Marie she hoped as well so all was being set in motion for her to go to Marseille. Before she had finished asking, David had agreed. From Edinburgh he would return to Marseille and then if she wished would join them in travelling back to Morocco. David had already resolved to share his ambition to offer to marry Jamila with his mother and ask for her blessing.

*

Over the next few months Jamila tried not to notice that David had gone. She made herself busy from day-to-day helping on the stall and in the café and everybody came to know that she was pregnant and was planning to have the baby in Marseille. There was general ascent around the village that this was a good thing and admiration for Jamila as she took matters into her own hands. Ismail was increasingly forgetful and did not really understand but the rest of the family soon realised that Jamila intended to return to Morocco from Marseille with her baby and Zohra and Nada soon guessed that David may well accompany them. And so it was that with only a few weeks to go before the baby came to term Jamila and Zohra travelled to Marseille.

*

A few days after they arrived Marie arranged a visit from a doctor she knew from her own pregnancy, and they agreed

Jamila would come to the maternity home when her contractions started. After a few quiet days Jamila began to realise that her baby wanted to be born and at the same time she felt herself in a kind of retreat from reality. She told Zohra that she had started to feel a light pain and a churning, 'like rubbing the washing through the stones by the river,' she said. Zohra chuckled and said that sounded unlikely. Marie was quick to chip in. 'Well, Zohra, you're not having a baby so how would you know?' The three girls laughed at their new understanding.

Later that day Jamila lay on the hospital bed and she knew her attention was starting to dissolve. Everything seemed to be disappearing except her and her own throbbing pain pushing on her body as it seemed to tighten on the inside. Over the next few hours Marie and Zohra came and went, mopping Jamila's forehead, holding her trembling hands, calming her, loving her whilst to Jamila her experience seemed out of her body where time had no meaning, minutes dragged and yet hours passed without her recollection. Marie and Zohra were just pleased to be there in the hospital and able to help when the time came. Jamila felt that if she could look away the intensity would decline and yet the less she paid it attention the more this concentration increased and consumed her.

'I can feel a band wrapped around me,' Jamila protested to Zohra in the intimacy of the night. 'Loosen it. Please, it hurts.' Zohra called the nurse, and she massaged Jamila's belly and her arms as she struggled to be comfortable and could not be so. 'I want to get out of bed.' Zohra smiled with the nurse.

'Of course you do,' she said. 'All in good time.' Somehow Jamila had formed the notion that if she sat up, everyone would go away so she could go back to Morocco, to the leather stall and sell leather to the travellers in the morning. Instead, the waves of discomfort were worse and worse again until roaring crests broke across her and she felt the water around the sea ferry tumble against her as she sensed she was dropping down, drowning, just riding in huge rolling breakers of pain like an angry sky, out of control, terrified for what seemed like an endless moment. Then the breakers came again and again until out of nowhere an indescribable high consumed her when she realised the child was there and the nurse was holding a tiny scrap of messy flesh before her and saying, 'It's a girl, Jamila, you have a daughter,' and then Jamila sensed her own power as if there was no one else who had ever done this, no one else had ever turned pain into such pure relief and happiness. Zohra had brought Latifa's shawl, the charmed gift from Nada to Jamila and when the nurse had wiped a little of the blood and mucus from the child, she wrapped her in the soft shawl. Now exhausted and smiling she cradled her child close, and the mother and child slept, stirred, moved into each other's spaces and slept again.

In the new hours that followed, her child felt for Jamila a resolution for the pain and sacrifice of her own real mother. The granddaughter's restitution for the suffering of the mother for the daughter, unknown and unrequited love, love wrenched from the mother as the child was embraced by the living love of Habiba. 'I shall call her Latifa,' said Jamila. 'Her grandmother's name, so we will always remember my mother, through her granddaughter.' Wakeful dreaming separated Jamila from the duplicity of Latifa's father, mirroring grandmother Latifa's probable detachment from Jamila's own father, a detachment Jamila would sustain. Where Jamila had imagined she might find a new truth in her unplanned travels to Scotland she had now found a greater hypocrisy, shamelessness embedded in the elevated artificiality of Donald's culture where fatherhood could be denied and unselfconsciously overlooked rather than condemned by consistent morality within the community. The irony resided in the new Latifa's birth. In her own child Jamila had found her own mother and reconciled herself to the absence of a father, a shared condition for mother and child. This emotional realignment was more subconscious than otherwise for the new mother, a curious recreation of roles. As she nursed her child Jamila could not help but wonder at the shamelessness of Donald Lansdown when faced with his own children, the incontrovertible evidence of his immorality, set against the remorse and penitence of Nadeem in the face of his rejection by the community. This newfound understanding was to underpin Jamila's life as she brought Latifa into a more complex world than she had known as a child. The old platitude history repeats itself was manifest.

Throughout the days around Latifa's birth Zohra and Marie had been wonderful. In her heightened state after the birth Jamila regarded them as guardian angels, miracle workers. Then another miracle; the day after Latifa was born David returned to Marseille. He was quietly fearful of meeting the baby Latifa, alert to her provenance and its complex relationship to what was now his past. There was no doubt that Donald had forfeited any claim over the child given his treatment of Michael and Sasha, but even so David's strongest wish was that he should never have to see Donald again. Jamila's delight at David's arrival filled him with warmth, still in no doubt as to how she felt about him and as he gently held Latifa to his cheek he felt himself suffused by a profound urge to protect her. In these few moments Donald became an irrelevance for David. His Protestant past niggled away at him from time-to-time but practical common sense and his mother's generosity of spirit towards Jamila's circumstances left him self-assured, ready to make the compromises that would be needed if Jamila and he were to make a life together.

Above all Marie's down-to-earth approach impressed them all. She reminded David of Charles Dickens' ever loyal Peggotty, so much so that David searched out an old edition of David Copperfield in a second hand bookshop he'd discovered behind the Notre Dame de la Garde and gave it to Marie. 'If you read this,' David said, 'you'll find a character just like you. Please will you tell me when you have decided which character I mean?'

'How strange,' said Marie. 'Jamila gave me Little Dorrit to read because it starts out in Marseille.' David was delighted by the coincidence.

As they both sought the best for Jamila, David and Zohra were immediate friends and within a few days they were planning their return to Morocco whilst Marie saw to it that Latifa's and Jamila's papers were in order. Zohra needed to leave once Latifa was settled as she was worried to neglect Ismail for too long. David had lodgings near to Marie for a fortnight and he and Jamila agreed that after the two weeks were up and assuming all was well with mother and child, they would all return to Morocco.

Now nursing her baby Jamila remembered how shocked she had been that she was pregnant but having overcome the fear and the anger she now found herself excited and a little surprised to have a baby. The intense hours during which she was giving birth had given way to a calm love for Latifa as well as a passionate high regard for her friends who had been there to support her at her moment of greatest need. As she nursed Latifa she went over what she could or couldn't do next and she felt no doubt that she wanted to return to Morocco to her family home and to go with David. Her own feelings were overwhelmed by what she now saw as a growing love for David and his unbiased and non-judgemental support deserved nothing less. Her life had changed and would never be the same again but her view of her friendships and family had been enriched by this process in a way that she could never have imagined. She was swift to see that whatever she decided would have a significant impact on Latifa's life and she was already in no doubt that any return to Edinburgh or notion of going back to Scotland was completely out of the question for her. The help she'd been given had been magnificent and in becoming a mother she was beginning to discover a whole new self-confidence. She and David had already begun to plan together what they may or may not do and this left her feeling calm and quite sure that David had her best interests at heart. In his turn David felt the same way about Jamila. She was no longer one person and the arrival of Latifa seemed to have strengthened her bonds to her friends and he could see that although she was tired from nursing her baby and taking care of her needs, that tiredness was an enrichment not a burden, a privilege she cherished. Any needs Jamila experienced were solved through her friendships and so it was that the few days she had in Marseille had become a reservoir of kindnesses which she would find sustained her for many years. Her remaining worry was money but she was quite sure that she could contribute to life in her village back in Morocco and find a way through.

*

Three weeks later David, Jamila and Latifa joined Zohra back in their village. Baby Latifa had slept across the ferry and David had loved being on the boat. When they arrived back in the village they found that Ismail had been fine, a great relief to Zohra and as soon as possible Jamila joined Zohra on the seat next to Ismail, with Latifa snuggled beneath her clothes. Ismail was propped on a few cushions wearing his most comfortable shalwar kameez and loosely covered in a cotton sheet. He stayed thin and weak and still at times looked unwell, but he was better than he had been, and his chair was now placed beneath the bamboo canopy that sheltered the café and the leather stall from the sun. He always felt better outside in the cool mountain air, warmed by the summer sun.

'You asked to see Jamila and her baby. They are here. I promised you we would come, Papa, when you were awake and comfortable.'

Ismail gestured with his hands that he understood, and he tried to smile, enough for Jamila to notice and feel pleased. 'Papa,' she said. 'For you are my Papa. I would like you to hold your grandchild. I have called her Latifa, my own mother's name. Will you hold her? Please?'

Ismail gestured that Jamila should bring Latifa closer to him. She stood and drew the child from beneath her shawl, peacefully asleep, Latifa's finely drawn pink fingers resting on Jamila's hands. She was making almost imperceptible sucking noises and Jamila bent to kiss her as she carefully guided her towards Ismail. Zohra helped Ismail to sit up a little and between them they rocked the baby onto his arms. He wrapped his weathered hands around the child, smiled through his watering eyes and using just two crinkly fingers stroked Latifa's head. He whispered an Arabic blessing 'بنا يحميك. God bless you.' As he cradled Jamila's baby, the new Latifa, he remembered the events that had surrounded Jamila's real mother, her departure from the village and Habiba's adoption of the child. He had never felt easy with what had happened to Latifa, but he at least felt easy about their own adoption of Jamila and the chances they had given to her. For her part Jamila felt her heart bursting to see them together. She had always loved Ismail, even more now that she understood her own history. The excitement tired Ismail, and Zohra lifted the child from his arms to return her to Jamila who pressed a purse of coins into Ismail's hand, kissed his forehead and whispered 'thankyou'. His eyes sparkled for Jamila as she held her baby and behind them both and inside on the wall, Habiba's likeness smiled down at Jamila and Latifa, knowing that her unconditional love for Jamila had born rich fruit.

*

Within days David was working the leather stall. Since Jamila disappeared and Nadeem fled to fight in Chad 'Hammed had gradually taken on the responsibility for keeping the stall and café in good heart and it was a role he relished. 'Hammed enjoyed showing David techniques for cutting, shaping and marking the leather for belts and straps, purses and wallets and he proved to be a good student. When Jamila was away 'Hammed missed her vitality, whilst in many ways he felt calmer without Nadeem there. Nadeem bullied and blustered although his skill with working the leather was badly missed. Now Jamila had returned 'Hammed was delighted that her partner seemed a natural at the stall, good to customers, well organised and best of all reliable. David was enriched by 'Hammed's warmth towards him and pleased for the companionship whilst Jamila enjoyed seeing them together, pleased for them both. Jamila had not yet declared that she planned to try to stay together with David, but the family were quickly attached to him and easily guessed Jamila's intentions. David thought of nothing else but struggled to know what to say and when to say it.

'Have you decided when to visit Marrakech?' was Nada's innocent question to Jamila. 'Is it time maybe, to try to trace your own mother? Perhaps you could go with David?' Jamila couldn't understand why she hadn't thought of this before and so it was Nada whose sparkle saw that the two of them had the time together they needed.

23

David and Jamila walked through a broad arched gateway decorated with ever expanding geometrical shapes and the marketplace opened out before them, wide, broad and long. Everywhere David looked small groups were gathered and people wandered thoughtfully or strode with determination. He was fascinated by Djemaa El Fna. Jamila explained in translation the square would be called *The Assembly of the Dead* and it was like the town market square of Marrakech. 'Like the Grassmarket in Edinburgh but larger,' said Jamila.

David laughed. 'I think they used to hang people in the Grassmarket,' he said.

'I expect they've hung people here as well,' said Jamila.

The tall tower of the Koutoubia Mosque watched over the market square like a patriarch, its narrow windows and balcony scanning the horizon. Five times a day the Imam called the faithful to prayer from the minaret that had stood guard above the old city since the 12th century, a minaret splendidly ornamented and with scalloped keystone arches, jagged regular ornamentations and constructed in mathematically precise and disciplined proportions. The alignment of this minaret with Mecca was exact. The Mosque dominated the city landscape as well as Djemaa El Fna. It was only possible to imagine the expansive view from its tower across the square and beyond it to the city of Marrakesh and no doubt the Atlas mountains and the plains of the Moroccan Sierra beyond. Jamila knew how cool the interior would be and how grand the arches and could imagine the beautiful shafts of sunlight falling across the richly tiled floors because her brother had told her, her brother had prayed there and was proud to have done so on the few occasions he had visited Marrakech.

Jamila carried Latifa across her back, tied with a gayly coloured scarf and David felt she looked as though she belonged here, it was her special place. David's instinct was warmth towards the baby Latifa. He was always there to help, to hold and to cherish. If Donald ever came to David's mind he soon disappeared again, unremarked. And so it was for Jamila. She felt David as a guardian and loved him as a friend to them both.

David scanned the square. Male figures, a few in jumpers and trousers, most in traditional Muslim dress strolled across the square crossing and recrossing whilst a stream of women, hijabs flowing in the wind with child boys often dressed as you would see children in a market square in Edinburgh, casting sparkling dark eyes at the sights and flicking their shining hair, with sun brushed faces smiling, running, chattering. Some of the child girls already had their faces covered. An occasional motor scooter dashed across the square invariably ridden by a man. Women and men carried burdens on their backs, bags of grain, clothes, foodstuffs. David noticed several men had traditional knives strung around their waists and they tended to be the men wearing the shalwar kameez. Many women carried sleeping babies on their backs slung into cloaks, like Jamila. David thought it looked a very comfortable place for them to be. Many of the men wore a traditional Muslim cap and some of the older men particularly were dressed in a heavy cloak and a scarf wrapped loosely around their chins usually revealing a fulsome grey beard, eyes shaded from the sun by a floppy hood, looking like he imagined Gandalf from Lord of the Rings. One or two white men could be seen standing with cameras slung around their necks wearing khaki shorts and shirts and sporting wristwatches, silent observers on foreign soil.

Presumably it was the wealthier Marrakech residents who crossed the square on the horse drawn carts, upholstered seats, gaily flagged and dressed, seated women in the full hijab, some with their faces partially covered by a scarf and their hennaed hands clasping the dark leather rails. Then around the edges of the square and into the souks the stalls and the entertainment began to emerge. David was fascinated. This city square was a crossroads, a place of mingling, a space where ethnic groups, social classes and generations came together and exchanged their cultures and their customs. From storytellers to musicians and trance dancers, via snake charmers, monkey trainers, herbalists, preachers, fortune tellers, acrobats, conjurers and healers, the square was the perpetual fountain of the art of communication, a scene characterised by gentleness, by respect and a generosity of spirit that was almost tangible. David had never seen anything like it.

Every city has its agora, the place where the heart of its population beats. David could feel that for Moroccans Djemaa El Fna expressed Marrakech, was its icon, its symbol. He needed no imagination to know that this colourful crowd buzzed day and night, magic happened where this crossroad of the worlds met, where nomadic humanity took the time to stop its frantic race, to share a moment, to fill its leather satchel or to sell its abundant contents.

In one corner a man stooped over his pen and paper writing to the dictation of another in Arabic script, curls upon curls, curves upon curves, an art in itself, with his paper resting on the covers of a worn leather bound notebook, scratched, torn but probably his most important possession. Jamila pointed. Animated storytellers squatted on the stones, palms upwards, spelling out their magical stories to rapt audiences, sometimes of children, sometimes of adults and often of both. Child acrobats tumbled onto and off their father's shoulders to the applause of an enraptured crowd whilst others juggled and magically made coins disappear as they strung them through their fingers.

Dancing bands, with pipes and tambor, drum and trumpet wore bright ivory and mother of pearl encrusted cloaks, costumes from other North African cultures. Summersaulting monkeys raised cheers from the crowd in one corner whilst in another the snake charmer had his snakes curled on a rough, woven rug, with a small group of tambourine rattling supporters to heighten the tension and strengthen the drama, as he started with one black cobra and reached his finale with four snakes all held, swaying and dancing at the same time, face-to-face and tongue-to-tongue and David stood transfixed and loving it. He could say no other words but thank you.

Smoke curled and thickened in the distance of the square from the food stalls whose main delight seemed to be steaming snails, no doubt a throwback to the French. Fresh mint tea was poured high from shining copper kettles, always frothy and if you didn't mind paying, accompanied by a sweet, scented rose.

Once they had crossed the open square Jamila and David strolled into the souk. Here they were to search for a single stall, with the family name that Nada had suggested Jamila's mother Latifa would have used, Harrak. Nada thought they should look for a cotton clothes shop and it wasn't long before a friendly spice trader had given them directions. As they dodged through the teeming market Jamila found herself remembering Donald's mother and her stupid comment that a 'souk' was like a hot bath! 'Do you remember what Donald's mother said you'd find in a souk?' she asked David. 'I do,' he said. 'You've never mentioned her before. Ghastly woman. How could I forget?' Jamila smiled. She was ghastly. David was right.

The spice trader's directions worked. Round a crowded corner of cotton shops and leather stalls they found their stall. 'Elmahadi Harrak' sketched in striking blue letters above the front of the store. Jamila had concluded from her discussions with Nada that if the store was still there it would be her mother's brother running it. An elderly man sat just inside the stall, waiting for custom. A sewing machine and scissors rested on a table beside him. Jamila was surprised how calm she felt. This could be her family. David gently guided her past the stall, and they sat to take some tea whilst they found their bearings and gave themselves time to talk. Latifa slept on Jamila's back, oblivious to the noise and bustle. Cane mats were strung from side to side of the narrow market street to keep out the worst of the midday sun and the incessant calls of 'You buy. You buy' rose from every stallholder on every bend and every corner. Just past where they sat a stone arch, like a giant keyhole, led the way from one lane to another lane. Bicycles stood unattended waiting for their owners to return. Opposite where they sat a stall was laden with leather goods, handbags, ornate decorated mirrors, frames of leather and coral, fire bellows, waterpots, coats and jackets, gloves and hats. 'You buy. You buy.' Next door copper and chrome sheesha pipes and jars with the omniscient curved dagger hung in an endless supply at stall, after crowded stall.

A young man fashionably dressed in tight purple trousers under tight blue sweater strolled down the Market Street for all the world dressed as if he was in the middle of Edinburgh and yet he carried in his hand a tray with a delivery of mint tea and lemon.

'So,' said David. 'Do you think the man with the sewing machine might be your uncle?'

'I think he might be, David, so I shall have to ask him. He will know the fate of my mother if he is my uncle and I hope he will know where I can find her burial. Let's sit over there while I feed Latifa.' While they had taken tea Jamila had discreetly suckled Latifa who slept on quietly. David marvelled at Jamila's skill with her baby and the easy way in which the child had become an extension of the mother. Since they had left Marseille Jamila had managed Latifa's needs with a natural flair that left him in awe of her resilience. 'I can only love Latifa as Habiba and Nada have loved me,' she said when David praised her. As he looked at Jamila, David was feeling ever surer that he loved her and her child. 'Let's go back to the cotton stall now, David,' she said. 'I am so glad you are with me.'

David could only observe the lively conversation that occurred between Jamila and the man with the sewing machine, whose own apparent unconcern soon gave way to interest and then animated dialogue. Jamila, eloquent in her native language, gradually turned his caution into excited engagement. David quickly understood by the waving of arms and pointing to watches that arrangements were underway for another meeting in another place later today. David was introduced, they shook hands and were away.

Jamila's eyes sparkled. 'It is him,' she said as they walked back through the souk. 'He is my uncle, and he knows where my mother's tomb can be found. My mother stayed with them here in Marrakech after I was born and until she died. She cooked for them and kept the stall clean. He thinks she never recovered from losing me.' As Jamila spoke, she started to cry, deeply drawn breaths and heavy tears. They stood still in the midst of the flurry of commerce and David embraced Jamila, gently at first then more firmly, resting her tearful face on his shoulder and carefully lifting the light weight of the still sleeping Latifa onto his own arm. Jamila felt the embrace drawn around her, lifting her spirit with its tenderness as she sank into David's love. 'My mother's body rests in the 'Cimetière de Bab Aghmat'. It's not far from here. Elmahadi will meet us there at six o' clock to show me the place.' Again, she cried; again, she leant her weight on David. She felt safe.

They stood together for a while and then David broke their silence. 'I promised 'Hammed that we would visit the Chouara tannery. He said I needed to see it. Shall we go there now? It's not far from here. We've a couple of hours to spare.'

'That's perfect,' said Jamila. 'Thank you, David.'

*

In the heart of the souk, they found the tannery. It processed the skins of goat, cow and sheep; labour intensive work their guide told them, that had stayed in families for years despite the dangers, from chemicals which smelt unpleasant, the cow's piss in particular, so unpleasant that David and Jamila as visitors to the tannery were given fistfuls of mint to hold to their faces to mask the smell.

'Will Latifa notice the smell do you think?' asked David. Jamila laughed.

The beating, tub-thumping courtyard of the tannery was floored with dozens of deep, cylindrical dye vats each full of myriad coloured dyes; amber, oak, grey, blue, red, gold, and green, where men stepped nimbly between the vats stirring and treading, dunking and squeezing the hundreds of hides, pressed, cleaned, trimmed and so left to soak in their ordained colour. The high sun shone, beating down onto the vats and the men below as the process advanced and was completed and the skins were dragged from the vats, rinsed and hung along numerous balconies so they festooned the inner walls of the courtyard, each skin trimmed leaving traces of animal neck and limb skin hanging, drying in the fierce sun.

As they walked with the guide they could see men in covered halls surrounding the courtyard sat at blocks and tables brushing the dried skins to re-soften the cloth and enrich the depth of the colour, whilst in workshops that filled all of the available free space yet more men sat at benches, cutting, trimming, slicing and pairing strips of leather on their way to being designed into bags and hats and straps and shoes. David was fascinated. This labour was intense, focused, physical and for all there was ardent concentration and determination; a singular silence was pierced by the noise of the marketplace that surrounded the whole building and it was in this marketplace deep in the souk where many of these items were sold to dealers and tourists alike while others were taken away on carts and vans for export across Morocco, on to North Africa and into Europe.

Throughout the tannery the atmosphere was penetrated by concentration, resolve and patience, where repetition had perfected each task and where each task had a significant part to play in the final product, where little energy was wasted on the niceties of life.

The guides passion for his subject hooked David. He lapped it up. For some leather workers there were templates, for others there were knives to cut and the freedom of their own imaginations to create artefacts for sale. David pointed, drawing in Jamila's attention as he admired cutting and sewing machines of various shapes and sizes which were scattered according to need and each had been added to and subtracted from over the years to make it fit for a particular task at a particular time in the process; machines whirred where hands had for several generations turned them in the same place in the same way for the same effect leaving them with shining, worn surfaces. 'Look,' exclaimed David. Over there excess stitching was burned away by an old, bearded man and a brass oil burner and beside him surplus leather was chamfered with a fierce looking carving knife; noisily nearby stumps of timber wrapped in leather were pummelled on the leather sheets to soften the product, soften its tissue, secure its design and pattern, seal its edges and bring it to a shining perfection. Final stitching brought the edges and corners together and with a deft push of the hand the inside popped out and the perfection of the product was instantly visible. David noticed there were no supervisors, nobody barking orders but there was a product of timeless beauty and endless fascination drawn from the simplest of resources with the greatest skill and art, conceived with creative, intuitive teamwork where the whole was far greater than the sum of the parts and where each person's role was clear, uncomplicated and probably the product of generations of duty from the same family. The work looked exhausting physically, even though mechanisation had taken over some aspects in the previous few decades. David could see that there was no ornament to this labour, no soft chairs and no water tap in the corner but there was a sense of purpose and commitment, determination and honour, which ran deep and was sewn into every stitch and beaten into every corner of every product. He was delighted and transfixed.

*

After the tour of the tannery both David and Jamila were tired, so they shared a tagine in the market square, watched another snake charmer at work and soon began to feel refreshed. David was overflowing with excitement at what they had seen although Jamila was tearful again and David gave comfort and understanding in equal measure helping to restore her self-confidence and reassure her self-doubt. 'It is right you are here,' he said. 'You need to seek your mother and to get as close as you are able and Latifa in her own time will share your newfound understanding and it will enrich her own sense of herself and her history.' As he spoke David had taken Jamila's hand in his own. She recognised in herself new sensations; comfort, trust, faith in another. 'With Elmahadi's help we will find your mother's tomb and close that part of your search. Then we can move on.' Jamila liked the 'we' in what David said.

*

Several donkeys rocked from hoof to hoof and flicked flies with their tails as they stamped the stony ground around the crumbling gate of the cemetery. Woven baskets littered the entranceway and a few beggars squatted in the little shade afforded by the stone walls. Jamila noticed Elmahadi sitting in the shade of a nearby tree and as he spotted them, he came over, smiled and greeted Jamila. David held Latifa. Elmahadi looked at the child and then at David. He spoke to Jamila. 'He wants to know if we are all going in,' she said to David. 'I told him we were.'

David thought Elmahadi was about to speak again but then he seemed to change his mind as he turned and walked slowly through the gateway. As they emerged at the other side David was surprised by what he saw. Myriad rounded tombs stretched out before them, dusty, plain, many peeling and cracked, endless and seemingly identical steppingstones stretching into the distance. On a very few there was a sparse Arabic script, but most were unadorned. There was hardly space to walk between the tombs, but Elmahadi was walking with determination to a spot David guessed he would recognise. When he did stop David could see no difference to the dozens of tombs they had already passed. Elmahadi spoke with Jamila, their tone hushed and their eyes downcast, diffident. Jamila turned to David. 'This is my mother's tomb.' She stooped and touched the dusty brown of the tomb's cover. She stood a while then bent to the ground and took a stone, kissed it and placed it on the tomb and then looked around her. David held Latifa, rocked her gently. He felt he was witness to a renewal as Jamila pondered the stone before her and the secrets it held.

Jamila took Latifa from David, kissed her forehead and rested her gently on the tombstone. 'Surely we belong to Allah and to him we shall return,' she said. Jamila stooped as she held Latifa against the dusty stone and David saw that silent tears were running across her cheeks and falling onto the baby's shawl. 'A soul belongs to Allah. It will return to him in time. Everything in our world is temporary.' As Jamila spoke, she lifted Latifa, kissed her gently and offered her to David, who carried her carefully as Jamila turned back to the gateway. Elmahadi had already gone. 'He said that he didn't want me to come back to his stall. People would talk and ask questions and Latifa was a part of history for him now. He did tell me that he thought my father was English but that nobody ever saw him, and he never tried to make contact. My mother died of a broken heart, he said. I think he knows more but would rather keep his council. I respect that.'

*

The following day David asked Jamila if she would marry him. 'I will,' said Jamila. 'I would like that very much.'

24

Several months had gone by since Latifa's birth and their trip to Marrakech and David had returned to Edinburgh to see his mother and sort out his affairs. She was delighted that he planned to return and make Morocco his home. Jamila had arranged with Marie that she would visit when David was away, so Pierre and Jean-Luke were there to share Jamila's birthday, spend time with Latifa and introduce Marie's baby Jean-Luke. Like Jamila before them they had travelled by boat, train and bus from Marseille. Pierre had enjoyed the journey and was soon working out how he might start up another café in the village to cater for the increasing numbers of travellers passing through. He loved making plans. He was destined to do the same in every town he visited. Musing on opening restaurants was his favourite past-time. His family were spread around the Mediterranean where Marie's were embedded in Marseille so living elsewhere felt easier for him. 'Let's just have this time here first, before we decide to uproot ourselves,' she pleaded. 'Have your dreams, though, Pierre. Who knows what might happen.'

'You and Pierre work well together,' said Jamila as she and Marie walked arm-in-arm down the steep slope from the village to the river. 'I feel it's like that with David. We just fit well together.'

'Pierre's a good man,' said Marie. 'He deserves his ambitions. Your David is the same, isn't he?' Jamila thought of Moira's advice about 'good' men and the treasure they are when you find one. She had been wrong about Donald and so had Sophia. This still bothered her.

As they walked Jamila pointed to the cliffs beyond the river where the afternoon summer sun shone onto the rocks and crevices of the harsh mountain landscape. 'Look, Marie. There they are. The Yellow Rock. That's where I was born.' Marie felt awed by what she saw. The deep shadows of the limestone caves were bathed in sunlight but whilst Jamila was joyful to show her, to Marie they appeared inhospitable, apparent emptiness set against the endless reach of the granite mountains. She decided it would take her a while to love this landscape. Pierre might have to wait a year or two to open his café.

'I know so much more about myself now, Marie. You were right; coming back and seeking my own history has changed my life. But I needed to go away first. It's the coming back but seeing things in a different light that has released me to be myself. And then there is David of course.'

'What about Donald?' asked Marie. 'Does he know what's happened? Has anyone told him anything?'

'No. I don't think so. He'd already deserted at least one woman and two children when I was stupid enough to fall for his charm. I don't think he'll be chasing me. David taught me an expression, Marie: "I'll cross that bridge when I get to it". Jamila felt pleased that she could so easily answer Marie's concerns. That was David talking, she thought.

They had planned to cook by the river and barbecue some lamb. Today the leather stall was closed. By the time Jamila and Marie had reached the river Pierre was already collecting driftwood to make a fire. 'The French cannot resist a picnic,' laughed Jamila. She had made pitta that morning ready for the feast and Zohra had created the falafel, both noted specialities of their café. A kettle of lemon and mint tea would accompany the feast. Jean Luke was asleep on a blanket so while Marie held Latifa, Jamila joined the wood search.

Zohra had walked down to the river with Nada. They were both proud of Jamila, thought she seemed a natural mother and were keen to praise her and encourage her. Since Latifa's birth Jamila's fondness for Nada had grown so that by now they shared many confidences. Jamila had told Nada about Donald's behaviour, and she was unequivocal. 'He deserves to be left,' she said. 'He took advantage of you, and you owe him nothing.' Zohra found it difficult to imagine a man who could go off and leave his own children and so she worried about Jamila being on her own with her child, who seemed destined never to know her father. David's appearance had impressed her and his capacity to give himself to Jamila and her baby with such goodness and heart, but she still wondered how the baby Latifa would regard her father; she could not help reflecting on Habiba's role in Jamila's life. In these thoughts Zohra was ahead of Jamila, who had not yet worked out how to direct her emotions as they played with notions of Donald as a father, failed already. As for what Latifa might think about her father that remained a long way off for Jamila.

As they all enjoyed the picnic it wasn't long before Marie and Nada were good friends and chatting away about babies. Nada had never had children but as she knew all Habiba's children and many of the village children as well, she had plenty of knowledge of childhood and its complications and pleasures. Marie admired her and was to spend time thinking about her after their visit. 'I wish I had a Nada of my own,' Marie had said to Jamila the following morning. 'Living in open spaces where families and children easily mingle gives everyone so many possibilities as friends and companions.' She would like that for Jean-Luke she thought. Suburban life in Marseille was very different. Her brother loved Morocco and now Pierre the same. She kept her counsel.

The lamb smelt delicious by the time Hammed and Adel arrived with Ismail. Its sweet scent of roasting rosemary rose up the side of the valley as they descended. After his morning sleep they'd carried Ismail down to the river in a cane sedan chair kept by the steep track to be used on these occasions by villagers. Going back up was always easier than coming down. They carefully secured the chair where they were all gathered, Zohra wrapped Ismail in warm blankets and he let his waterfall eyes search the river water and the familiar skies, remembering, examining the distant hills, tracing ancient images along familiar trails, gazing away the afternoon. Tears spilt. Images blurred his thoughts. On his lap, under his crooked hands, where his children once rested, was hidden a silver tinder box. He carried the single first lost tooth of each of his children, saved for him always by Habiba, where even Jamila, neither their blood nor their flesh, was no exception. Holding the warm box he sensed each life, each new child an adult now and a witness to his own youth. Ismail closed his eyes as his thoughts wandered.

'There,' Nadeem pointed. 'There's the buzzard. There it is papa, above the Yellow Rock. I wish I could spot its nest.'

'One day you will search and find the nest.'

'Will you help me, Papa? Please?'

'If I can, I will,' Ismail had said. He knew Nadeem had always remembered how delighted he was to see the fine creatures fly free and how as he stepped along the tracks with his father they chattered, laughed and smiled, shielded their eyes from the blazing sun and again and again glimpsed the buzzards soaring on the warm air of the mountain's day. Years have been dispatched yet in his heart, the old man still strides, whilst by his side the children trot, panting at the pace, skipping across the ridges, dipping, squealing into the pools of icy water, scrambling deftly across the rocks. But he has lost his firstborn. He has lost Nadeem. Jealousy and guilt sent Nadeem into an exile from which he has never returned but today the others are here still, breathing the same crisp air, sharing a meal from the same basket. Jamila, stretched out on the hill before him, Marie, her French friend by her side, his stray child just returned to the mountains who now knows the uncertainties of her birth, her mother's offence, the truths of her conception and the caves of her birth. And now Latifa has re-joined the family and Jamila has brought David and he is welcome.

All those years ago Ismail often felt a guilt when he considered Jamila, guilt that stays with him still, that surfaces whenever he sees the buzzards soar on the evening warmth, carrying his sometimes desolate whispers to the distant hills, a guilt that pursues him even today where the twilight marks the fragility of his condition and the loss of Nadeem a drain on his spirit. Soon 'Hammed and Zohra will cart him up the steepening slope to his village home, still shared by all his children bar Nadeem, lost, Ismail must believe, destroyed by his own irreconcilable envy of the child Jamila; Nadeem, who when scarce made man, faced a reckoning unbidden; he had struggled, ashamed to speak, lost and alone, carried his covetousness on his tired back and stumbled, crumbling into the stream of a war he chose, unseen as he tramped into the flow and rush and drag of the battle, onwards, drawn away and drawn down. He did not search for the buzzard's nest. Ismail had no son to bury then or now, his memory a chimera, the truth still unknown.

*

As Ismail rested by the river and dreams of Nadeem's youth, Jamila and Marie set out to climb to the caves where

Nada had recounted Jamila had been born. They left Pierre and Nada to keep an eye on Ismail as well as the sleeping babies and they ascended the winding track to the Yellow Rock. Marie knew Jamila better than anyone, understanding the immense apprehension that would invade her as she made this journey. Jamila now knew the answer to many of her questions so her return today to the place of her birth stirred her sense of self, her respect for her own mother, for Habiba, her understanding of Nada.

The two friends spoke little on the way; the climb was steep, and it wasn't many minutes before they were coming to a halt at regular intervals to catch their breath. For Jamila this journey was already a bittersweet experience. Now she was here it was hard to imagine how her mother had made the climb not only bearing the burden of her unborn child but also the fear of her circumstances; it was equally hard to imagine how she was able to turn her back on the village and depend on her own resources and the kindness of a few women to survive. As she climbed, Jamila mused on the accident of her own conception, her mother's chance encounter with a stray soldier, her mother's search for safety, the pain of the birth and the consequences for them all as Latifa had made the infant and Habiba had made the child. Jamila felt twice blessed, despite the spectre of Nadeem in the valleys of her childhood that also invaded her consciousness as she climbed.

Reaching their destination, panting and perspiring, the two girls rested outside the entrance to the caves and scanned the rugged landscape. 'It's beautiful,' said Marie. 'The village from here clings to the hill and feels as if it has been there forever, built the colour of the rock and the sand, your village Jamila with all its splendour as well as all its faults. I'm glad you've returned to where your heart must be filled with love.'

'You're right, it is filled with love.' Jamila again recalled Moira and David talking of Donald and the lines of the old truths she had uncovered and how Moira helped her see that as she kicked them away new truths emerged and had to be embraced as new lines settled. She smiled to herself; David and his mother had both understood. Jamila turned towards the cave entrance. 'Nada told me a Berber family lived here before the war. They left the caves and found a new home in a nearby village. They had diverted water from higher on the rocks but otherwise they had to carry everything from the valley. How lonely they must have been and how lonely must my mother have been.'

Marie peered into the cave. 'You were born in there?' She was smitten with admiration for Jamila's mother. 'Your mother had courage, Jamila, a courage you also carry within you.'

'Nada said my mother had courage. I find it hard to imagine I was born in that dark and cold place before my mother carried me out into the sunshine and down the mountainside. Habiba stood here and she helped my mother walk away. My mother chose this space to bring me into the world. A safe cave in the mountains above a glorious valley.' Marie watched Jamila's eyes as they searched the landscape and observed her slow tears. 'Now I know, this is my safe place, Marie, I came from here.' She pointed to the swift waters below, seeing in her mind's eye Nadeem's attack. 'But down there, that was not safe, by the river, not when Nadeem was seeking evil.'

Marie wrapped her arms around Jamila. 'What will you do with your courage, especially now there are two of you?'

Jamila smiled and settled within the shade from an immense rock, leant against the cool stone, quiet for a while, listening to her heart still beating hard after the climb, listening to the goats tearing the rough grass around the caves, watching the kites swoop in wide, gentle circles, searching over the hills for carrion. Marie's tender words ran within her, 'Now there are two of you.' She looked down to the river where Nada and Pierre waved up at them and she watched 'Hammed and Adel chasing, splashing each other just like they had as kids, just like she and 'Hammed had been running around the leather stall when Nadeem had hit out at her, with pent-up aggression, abuse and assault. *'You're the child of a whore, Jamila. That's what they all say but you never hear. You're a whore's bastard child!'* Nadeem's malevolent words were indelible. Jamila was startled to perceive an unwelcome irony. If Latifa was a whore carrying a bastard child, then so had she been. Her Latifa was a bastard child. *'Now there are two of you,'* Marie had said. *'You're a whore's bastard child,'* Nadeem had shouted. Jamila, like Latifa; her daughter was fatherless.

Resting beneath the shaded rock Jamila closed her eyes and pictured bright woven mats hanging outside their home, Nadeem alone and working at their stall by the road, sitting hunched and serious, tooling the leather with intricate designs whilst Ismail stood beside him, holding a finished shoulder bag and polishing with a cloth whilst they talked of knives and straps and purses and threads for Jamila's blanket making. She hears Ismail praising her intricate stitching to Nadeem and Nadeem's usual tirade rings again in her heart. *'Whatever you say, father, I will not work with her,'* she can hear him say. *'Why did you let mama slave over her, Jamila should go, be sent away, it was Jamila that wore out our mother.'* She hears Ismail declare that Jamila will only go when she chooses and Nadeem mutters, spits out the whispers, *'You love her more than the rest of us, Papa, and you always have.'* Jamila hears Ismail grunt angrily and in her mind's eye the men stop talking and bend to their work as Mohammed sits nearby reading, Adel plays cheerfully in the shade of a bougainvillea, Zohra sits with her, grinding corn, talking of men and marriage and Jamila thinks why should I marry when I see men like Nadeem?

She remembers Zohra's words. *'All men have a cruel and selfish side; it's the way of the world. We women must grin and bear it. It is better to go with the grain than fight the natural way of things, Jamila.'* Jamila remembers she argued, *'Why? Come on, Zohra. Why must we accept this? Why does it have to be like that? Why don't we deserve respect? Habiba understood that so I want to be like her. Habiba loved me despite everything. Why should I tolerate less from lesser men?'* And then she remembers how 'Hammed, in those moments, brought his book over and stood by her interrupting the conversation, pointing to words he couldn't grasp. *'Please Jamila, I need your help, what is this phrase, I do not understand? I hate French.'* And Jamila read 'Petit a petit, l'oiseau fait son nid.' *'Ah! 'Hammed,'* she said, *'Little by little the bird makes its nest,'* and 'Hammed protested, *'What does that mean? It's just words.'* And Jamila explained. It means, *'Patience wins through in the end, little by little'* and adds in Arabic أول الشجرة بذرة. (A great tree begins with a small seed).

She put her arms around her brother and joked with Zohra. *'You see, Zohra, just like I said, men are always needing help.' 'Maybe you are right,'* said Zohra, *'but now you must see, Jamila, men are always needing help from us women, and that's how we use them to get our own way,'* and then 'Hammed said, smiling, *'You always study so hard Jamila, you are lucky to go have French lessons, how can you know all these things?' 'Ah! 'Hammed, little by little,'* Jamila said, and they both laughed and play-chased around the stall, skipping, dodging but then she stumbled and knocked the stall sideways, Nadeem's carefully crafted leathers spilling to the ground and that was the moment his rage was unleashed as never before. *'Whore's bastard.'*

These words are scratched into Jamila's heart and still echo in the hills and run free when she lets down her guard. She can hear them now as she opens her eyes again and casts her sight over the distant rooftops of her village and the glorious mountains, whilst Marie stands by, silent and loving. They had also been Ismail's words as Jamila now knows.

For Jamila the layers of these recollections are fused by the violence of Nadeem; his hate and his obsession with her birth are a harsh bedrock of her old truths alongside the love of Habiba and her family whilst the lines of her new truths run through her own unknown and absent father and past Donald another absent and unknown father to his children and back through to her own, now known mother Latifa and Jamila's own child, Latifa. These new lines must also embrace the lives of Sophia and her children, Sasha and Michael. Maybe by now they are in Australia. Her Latifa is a part of their family. New truths. She wonders if she might hunt for her own father to find his lines and concludes that he surely hardly knows and as far as she can tell he's never returned so he surely has never cared. She has no more need of him than he does of her. But she has found her own mother; learning her own story has now taught her to love her mother Latifa who even in her death carries a new line of truth. Maybe to know her own father would release more truth.

Marie smiles at Jamila, lost in her thoughts, gazing across the wildness then below her in the valley she hears laughter as their families splash in the shallows of the stream. 'That's Ismail I can hear laughing,' she says. 'And I think I can hear Latifa crying!'

'No. It's Jean-Luke, surely. Latifa doesn't cry.' Jamila and Marie laugh as they start the climb back down to the river.

*

Jamila felt her own experiences were tough enough but now she saw that was not half as tough as running away from them had been. She had found out for herself that only when she was brave enough to search the unknown did she uncover her strength. Embracing her weaknesses, failures even, was perilous but not nearly as risky as giving up on sharing love, belonging and even giving of itself. She knew this openness exposed her, but she felt herself created to connect, risk or no risk. As she looked at Latifa she saw how the infant used her connections to survive and for the first time understood this in herself. Jamila also saw how as she had grown older these connections enriched her emotions, strengthened her spirit and sharpened her thinking. By cutting herself loose she had learnt how to belong and discovered how to value herself not for what she might be but for what she was. Nadeem had violated her physically and emotionally and she had run away only to learn that facing him was her only route to recreating her own confidence. His absence felt as if it had cheated her; she felt the irony that now she wanted him to be there. What she felt as her shame, now enriched her as she took on the mantle of motherhood with Latifa. The tunnel vision that sent her scurrying away had been replaced by a clear-eyed and fertile sense of self-worth from which to view the possibilities of her new life with David. Her failure with Donald was a failure of judgement; her trust in David was secured by the lessons that failure had delivered.

'We're coming down.' Jamila's call echoed the hills as she and Marie began their descent to the sparkling river. They arrived panting at Ismail's side. 'It's beautiful by the caves where I was born. I am so pleased I know at last and have realised the place. Thank you, for your kindness to me and to my child, to my Latifa. I love that I can show her the cradle of our secret lives, the source of our creation. She will grow to know and love this place.' Ismail smiled. Jamila loved to see that smile, feeble as it had become, for he had been the father of her fate and she respected his love, his care and patience.

Marie took Jamila's hand. 'Do you miss Edinburgh? Will you tell Latifa's father where you are?'

'No. I do not think I will.'

'Will he not search for you both?'

'He does not know I have a baby and I know he would not care. He cares only for himself. I know that now. I regret that I overlooked your warnings, Marie.'

Marie was thoughtful. 'Latifa may wonder who her father was.'

'I know. I try not to think of that.'

'Maybe that will change. Your sister is very kind. She is lovely with Jean-Luke.'

'And with Latifa, she always smiles when Zohra comes close.'

Marie and Jamila laughed. 'Do you remember on the dig?' said Marie. 'When you told me you planned to go to Edinburgh and that Donald said he would pay. You said you had to take some chances to make a life. You weren't thinking about having babies then, were you?'

'Too true.' Jamila laughed. 'The thing is, Marie, you always understand but you don't always say so. That's good because it leaves me free. You help me to ask the right questions. That's a true friend. I'm sorry you must return tomorrow but it's been a wonderful few days.'

'We are both lucky,' said Marie. 'Lucky to share our friendship, our children and our friends.'

*

Marie and her family left the following day, back to Marseille and their busy life. Jamila loved Marseille but it was not for her a home. Marie was keen to seduce Jamila back to the energy and excitement of the city streets, but Jamila was firm in her resolve. She had returned to Sidi Sayfa as she had departed, through the city ports of Algiers and Marseille and after nearly a year of self-imposed exile in Edinburgh had rediscovered her village, its dark mountains and sparkling valleys, its tough and clear talking people and the tolerance and passions of her adopted family. She felt embraced by all she had recovered by returning. The events of recent months had dented her sureness. She had been wrong about Donald, wrong about Nadeem's motives. She had trusted where that trust had been abused. But she found no fault in herself, simply a sense of disappointment that there was a price to pay for some lessons learned. It wouldn't happen again.

*

'What was it like for you Jamila when you climbed to the Yellow Rock?' Nada's question had so many answers Jamila didn't know where to start. Only now did Jamila grasp that it was Nada who held them all together when Habiba died, Nada who helped Ismail to grieve and the rest of the family to pick up the traces. Only since she returned home had Jamila understood Nada's love for Habiba and for her family and discovered from Nada that Nadeem's jealousy and harsh treatment of her had started when she was born and whilst Jamila had always wondered what the circumstances were, she had never imagined the reality, her birth in the mountain cave, her mother banished and the new-born baby, Jamila herself, taken on by Habiba as she weened 'Hammed and became Jamila's mother; her wet-nurse with an ocean of love. Nadeem had so often chanted,

'Jamila! The whore's bastard child!' but Jamila had never imagined that this could be the truth although she always suspected she did not know the truth. Why had she not made the connections?

'That's the right question, Nada and there are so many answers now I know so much begins with the Yellow Rock. We've talked about how it was with Nadeem when I left the village after he tried to attack me by the river and how I came to travel to Marseille and then Scotland. Ever since I could dream, I had imagined that Habiba was my mother, Ismail my father and Zohra and the children my own kin. It is only a few weeks since you told me the truth, Nada, so when I reached the caves with Marie it was a journey into part of my own past that had never featured in my present. Now I have stood where I was born, I have begun to absorb the truth, to respect my real mother, to develop a perception of her courage that overwhelms me and a fascination with her history and whether living or dead to connect my life and my daughter Latifa's life to her own grandmother. Finding the caves has been finding my own beginning. Finding my real mother's resting place in Marrakech is the last piece of that puzzle.'

Jamila was sitting with Nada by her window, overlooking the narrow lane that dropped down towards the river tracks, wrapped in the sweet scent of her roses tumbling around the shutters. Since she had returned to her village this space in Nada's home had become a shrine, an irreplaceable space of peace and understanding for Jamila. 'Tell me, if you can, Nada, why my mother paid so dearly for conceiving me and yet for me, with my own baby, I am welcomed?'

'Times change,' said Nada. Her eyes searched for words but she found none.

'Maybe the lines have been redrawn,' said Jamila.

Nada rocked her head and smiled. 'Redrawn, as you say, Jamila. Reimagined and redrawn.'

Warm in their companionship they were quiet. Outside the safe sounds of the silence of the valley; the distant wash of the river; the rumble of a truck through the village; subdued voices nearby sorting the business of the day. Beside them the slight breath of Latifa, resting beside her mother.

25

As the driver twisted the rattling jeep along the uneven mountain tracks Nadeem's eyes closed in uneasy sleep and he was trapped again at a junction between roads in a now distant place that had been a town and was now bullet scared and shell crushed buildings; nationalist graffiti scrawled over every broken surface and posters for the President defaced with obscene messages of eternal hell or pasted over with Chad's National Front propaganda. Everywhere was rubble, battle broken homes and shattered lives. The evil sun beat down on him through the bone-dry dust of this landlocked hell. Scattered around him the armed militia he had joined to purge his guilt, snipers and their targets, were dug into part formed part sheltered positions, pinned down by each other, desperate, evading sporadic fierce gunfire. Nadeem could not recognise himself, in rebel battle dress, dirty, salt sweat drenched, wild, angry and terrified, fighting alongside Ahmed, his battle partner, a stranger none the less, consumed by the same anger and the same hopelessness, swathed in vitriol against an enemy he also hardly knew.

Snatching his breath as the jeep thuds onto a deep crack in the track Nadeem sees himself again ducked down, panicked, alongside the familiar stranger Ahmed, both squeezed into the corner of a ruined ground floor room, the shelled and pitted walls open to the destruction around, a beaten dirt road between them and the unknown enemy, skulking in every nook. In his edgy sleep he hears Ahmed's rasping whisper. 'We need to break out now before we get trapped. You go first, Nadeem. I'll cover you 'till you crash that corner. Go. Go now. Inshalla.' Ahmed points urgently across the road to another ruined wall of another ruined home. It could be a few gained paces in a few frantic moments. Nadeem wonders why, what is the point of this madness.

'Okay, Ahmed.'

'When you reach the corner, count to ten, then you cover me and I'll join you.'

'Inshallah. Okay. Just do it.' Nadeem hears himself spit out the words with no idea of why.

The two men touch hands. Nadeem prepares to run. Ahmed prepares to fire. A tangle of images wash over Nadeem as Ahmed drops his weapon into a shattered window space, pauses, looks towards the sky as if invoking all the gods and starts to fire, splattering the adjacent building with shot from his automatic. Here it comes again, sleep drawn terror, as Ahmed fires, Nadeem runs. All hell. Enemy bullets bite the ground around him as he successfully hurls himself towards the cover of the next corner. He rolls to his knees, wipes more sweat from his brow onto his filthy sleeve, checks his automatic, and he turns his own weapon on the opposite building and at his count of ten starts firing. As he does so, Ahmad breaks cover and throws himself across the same open space, but at the moment Ahmad runs, Nadeem struggles with his gun which jams, goes silent and within an instant bullets from the adjacent building tear into Ahmed who falls, rolling over and over again, across the road dirt within spitting distance of Nadeem. Just as Ahmed's slack body collapses, Nadeem's gun clears and he's firing again as more enemy fire tears into Ahmed who now lies, motionless in the road before Nadeem. In the sudden silence, through a crack in the bullet splattered wall Nadeem sees Ahmed's hot blood drain into the dirt, flies already feasting.

When he closes his eyes, day or night, Nadeem sees the same; Ahmed's lifeless body, face up in the middle of the decimated landscape, his skin caked in dirt, sweat, dust, blood and insects. Nadeem sees Ahmed's right arm reaching out towards him across the dirt road, bloody fingers clawed into the gravel. He sees himself reflected in Ahmed's dark glasses as the moment of silence is shattered by the unforgiving clatter of guns being reloaded. Nadeem reflects in gratitude: Allah has not chosen him.

*

Somehow Nadeem had found himself in Chad, ushered by his guilt out of his village, choosing to offer himself in a civil war he hardly understood, choosing to escape the censure of his village and lay himself out as a sacrifice if Allah chose to take him. The last of his battles and the slaughter of Ahmed, seeped through Nadeem's mind over and over. Somehow, he had survived and escaped and travelled back. The long-distance jeep that had carried him from the Moroccan border to his own familiar mountains ground up the long hill and Nadeem was shaken awake by the irritated driver. He climbed down in the village square shrugging off his tortured sleep, touched the ground again not so many months from his flight whilst his escape from the battle still soaked into his heart, where Ahmed lay abandoned as Nadeem fled terrified from the scene leaving his useless, accursed gun behind.

Nearby, as the jeep drove into the square, Zohra was attending to the leather stall. Ismail was asleep in his rocking chair beside her and little Latifa lay naked on her shaded mat kicking the air. Zohra noticed a jeep drive into the square and then an almost familiar figure climb down and start across the dusty road towards them. She considered the uneven set of the jaw, the shuffling walk and gasped as she perceived her brother, vanished, but now could it be him returned and she dropped the leather bracelets she was rearranging and looked again hardly believing. 'Nadeem,' she whispered afraid to speak the name she thought was lost. 'Nadeem.' She glanced across to Jamila, who was sweeping the dusty floor. Zohra stuttered the name again as she crossed the square and approached the figure. Seeing Zohra leave the leather stall Jamila had looked up and taking in the scene before her, studied the figure who staggered across the square towards them and in that moment recognised Nadeem. Jamila watched as Zohra reached out to grasp her brother. She watched as Nadeem with dark, sparkling tears flowing down his parched and scabby cheeks, stretched out his scared and grimy hands towards Zohra.

'Zohra,' Jamila heard Nadeem plead as he stretched out to his sister and clasped her to him as if taking his own life back into himself. 'Zohra,' he repeated, clinging to her as he may never have done before. He cried, sobbed onto her shoulder. Jamila held back. Zohra smelt his pain and felt his bones and shuddered, horrified by what she now knew she did not know.

Acknowledgement

My thanks to Elizabeth Speller and Craig Baxter of the University of Cambridge Institute of Continuing Education who through their support and friendship have helped me to better understand the complexity of the continuous written word and have encouraged me to make my own marks on a page.